THE HUNGER
AND THE HUNT

All that night, all that lovely night, Lamashtu, the fierce lioness—Demon Goddess of Death and Disease—prowled the city in Sedgwick's body, not yet attacking, merely enjoying the novel experience of . . . anticipation.

So much promise here, all these nice, fresh lives about her, more than she had ever seen in one place! Lovely, sweet, rare, and intoxicating. And all she would need to do when she was sated with this new and thrilling act of waiting was reach out a hand. . . .

But to her disgust, Sedgwick's body, being mortal, was wearying. She must, Lamashtu realized, let her host eat and rest. . . .

Rage stirred within her, hot, sweet, aching to be loosed.

Tomorrow, Lamashtu mused. After so many ages of timeless boredom, tomorrow she would get Sedgwick to obey her more efficiently. Tomorrow, too, she would see about eliminating the troublesome human, the scholar-woman who knew too much about her.

Tomorrow, Denise Sheridan would die.

ROC

FLIGHTS OF FANTASY

☐ **THE BROKEN GODDESS by Hans Bemmann.** When a beautiful woman demands to know whether or not a complacent young teacher believes in fairy tales, his life is forever changed. He follows her out of the everyday world—and into a fairy tale. So begins a strange quest in pursuit of his elusive princess, through a realm of talking beasts and immeasurable distances, of deadly dragons and magical gifts. (454871—$4.99)

☐ **A SONG FOR ARBONNE by Guy Gavriel Kay.** "This panoramic, absorbing novel beautifully creates an alternate version of the medieval world.... Kay creates a vivid world of love and music, magic, and death."—*Publishers Weekly* (453328—$6.99)

☐ **THE DEEPEST SEA by Charles Barnitz** It is A.D. 792, a time of violent uncertainty. In Ireland, the Cross of Jesus vies with Thor's Hammer; the new ways of the Church clash with ancient beliefs. Bran Snorrison, carver of runes and composer of verse in the Viking town of Clontarf, has fallen in love with the village beauty and sets off on a journey to prove his worth in gold. But the fates have much more in store for him. (455045—$5.99)

☐ **ARCADY by Michael Williams.** With one brother locked in the Citizen's war against rebel forces and the girl's own father immersed in grief, Solomon Hawken must turn to a magic he can scarcely control in an attempt to save his family—and perhaps the entire world. (455002—$12.95)

*Prices slightly higher in Canada

RCF51X

Buy them at your local bookstore or use this convenient coupon for ordering.

PENGUIN USA
P.O. Box 999 — Dept. #17109
Bergenfield, New Jersey 07621

Please send me the books I have checked above.
I am enclosing $_____ (please add $2.00 to cover postage and handling). Send check or money order (no cash or C.O.D.'s) or charge by Mastercard or VISA (with a $15.00 minimum). Prices and numbers are subject to change without notice.

Card #_____ Exp. Date _____
Signature_____
Name_____
Address_____
City _____ State _____ Zip Code _____

For faster service when ordering by credit card call **1-800-253-6476**

Allow a minimum of 4-6 weeks for delivery. This offer is subject to change without notice.

SON OF DARKNESS

Josepha Sherman

A ROC BOOK

ROC
Published by the Penguin Group
Penguin Putnam Inc., 375 Hudson Street,
New York, New York 10014, U.S.A.
Penguin Books Ltd, 27 Wrights Lane,
London W8 5TZ, England
Penguin Books Australia Ltd, Ringwood,
Victoria, Australia
Penguin Books Canada Ltd, 10 Alcorn Avenue,
Toronto, Ontario, Canada M4V 3B2
Penguin Books (N.Z.) Ltd, 182–190 Wairau Road,
Auckland 10, New Zealand

Penguin Books Ltd, Registered Offices:
Harmondsworth, Middlesex, England

First published by Roc, an imprint of Dutton NAL,
a member of Penguin Putnam Inc.

First Printing, May, 1998
10 9 8 7 6 5 4 3 2 1

Copyright © Josepha Sherman, 1998
All rights reserved
Cover art by Royo

 REGISTERED TRADEMARK—MARCA REGISTRADA

Printed in the United States of America

Without limiting the rights under copyright reserved above, no part of this
publication may be reproduced, stored in or introduced into a retrieval system, or transmitted, in any form, or by any means (electronic, mechanical,
photocopying, recording, or otherwise), without the prior written permission
of both the copyright owner and the above publisher of this book.

BOOKS ARE AVAILABLE AT QUANTITY DISCOUNTS WHEN USED TO PROMOTE
PRODUCTS OR SERVICES. FOR INFORMATION PLEASE WRITE TO PREMIUM MAR-
KETING DIVISION, PENGUIN PUTNAM INC., 375 HUDSON STREET, NEW YORK, NEW
YORK 10014.

If you purchased this book without a cover you should be aware that this
book is stolen property. It was reported as "unsold and destroyed" to the
publisher and neither the author nor the publisher has received any payment
for this "stripped book."

ONE

The Art of Making Art

The shabby little man in the worn brown suit paused nervously on the corner of Madison Avenue and Seventy-eighth Street, glancing about him in the early-morning sunlight. The weather was warm for this early in April, but he hardly noticed. People hurried by on all sides, latecomers heading to work with grim, determined expressions since it was already after nine o'clock, but he hardly noticed them, either; they, in true New York fashion, summed him up as Object, Non-threatening, and kept going.

It was the stores that the little man was studying. The buildings here were good and solid, mostly stone, little of that sleek modern stuff you saw farther downtown, though there were just as many storefronts as downtown: expensive boutiques and elite art galleries.

Never mind the other stores. There was *the* gallery, there on the west side of the avenue, just as he'd been told.

Clutching the small, newspaper-wrapped package more securely, the little man scurried across Madison, dodging the flow of traffic, not even hearing honks or the squealing of brakes, coming up short on the sidewalk in front of the gallery's wide window. Heart racing, he stood looking at the window display, trying to calm himself, trying to pretend that all he had in mind *was* looking, even if the gallery wasn't officially open yet.

Nothing alarming in the display: a few small, elegant statues—Roman, he guessed, and maybe even all real, it was *that* sort of gallery—and one equally elegant bronze vase that looked like maybe it was Chinese. No name on the window, but a refined bronze plaque by the door stated that this was, indeed, the Highborn Gallery. Belonging, the little man recited to himself, to one Ilaron Highborn.

Ih-LA-ron, he repeated silently. Get the name right; more professional that way.

Aie, aie, what was wrong with him? Why was he hesitating? He was used to being the go-between in sales of maybe not exactly authentic artifacts. Never been in trouble over it yet. But . . . well . . . maybe it was just that the man who contacted him last night had been so *friendly,* with such an eerie smile, all sharp teeth and little humor.

But the stranger's cash had been good, the little man reminded himself, and there was a nice bit more of it waiting if he did as he was told.

And he was not going to get paid for dawdling.

The door was, of course, locked. Swallowing drily, he rang for admittance. At the skeptical looks from the staff within, two sharp-faced kids, young man, young woman, both nicely dressed—making him feel, in his well-worn suit, maybe a little bit shabby, yes, maybe a little bit resentful, too—he held up the package, then pointed to the time: Yes, he was expected.

A third staffer joined the two, this one a well-groomed, middle-aged woman (nice, he thought nervously, good curves to her, good face, too, but an expression that said, try anything and die). She disappeared into the back of the gallery to check, then returned to the door, nodding to the other two: He was telling the truth. About this, her suspicious glance told him, at least.

The little man slipped into the gallery through the

half-opened door, carpeting soft under his feet, the traffic noise suddenly shut out as the door closed. Elegant place, yes, money here all right: quiet color scheme, all soft beige and tan, precisely placed lighting, nothing to detract from the art itself.

Odd collection, though, no one theme. He saw a fragment of what had to be an Assyrian relief, eighth century B.C., maybe, nice and brutal scene, too, displayed beside a very modern abstract painting, bold reds and blues. Yet they did not look so bad together, not bad at all.

He would have liked to stop and take a better look at this weirdly nice mix of art, but the wary-eyed young man and woman were watching him, so he nodded, smiling, and hurried on. Never draw attention to yourself, no, safer that way. Much.

And you did not, so he'd been warned, keep Mr. Highborn waiting.

His guide stopped, knocking on a door. "Come," said a voice.

The woman stepped aside to let the little man enter, and his heart started its panicky racing all over again. The office in which he found himself was windowless but very modern, very chic, softened by subdued lighting that was just this side of dim. Nothing alarming here, he saw as his eyes adjusted, not really, but:

A man who could only be Ilaron Highborn himself sat behind a sleek wooden desk, leaning back in his chair with casual grace. And at the sight of him, the little man felt a whole new surge of fear.

Highborn was tall and slender, his long black hair, drawn back in a fashionable ponytail, contrasting starkly with a pale, sharply planed, coldly beautiful face, completely ageless and not like any other the little man had ever seen. Sunglasses shaded all but a hint of Highborn's eyes, adding to the air of quiet menace, and for a moment the little man ached to turn and run.

"Sit," a cool voice ordered.

He did, plopping down in the chair across from the desk and unwrapping the package with trembling hands, making a bad job of it. Highborn waited with unnerving patience, not even stirring, and at last the little man managed to free the statuette from the newspaper and held it out with wary reverence.

"Sumerian. Very old. Very nicely carved. See?"

The little statuette certainly did look authentic. Even he had been fooled at first. But Highborn frowned, then closed a long-fingered hand about it, silent for a disconcertingly long moment, eyes shut behind the sunglasses.

What is he doing? Is it a trick? Or . . . or . . .

But then Highborn's eyes snapped open again, and he drew his hand back as sharply as though the statuette had scorched him. "A forgery," he hissed.

"N-no, no, sir, I could not, would not—it is genuine, I swear—"

But there was something about Highborn's face, something almost . . . terrible, that choked the words in his throat. Babbling apologies, he jumped to his feet to leave, but Highborn was on his feet, too, and that same graceful hand closed with inhuman strength on the little man's shoulder, forcing him brusquely back down.

"This is more than a foolish attempt at fraud," Highborn said flatly, standing over him. "You were sent. By whom?"

"I—I don't know." The little man twisted about in his chair to stare beseechingly up. "Truly, truly, I do not! He was—he is—is a stranger, someone w-who offered me money to act as go-between. I swear this, on my mother's grave I swear, I did not know—"

"Describe him."

"He, uh, was small, yes, small. No taller, me. Not much meat to him: skinny, like you know, weasel, ferret maybe, all wiry."

"What else?"

"Else? Else? I don't know. Clothes, nothing cheap, nothing flashy. Ordinary, just ordinary. Wait, wait, and he had, well, yes, a weird smile."

His words became increasingly more panicky as the tall figure loomed over him in terrifying menace and even more terrifying cold . . . amusement.

And suddenly it was all too much to bear. Without a thought to his money, the little man snatched up the fake statuette and ran.

Ilaron, he who these days called himself Ilaron Highborn, a free translation of his true name, stood frozen, face showing nothing but coldness, no trace at all of the fierce battle he was fighting with himself.

That stupid little rabbit of a man! Trying to fool him so simply—

Yes, yes, and worse, the man had been radiating that so very intoxicating aura of fear! Aie, yes, it had roused the ancient night within him, the Darkness whispering hotly of *the hunt . . . the terrible joy . . . the wild delight of drinking in the victim's fear, despair, pain—*

No!

No.

He was no longer what he had been.

So, Ilaron thought with bitter humor, *I claim each time. And each time am mocked anew.*

Grimly he willed his heart to calm, his mind to clear.

And, with his mind clear, Ilaron suddenly straightened, realizing—

Yes, curse it. Why hadn't he seen? There *had* been something more than fear shadowing the little man. And if he hadn't let himself be so overwhelmed by the taste of that fear, by the Darkness, he would have immediately known and not let *the prey*—no!—the man escape—

With an angry hiss at himself for his weakness, Ilaron raced through the gallery, waving aside the startled cries of the staff, and out onto the noisy, crowded street. The enemy sun hit him with the force of a blow, and he staggered back against the door, blind, deaf, stunned.

But he was used to the sun, if not inured to it, used to the garish loudness of this city. In the next instant, the sudden shock was past and his senses had cleared. With a great surge of will, Ilaron straightened as though nothing was wrong, his face forced back into its usual elegant mask.

No one, praise the New Yorker's gift for selective vision, had noticed.

The little man, of course, was long gone.

Cursing himself for a fool, Ilaron turned and reentered his gallery.

"Mr. Highborn? Is everything—"

"Was he—did he try to—"

"—a thief?"

He glanced at them, at Ms. Daniels, his solid, dependable second-in-command who had been with him since the gallery's opening nearly six years back (stroke of astounding good fortune, finding her), and the two younger staffers, Sharon and Kevin, earnest, ambitious youngsters who'd joined him a year ago.

Why should they care? Ilaron wondered, as he always did. *Why should they be so concerned?*

Granted, he was the source of their employment, but there was more to their alarm than mere worry about . . . what was the phrase? . . . job security. Odd, Ilaron thought, as he had so many times before, that something as simple as treating them with courtesy, paying them honestly for honest labor done and listening to their opinions, should rouse such loyalty.

Odd, and yet rather agreeable.

Once there had been slaves, not free workers, and nothing of loyalty or gratitude . . .

Quickly blocking that unwelcome memory, he assured the three, "No harm was done," and strode back to his office, hunting. Surely the little man had, in his haste to be out of there, forgotten something, left some tangible evidence. . . .

Ah, yes. Merely some scraps of the newspaper in which the statuette had been wrapped, but they were still moist with the little man's nervous sweat. Evidence enough.

But there was nothing more he could do about this now. Even in this windowless room, it was still too strongly day. Certain procedures could be worked regardless of the hour, but Ilaron knew from long experience that what he needed must wait for the added strength of the night.

Could it wait? The tiniest new prickle of alarm stabbed through him. Who *was* the stranger behind the little man? That description: small, wiry . . . a sharp smile . . .

Bah, that could fit a hundred in this city. Was the stranger a mere "con artist," as these people so charmingly put it? In the six years since the gallery had opened, Ilaron had caught a fair number of idiots pretending to be refugees, impoverished nobility or even agents for unnamed governments, all of them trying to sell him forgeries or stolen property.

Yes. Just another con artist.

Or . . . was he . . . ?

"He had a weird smile."

No. *They* could not have found him. He would surely have known the moment they entered this realm. And yet . . .

A wary knock broke into his uneasy thoughts. "Ms. Daniels?" His voice feigned calmness perfectly. "What is it?"

Once, soon after the gallery had opened, Ilaron had slipped and carelessly identified her before she'd entered or even knocked. Then, he had concocted a quick fiction of having recognized her by her footstep. By now, he no longer needed to pretend. Whether or not she had ever believed his story, whatever she thought of him now, Ms. Daniels was quite used to her employer's quirks—such as his not needing any visual clues to identify her.

Opening the door ever so slightly, the woman said apologetically, "Sorry to disturb you, Mr. Highborn, but it's almost ten-thirty. Have you forgotten your appointment?"

"Ah, yes. I had." He remembered to add, "Thank you." Courtesy to underlings, again.

Once she had left, Ilaron wrapped the bits of newspaper in a clean scrap of chamois cloth, then, after a moment's thought, put the little package into a desk drawer. Others used a small safe for such valuable items; he found this method quite effective and less troublesome. A tap and a whispered word ensured that the drawer would stay locked till he returned.

Getting to his feet, Ilaron opened a second drawer with a touch and a whisper. Taking out a small box, he slipped it into one pocket.

Denise Sheridan, Ilaron thought, and smiled in spite of himself.

He could, of course, always have sent an underling. Any of the three waiting outside would have been quite competent to handle such a matter. But the woman was charming in a refreshingly blunt way, witty and intelligent. She always provided a welcome touch of sanity.

And right now, such sanity seemed like a very good idea.

So. He straightened his jacket, adjusted the clasp about his hair, checked his appearance with a quick glance in a hand mirror.

Yes.

Looking the very model of elegant calm—which, at the moment, Ilaron knew, was a very deceptive appearance—he set out for Fifth Avenue and its most prestigious tenant: The American Museum of Art.

TWO

The Letter

Denise Sheridan, Curator of Mesopotamian Art and Archaeology, was feeling far from sane this morning. Far from awake, too, despite the freely flowing coffee. A first-thing-in-the morning meeting was *not* her favorite way to start the day.

A glance about the long, dark oak table at the other curators in the dark oak-paneled conference room showed that most of them felt the same way. Robert Branford of the Egyptian Department, a neatly dressed fellow more or less her own thirtysomething age, was stifling yawns; solid, sensible Olga Margolis of European Paintings looked rather dazed; while poor Edgar Williams of Musical Instruments (who, it was rumored, despite his seventy-odd years, still led a deliciously active night life) was, if Denise wasn't mistaken, downright asleep with his eyes open.

The only one who looked bright-eyed and disgustingly awake was, of course, Alan Atherton, sitting there like the tall, refined, quite literally fair-haired society pet he was—as well as the museum's director. It was Alan who insisted on holding these monthly curatorial meetings, and on holding them the first thing in the morning, as he said brightly, while everyone was still fresh.

While everyone is still too groggy to argue with him.

"Very well, people," Alan said almost cheerfully, his accent as always a little too crisply British to be *quite* credible, "shall we begin? Any opening comments? Anyone?"

Of course there were none. They were all waiting to hear what he was going to say.

And don't you know it, eh, Alan?

"Very well," Atherton repeated. Rustling an impressive stack of papers, he asked, "Do you see these? Museum receipts. The good news is that attendance is up by a little over five percent since our last meeting."

Some faint cheers. Williams came awake with a start, glancing guiltily at Denise, who gave him a reassuring little grin.

Unfortunately, she'd done it a bit too obviously. "But," Atherton continued severely, frowning slightly at Denise, "but I don't have to tell you that we are still not where we should be. Indeed, we are still running very much in the red."

"Ah, isn't that true of every museum?"

Damn. She hadn't meant to say anything. Blame the early hour.

Atherton's frown deepened. "We are not 'every' museum, Dr. Sheridan. We are a world-class institution. But if, and mind you, this is a worst-case scenario, if we cannot find another way to increase revenue, cut costs, if we do not at least make an effort to, as Dr. Sheridan has implied, leave the ranks of 'every museum' and enter the black, we just may, *may*, mind you, be forced to eliminate a department or two."

This was not a new threat. As it did every month, Atherton's gaze swept around the room, never quite stopping on anyone. Since as always he wouldn't exactly name names, each curator was left feeling sure Alan meant *his* or *her* department. The idea, Denise was sure, was simply to keep everyone on edge, make everyone work harder—be more productive, or whatever the proper management term was.

Ah, but now Atherton was shuffling papers again. Some big announcement was pending.

"I have been speaking with the Board of Trustees, and we have all decided that what the museum needs is another Special Exhibit."

Muffled groans. Special Exhibits—those huge events on a chosen theme—were all well and good, and they did bring in the crowds. Unfortunately, they also entailed mountains of paperwork regarding loans of artifacts and insurance hassles, and the hazards of moving often-fragile artwork.

"And who's going to be doing the dirty work?" Denise muttered to Edgar Williams, and got a rueful chuckle from him: Not Atherton, that was for certain!

Blast. Alan was looking her way again. "Dr. Sheridan, I know that your department is woefully short-handed just now. But if Professor Williams isn't complaining, surely a *rather young* woman like yourself can manage."

Right. She'd caught that emphasis. Alan had just managed to make it quite clear to her, without of course actually saying anything specific (not in front of all the other curators, give him that much credit for tact) that he considered her "rather young" to be in charge of a department.

"Rather young" meaning underqualified. Ha. If you only knew I read anything as . . . what do you call the genre? . . . as "unworthy of a scholar" as fantasy novels! You'd fire me on the spot!

That she knew his not-quite claim was just one step short of a lie—she certainly was not the first of her age to hold such a post, or didn't Robert Branford in Egyptian (he who was right now carefully not meeting her gaze) count?—that she knew this didn't make it any easier to bear.

Particularly since this month seemed to be her turn in the spotlight. "While we're on the subject," Atherton said delicately, "there still is a slight problem, you know."

The words shot out before she could stop them. "With what? My politically unfashionable department?"

No, you idiot! Why don't you just shoot yourself while you're at it?

Atherton's smile was downright . . . charming. "I wouldn't put it in such harsh terms, Dr. Sheridan. But you must admit that the department *is* devoted to a . . . well, shall we say, a volatile part of the world? And while we both know that there's a certain mystique attached to archaeology, you really must also admit that it *is* less, well, *glamorous* than art. Not enough gold and glitter and all that, and no famous artists' names to tout to the public."

With that, he returned to the subject of gallery space and Special Exhibits. No theme had been chosen yet, and so forth and so on, but they would all be notified in plenty of time.

Hah.

But Denise listened dutifully, dutifully jotted down notes, and, keeping her mouth determinedly shut, nodded in all the right places, just as everyone else was doing.

And then, as he always did to end these meetings, Atherton made a great deal of suddenly glancing at his watch—a Rolex, of course—and saying, "Enough, enough! Off with you! The museum waits for no one, least of all a curator."

When oh when, Denise scolded herself, *will you learn to keep your mouth shut?*

She was stalking back toward her department— which meant doing some basic broken-field maneuverings through the crowds. Denise, used to such tactics, dodged two Japanese tourists intently studying a guidebook, a pack of art students setting up easels, and a woman struggling with three small children and a stroller without once breaking stride.

Look at this. He's got his crowds! Why doesn't he just leave us alone to do our jobs?

Because, of course, that wasn't Atherton's way.

Idiot! Hidebound, sexist, ageist idiot!

No curatorial offices ever seemed to be in logical places. Hers, in traditional museum fashion, was nowhere near her gallery space. Denise took a shortcut through American Art, past nineteenth-century columns masquerading as Egyptian, glancing up almost thankfully at the blazes of color that were the cleverly backlit Tiffany windows. But for all her appreciation of those quick flashes of beauty, she was still fuming.

At herself again as well as at Atherton. Alan hated disagreement—and Alan was on a social level with most of the Board of Trustees, the real power behind a museum. So if he decided on a Special Exhibit, you smiled and nodded and made the best of it. Nothing wrong with his being a publicity hound, after all. Nine times out of ten, those grandiose affairs did bring in those much-needed funds.

"There's no business like show business," Denise muttered, galloped up the final little flight of stairs, and flung open the office door.

Sarah Thomas, the department's young assistant, fresh-faced and both blessed and cursed with the "dumb blonde" stereotype of big blue eyes and golden hair, glanced up in alarm from the floor, where she, surrounded by stacks of books, had been engaged in the never-ending job of reshelving volumes. "Do I, uh, dare ask how it went?"

Denise sighed. "Let's just say that we still have a department. And a budget. More or less."

Sarah, fresh out of the University of Chicago with her shiny new degree, was still as green as they came, but she made up for what she lacked in life experience with intelligence.

And tact. One glance at Denise's face, and she nodded and returned to her books without another word. Denise continued down the bookcase-lined hall into her equally book-filled private office, just barely keeping from slamming the door. No use taking out her frustration on Sarah!

After all, we share a perversion. We both like fantasy novels. Alan could get rid of two of us "unscholarly types" in one blow!

Oh, enough of this. Denise glanced out her one small window at Central Park, the trees and bushes of which were, with charming disregard for the petty ways of humankind, just beginning to show the greenish fuzz of early April, and took a deep breath. Alan was director, Alan was going to go right on being director, and Life Went On.

Determinedly pushing museum politics from her mind, Denise settled down at her desk to struggle with the usual mound of paperwork involved in running a museum department.

An understaffed one right now, more so even than usual—as Atherton had so tactfully reminded her— what with the one assistant curator, Ira Meyers, on research sabbatical and Warren, the departmental technician—as he accurately put it, "the guy who does all the lifting and carrying"—on medical leave from having lifted and carried once too often. Denise's request for a temporary transfer of personnel was, of course, still Pending. And would probably go right on being Pending till Warren returned.

" 'Gold vases, not potsherds,' " Denise quoted under her breath, " 'bring in the crowds.' "

Never mind that such a "volatile" part of the world as Mesopotamia was the cradle of Western civilization, as well as of three major world religions—no, there was more than that. Yes, her department had some flashy gold vessels and some nice silver statuettes. But the rest of the collection, even down to those simple potsherds, the bits of ancient weaving, those fragments of everyday life—that was every bit as important. The whole point of archaeology, what Alan would never see or never admit to seeing, was that it was about *people,* not gold or cold dates in a text!

A rather timid knock from Sarah interrupted her mental tirade. "It's all right, Sarah. I won't bite."

The door opened a crack, then a little more. "Ah . . . mail's in."

Denise raised an eyebrow. "You don't sound too thrilled. Let me guess: 'nut mail.' "

"I'm afraid so. Would you rather I—"

"Never mind." Just another aspect of a perfect day. "Let me see it."

There were always a few letters, even the occasional phone call, from those *sure* they were reincarnations of this king or that queen; there also were, fortunately less often, the occasional warnings of divine or political retribution. Harmless insanities.

And this? Her hand tightened ever so slightly on the familiar no-return-address envelope with the typed address. The postmark was, unnervingly, a New York one.

Warily, Denise unfolded the single sheet of cheap stationery. Ah yes. The "Children of Sumer." Lately they had been sending increasingly frequent warnings that they, whoever they were, were not pleased with the department's "liberal leanings" and "lack of proper respect for the past."

The Children of Sumer. Hardly a name for any traditional Near Eastern militant group, certainly not for an Islamic one. Though it was true that the museum had—or rather, used to have, thank you, Saddam of Iraq and the late and current ayatollahs of Iran—excavations in both Iraq and Iran, and who knew whose toes might have gotten stepped on. . . .

Can't worry about might-be's. Too many weird groups out there anyhow.

At least this one seemed content merely to write letters.

So far.

Denise rubbed her hands over her eyes, then sneaked a peek at her schedule, rather praying that the morning would prove free. Ah, no. Not quite. She'd forgotten about the appointment with Mr. Highborn.

At least *that* wouldn't be a problem. In fact, seeing him should make a welcome break in the way the day was going.

Whoa, not Mr. Highborn, she reminded herself. *Ilaron.* They'd done enough business over the last few years to have arrived at a first-name basis. But it was still a little difficult to be so informal with someone with such natural dignity.

Such mystery, too. The man still puzzled her—partly because he wasn't like any other art dealer she knew, partly because even now she just could not figure out where he was from. What nationality *was* "Ilaron"?

Wherever he's from, I have to admit the man's a good conversationalist; he has an excellent grasp of what's certainly not his native language.

He was also highly intelligent and genuinely appreciative of the Arts, both wonderfully refreshing facts. And . . . well . . . Ilaron was a glamorous fellow, too, she had to admit it, the sort who seemed made for those sleek, expensive Armani suits he often wore.

A little too *glamorous for my tastes, thank you very much. I like my men a bit more, ah, human.* Denise grinned, very well aware that Sarah had quite a crush on Ilaron. *Not that I'd ever tell the kid I've noticed.*

But who Ilaron Highborn actually *was*, where he

was from, where he'd made his undeniable wealth—a mystery, indeed. At least, Denise reflected, the man was honest. The world of antiquities was rife with scandals about theft and forgeries, yet she'd never once known him to be involved with even the slightest of illegalities.

He also had an absolutely uncanny gift for separating the authentic from the forgery.

Too bad he doesn't work here. Oh, right. She could just see him abandoning the position of boss and taking the pay cut. No Armani suits on a museum salary! *But I certainly could use someone who could just—*

The softest of coughs made Denise start and look up, then start again.

Ilaron was there in her office, lounging elegantly in a chair, long legs crossed at the ankle, as suddenly as though the mere thought of him had conjured him up. His long black hair, caught back in its usual ponytail, contrasted sharply with his pale complexion, and his eyes were, as usual, hidden behind sunglasses—the man claimed light-sensitive vision.

"Pray forgive me," he said with a slight smile. "I could not resist a moment's drama. Ah, and don't blame that earnest young assistant; I slid past her when her back was turned."

Denise felt herself starting to grin involuntarily; that smile of his was just too charming. "She'll be disappointed."

"I know." Amusement tinged the words; he was well aware of Sarah's crush. "I'll bid her farewell on the way out."

As usual, his voice held the faintest and most unplaceable of musical accents. And as usual, Denise was taken by the intriguing, alien lines of his coldly handsome face—and as usual found herself thinking *dangerous* even though he had never shown her anything but courtesy.

Forcing herself sternly back to business, Denise reminded herself that both his artifacts and prices were invariably excellent. "What's today's item?"

"Today," he told her, opening a small box with a dramatic flourish, "I have a lovely little cylinder seal."

It *was* lovely, a delicately carved cylinder of chalcedony perhaps two inches long, showing what was probably, Denise thought, a representation of the Tree of Life, though she would have to roll it out on a strip of plasticine to see the entire design: Cylinder seals, meant to be rolled out on clay as the bearer's "signature," had been the signet rings of their ancient Mesopotamian day.

"Akkadian," Ilaron said, and Denise knew that, test it though of course she must, he would be proven correct.

"How do you do it?" she asked suddenly.

His smile was, again, quite charming, and absolutely unreadable. "What, identify artifacts? A gift."

And that, Ilaron Highborn, was as blatant an evasion as I've heard.

Ah well, she could hardly cross-examine the man. And the seal really was lovely. Of course Ilaron didn't name a price; dealing with such common matters, Denise had long ago learned, was something he seemed to consider beneath him.

And why is that, I wonder? Are you foreign nobility, Ilaron? Even exiled royalty? Or are you nothing more than a businessman who gets a kick out of being mysterious?

Whatever. At any rate, the sum eventually asked would, she knew, be fair; as far as she could tell, Ilaron got whatever prices he wished from the wealthy who patronized his gallery, but seemed to enjoy enriching the museum—protecting the human past, as he put it.

But suddenly he leaned forward, frowning ever so

faintly. "Something is bothering you. Badly. It is, I trust, nothing I've done."

Denise sighed. No mystery there. He'd probably read her uneasiness from her face. "No, of course not. Just the usual directorial hassles."

He "tsked" satisfactorily at that. "Bureaucracy is always maddening. But . . . I cannot accept that as all."

His steady stare behind the sunglasses was strangely persuasive. Reluctantly, Denise told him, "You know there's always 'nut-mail.' " At his hesitant nod (the slang had clearly puzzled him for the moment), she continued, "Well, lately I've been getting a steady stream of nut mail letters from a group—or, for all I know, just one creative loony—called the Children of Sumer."

He raised a brow. "Odd."

"Very. They . . . let's just say that they don't approve of the way we've been doing our exhibits. Not," she added hastily, seeing his frown deepen, "that they've actually done anything more than write a few letters."

"Haven't you notified anyone?"

"Of course. But, well, First Amendment and all: Can't stop someone from writing a letter or even a series of letters as long as no threats are made. No one higher up seems to be taking them seriously at all, and I can't really blame them, since, as I say, the Children of Sumer haven't actually issued any threats. They're just . . . annoying."

Now his "tsk," was decidedly disapproving. "The Children of Sumer." Contempt was in every syllable of the name. "Yet *another* extremist group. You are fascinating people, but you do find ways to complicate your lives. Might I see one of the letters?"

He'd segued into that so smoothly, his tone so suddenly, hypnotically persuasive, that Denise, hardly aware of what she was doing, handed the whole sheaf over to him. Her heart gave a little jump at the sight of his face as he read them: so suddenly, startlingly cold and remote, almost as though he was examining them with more than the ordinary senses. . . .

But then Ilaron sighed and returned the letters to her, shaking his head.

"What was that all about?" Denise asked. When he said nothing, she prodded, "What just happened? Or is it, failed to happen?"

"No. Not here. Not now."

"Then where? And when? Lunch?" Denise found herself saying. "Or maybe dinner? Somewhere out of the office, where you *can* explain?"

No, you idiot, not dinner, not with him, he's handsome as all get-out, but you don't need complications like that!

And why oh why are you reacting so strongly to— to whatever it was that—didn't happen?

Somewhat to her relief, Ilaron merely dipped his head politely. "Perhaps," was all he said on the subject. "And now," he added, "I really must be returning to my gallery."

His bow was as graceful as everything else about the man. Before Denise could say more than, "We'll be in touch with you about the cylinder seal," Ilaron Highborn was gone.

THREE

The Night Watch

Ilaron glanced subtly about from behind the screen of his sunglasses, aloof, and yet aware of every detail of the noisy, bustling world about him. Now, after 5 P.M., the traditional end of the New York workday, almost everyone, whether on foot or in those traffic-stalled cars and buses, was interested in one thing only—the quickest way home.

Not an unpleasant thought, home; it had been a long day for him as well. He hurried across Madison Avenue with a small crowd, holding his breath against the reek of exhaust from a delivery truck, keeping a wary eye on a turning taxi, thinking that every society had its downsides.

It could be worse. I could have rented that vacant gallery in the mid-forties. Perpetual nightmare, that, what with the never-ending crowds and traffic.

Eager to get home though he was, Ilaron, as always, refused to take the most direct route. Following a whim, today he wove his way through the commuters congested on the corner and turned south. He deliberately followed a different path home every evening, just as he went a different way to the gallery every morning. Unlikely that anyone could trace his aura, what with all the distorting iron and steel about, but why take an unnecessary risk?

"Just because you're paranoid," he quoted wryly to

himself, turning east at last on Seventy-third Street, *"doesn't mean they're* not *after you."*

Besides, this was a fascinating city, and, even after six years, Ilaron hardly begrudged the daily chance of seeing something new. The people themselves: such an incredible mix of types and races! Volatile, likely to quickly, irrationally, love or hate—so open with their emotions. The first time he had seen a couple strolling along holding hands, he had actually stopped dead, astonished to see anyone dare to show tenderness, to reveal an exploitable weakness at all, let alone in public.

Of course the crowds meant an indescribable mixture of aromas, particularly with the fumes of their vehicles added in, particularly in the humid days of summer. But all that activity, that wonderful, everchanging panorama of life, gave the city what came very close to its own life force.

A certain electricity, he thought, enjoying a private touch of irony. *Indeed.*

The architecture, he thought, was as much a mix as the people, three centuries of styles crowded in together, with unexpected treasures such as . . . ah, yes, look at that charming stonework on what these people called a brownstone (odd term, since the stone on such buildings wasn't always brown). Did those who dwelled within, Ilaron wondered, realize that the image of that being with the human face and the greenery for hair was a great deal older than the building the Green Man ornamented? Probably not; this was a city of a great many self-proclaimed realists.

Convenient. For me.

He turned left at random on Park Avenue, walked a block north, then crossed at a convenient green light and continued east. North again on Lexington, that more crowded, more hectic avenue, glancing at vastly overpriced flowers and tiny boutiques, then east.

At last Ilaron paused across the street from his own apartment house, a tall, narrow building—quite a fashionable East Side residence, as the agent had gushed when he'd first rented it—ostensibly waiting for the traffic light to change, actually testing the psychic air.

Nothing amiss. Good. He wasn't in the mood for any . . . adventures, particularly since he was facing an evening of strenuous work now that it was almost fully night.

The uniformed doorman held the front door open for him, and Ilaron spared the man a slight nod: courtesy to underlings, again. The building's lobby was a bit more ostentatious than he liked—marble veneer and gilded lamps—but by now he hardly noticed what was, after all, merely background. Pausing at the door to his private elevator, key in hand, Ilaron let his senses expand ever so delicately. . . .

Nothing unusual. But he kept his senses alert all the way up to the penthouse apartment: Elevators were convenient inventions, but they did leave one temporarily trapped. At least none of his foes were likely to attempt attacking someone who was in what was basically an iron box.

He stepped out, unchallenged, into the penthouse's small antechamber, doing a quick scan to be sure that the security systems were intact, smiling wryly at what others, again, would probably think paranoia. A second key let him into the actual apartment suite. A quick glance around, a second mental scanning of doors and windows, then Ilaron gave the softest sigh of relief, shaking his hair free of the restricting ponytail and pulling off his sunglasses—

Revealing eyes that were not by the remotest definition human. Slanted, their pupils were cat slits narrowly rimmed with gold, surrounded by jet-black irises.

Clever humans! Were it not for their invention of

such things as sunglasses, yes, and of that marvelous lotion known as sunblock, he never would have been able to survive in this realm.

Truthfully, he'd done more than merely survive. Ilaron glanced about, pleased. He had chosen this apartment mostly for its isolation and defensibility. It could be accessed only by that private elevator, was in effect a tower of iron, and was surrounded on all sides by a terrace garden providing no places to hide. But there was no reason for a home not to be comfortable!

And comfortable the apartment was, as much so as he could make it, thickly carpeted and furnished with tranquil elegance. Here a small but quite genuine Monet hung beside a Turkish weaving; there an abstract bronze soothed the eye with graceful curves. Ilaron, relaxed in privacy, dared a true smile, the action transforming the cold lines of his face into something almost tender. The charm, the vitality, the endless creativity of the human arts, never failed to entrance him.

He could afford to lower his guard a bit. No one came to this sanctuary without Ilaron's permission, and even the woman who visited once a week to clean never gained access without him being present (nor, for that matter, could she somehow really remember what she'd seen in there from one week to the next, knowing only that Mr. Highborn was a gentleman who paid her a good wage).

Once there were servants in plenty, slaves trembling in terror of not fulfilling my slightest command . . .

No. While he might sometimes regret the current lack of servants, he certainly didn't miss all the rest that went with the past.

At Ilaron's absent gesture, a sound system obediently switched itself on, filling the air with the fiercely elegant notes of a Beethoven piano sonata. *Rubinstein,* he thought with a moment's intense pleasure, and then, *a pity I arrived in this realm too late to hear him perform in person.*

He didn't bother lighting any of the lamps; mere darkness didn't bother him. But then Ilaron mused, drawing aside the thick draperies to gaze at the glittering city outside, there was no such thing here as true dark. Alien, even after all this time, alien . . . He could hardly feel nostalgia for his former home, and yet for a painful moment, Ilaron was very much aware of being without a land, without a people.

Grimly, he turned away from the view and cleared a space on his desk. Using magic in such a magickless realm was always, as the human phrase said, a double-edged sword; the advantages balanced the disadvantage of advertising his presence and abilities to anyone with Power. Still, he'd managed so far without any . . . interruptions.

Odd, this realm: The humans had almost no innate magical abilities, and yet their inventions had captured electricity, that source of Power which, Ilaron had discovered quickly enough, fueled his abilities quite nicely. Even if doing so did lead to occasional dips in power that puzzled the humans.

So. To work. Ilaron set a hastily made sandwich and cup of coffee at his side, but was soon too engrossed to take more than the occasional absentminded bite or sip. No physical clues of note from the scraps of newspaper from the little man who would have sold him the forgery; they came from a day-old *New York Post* that could have been picked up anywhere in the city.

Ah, wait! Before he called the magic, Ilaron pulled out the letter he'd taken from Denise Sheridan by sheer glamour: He'd neatly palmed it when handing her back the rest of the sheaf from the Children of

Sumer, and she, caught as most humans could be by his stare, had never noticed.

Phaugh. Once more, no physical clues—a cheap sheet of paper, this, that again could have come from anywhere.

And why, he wondered with a little jolt of surprise, was he even bothering with it? Could he really care what became of *humans*? Or was it just this one human in particular?

The puzzle, Ilaron decided. *It's the puzzle that intrigues me. Two puzzles, rather,* he corrected, glancing at the scraps of newspaper. *And, conveniently, the same spell should draw the truth from both.*

Sometime later, the dregs of coffee cold in his cup and the sandwich no more than crumbs, he wasn't so sure. Yes, there were tantalizing hints of strangeness, even of evil, to both. But there the similarity ended. The Children of Sumer were definitely human, idiots dabbling in Darkness like children in mud, while the little man . . . bah, nothing but the pettiest scraps of evil in him. But behind the *feel* of his aura was the barest, most frustrating suggestion of . . . of something . . . someone almost familiar . . .

Ah, useless! Suddenly wildly impatient, he swept the desk clear with an angry hand, then shot to his feet, pacing with short, restless steps. All that these hints of Darkness were doing was rousing his own inner Darkness.

No. No! "No!" he shouted.

Then he resumed his restless pacing, fighting the Darkness, fighting himself, fighting every instinct tearing at him, fighting—

Ilaron stopped short, throwing back his head in despair as the full force of Darkness tore free beyond all suppressing, screaming to him of what he had been, of what he was, screaming to him of the night, the night all around him.

Not again, no, not again! I will not!

But the night was calling, the night, the darkness, the hunt, the hunt, the hunt . . .

At last, with a strangled cry, Ilaron could no longer resist. Tearing off his costly suit, he flung on black slacks, a black turtleneck sweater. There must be a hunt, there must be a hunt—

But it will not be sworn to Darkness. Once again, it will not be sworn to Darkness!

Not even the wary doorman saw Ilaron slide past him. No one saw the dark figure prowling the night, a shadow amid the shadows, alone amid the crowds, unnoticed by humanity. He saw prospective victim after victim, but told himself fiercely, *no!* He would *not* harm the innocent, he would *not* slay those of the Light. Even though the Darkness burned at him until he could barely think, he held fast to this one resolution:

I offer no further sacrifices to the Dark!

But there was always evil enough to be found in a city this size. Ilaron let his breath out in a quick hiss of relief as he suddenly found his prey. There, ah there, that man, ordinary to human sight . . . ordinary, yet ugly evil clung to him, hints of rapes unpunished, of mindless hate, an emptiness of soul. . . .

Yes, yes . . .

Ilaron followed the man silently as he turned down a side street onto Third Avenue . . . no residences here, nothing but, frustratingly, stores still open despite the hour and office buildings fronted with glass revealing lobbies with wary guards within, but—

Yes, here, another turn onto a side street and blank brick walls at last with no one else about. Ilaron smiled, the cold, thin smile of the predator, as he realized that this human, too, was a hunter scenting prey, some woman leaving work alone.

Not this night, Ilaron told him silently, and sprang. The Darkness sought a ritual, burning at him to make this death slow, painful, but Ilaron, with the last shred of sanity left to him, refused the old, familiar, so seductive evil. He killed instead with quick magic, refusing as well to take pleasure in that kill or the feel of the life force draining, stopping the man's heart in an instant.

And in that instant Ilaron cried out not to Darkness but to Light, "For you!" not knowing if it was jest or prayer.

Slowly the madness ebbed. Ilaron slumped against a cold brick wall, racked by shudders, aching with despair. Had he really thought himself free? Had he really thought he could ever change? Even now, Ilaron knew it would be so very easy to slide back to what he'd been. There was so much possibility in this realm despite all its wonder, so much darkness hiding just beneath the surface. . . .

We are what we are, he thought wearily. *Like it or not.*

A sharp, high male voice said, "Well done, my liege"—and said it not in English but in Ilaron's native tongue. He straightened sharply, seeing red hair, pale skin, eyes as black and gold-rimmed as his own, a slight, lithe form like a two-legged fox:

"Reschet!"

"Ah, my liege remembers me!" The being performed an intricate, not quite mocking bow, dancing forward, though he stayed just out of Ilaron's reach. "I am honored."

Ah no, no, if he's found me, then the others have as well—

Fighting to keep all trace of that sickening shock

and horror out of his voice, his bearing, all Ilaron could find to say was a cold, "Don't call me that."

"My liege? But you are still that."

"I left such things behind. And you were never truly my subject."

Never mine or any other. Reschet had always been a tricky creature, switching alliances as quickly as thought—or whim—and loyal only to himself. "And what are you doing here?"

If they truly have found their way into this realm, I am doomed— No, if they've found me, surely if they have found me, Reschet would not be playing with me like this.

And Reschet answered lightly only, "Where great art may fail, simple craft and craftiness may succeed, and the small and clever may slip through cracks the mighty miss."

Damn you, Reschet! "Speak clearly. Or as clearly as your devious mind allows."

Reschet smiled coyly. "My lord need not fret! The others don't know of this sanctuary."

Until you tell them. "Enough delay, Reschet. What do you want of me?"

"Why, my liege! I wish only the best for my liege!"

Which, of course, could only mean one thing. Reschet must be anticipating a confrontation between Ilaron and those he left behind, and was, as the humans put it, hedging his bets, ingratiating himself with both sides, not sure which would be the winner.

But the tricky creature was so pleased with his own cleverness that he wasn't noting the sudden tenseness in Ilaron's muscles. He certainly wasn't expecting something as vulgar as physical violence. Ilaron, who had been among humans long enough to have learned from them, crashed into the being, pinning Reschet against a wall. Startled black eyes stared up into his own, more curious at the novelty than afraid—until

Ilaron dragged him along the wall to an exposed pipe. Reschet squealed at this sudden perilous nearness to iron and tried to wriggle free.

"My liege! My liege! If the cruel metal hurts me, it must be hurting him as well!"

Ilaron smiled coldly. "Is it?" he asked enigmatically.

Ah yes, now Reschet was genuinely scared, for one of the few times in his tricky life. "W-what has he become, my dear liege, what, if he is now invulnerable to the cruel metal?"

Ilaron wisely let him babble, giving only occasional alarming hints to keep Reschet talking. There wasn't much of use here; Reschet was beginning to enjoy the novelty of fright, and starting to say nothing but just so much intricately looping talk—

Save for one vital phrase. "That little man," Ilaron cut in, repeating it. " 'That little man' was the one bearing the forgery, wasn't he? Yes, of course—and *you* were the one who sent him."

Sharp teeth flashed in a snarl of a grin. "Yes, yes, so I did, clever me!"

Something cruel and delighted flickered in the being's eyes, and Ilaron knew in that instant that Reschet had afterward killed the human to leave no witness. "Why? Why send him at all?"

"How else was clever Reschet to track my liege? Only my liege could have known in one quick moment's touch that the statuette was false."

If Reschet could track him through negative evidence, so might the others. "Clever Reschet, indeed. And have you shared your cleverness?"

He gave his captive a punctuating shake, deliberately almost bringing Reschet in contact with the iron.

"Have you?"

A second shake brought the being even closer, a third—

"No!" Reschet gasped, curving his body frantically

away from the iron. "No. I told you, my liege, the others don't yet know the way here. Reschet won't tell them, either. That," he added indignantly, "would be no fun."

Suddenly, sleek as a rat, he twisted free, darting aside, out of Ilaron's reach. "But find it," Reschet added mockingly, "they someday will!"

With that parting shot, the being was gone into the night. Ilaron made an abortive leap forward, then stopped. Futile to try following the quick, cunning little trickster. But it hardly mattered. For all his guile, Reschet would be pretty much helpless in this realm of iron and sunlight.

As long as he stayed *in* this realm. And was the being telling the truth? Did the others know which realm he was in? Ilaron stifled a groan.

How close are they to finding me? Or is Reschet merely playing games? Trying to see what "the traitor" will do so he can report back to . . . whomever? Ha, yes, or is Reschet truly trapped here, caught by his own trickery?

Ah, ridiculous. Just the type of confusion Reschet had always delighted in creating.

Yes, and it was just a matter of time before one of the city's many law officers stumbled across the scene. He could not afford to linger.

Wearily, with one last, shuddering glance back at the human's crumpled body, Ilaron started for home. He had Warding spells to set and scrying spells to check.

It was going to be a long, long night. Much more so, thanks to what had just occurred, than ever he'd first suspected.

FOUR

Children of a Lesser God

His name, his mundane name, was Charles Sedgwick,
though his mother's family had come from Iraq. And
he knew that to those of lesser blood he hardly looked
memorable: medium height, medium build, a round
face framed by thinning black hair, ordinary save for
his one handsome feature, large, liquid brown eyes.

The eyes, he thought, *of royalty.*

Just as well that he bore such a . . . common seeming. No one who brushed up against Sedgwick on the
street or at work, where he was a minor employee in
an import company—a temporary setback, no more
than that—would ever suspect the fires that burned
within.

For here in their secret place of assembly, the basement of one member's somewhat rundown West Village town house—but what mattered the outward
appearance?—here, he was so much more than what
the fools outside might ever have believed. No longer
was he meek little Charles Sedgwick, no longer the
mundane, powerless nobody. Here he could reveal
himself in all his rightful, royal glory! Here was he no
less than Hanish, High Priest of the Children of
Sumer, the son of kings!

It was not a foolish dream, never that. Oh yes, his
father had been of inferior English stock. That was a
shame Sedgwick never mentioned. But on his mother's
side—ah, there, he traced his bloodline back through

the millennia all the way to the ancient Sumerian royalty, to the priest-kings themselves!

Only one other had ever known this secret truth:
late Uncle Haddad. It had been Uncle Haddad who
had originally told him about this wondrous, powerful heritage—

Uncle Haddad, who had been killed for his beliefs.
Oh yes, the rest of the family claimed foolishly that
Haddad had been "crazy Uncle Haddad," he who had
died under the wheels of an IRT subway train one
day when he went for a stroll on the tracks.

Sedgwick knew better. It had been a deliberate as-
sassination; there were those who did not wish to see
the ancient blood, the ancient powers restored.

Now Priest-King Hanish stood aloof, wrapped in a
woollen tassel-fringed robe dyed purest white, watching the others. Their robes, of course, lacked the royal
fringes and were simple brown. After all, they had not
a drop of the ancient, noble blood in their veins; he
would have known were it otherwise, just as he knew
that his rightful name was Hanish.

But even a king needed his servants! In daily life
they were an accountant, a clerk, an unemployed
something-or-other; such mundanity was hardly
important. What mattered, Sedgwick knew, was that
they were all as earnest as he, all as true to the faith,
to whatever could lift them from their hopelessly ordinary lives.

The ritual continued. As Sedgwick watched sternly,
the Children of Sumer chanted (softly so the neighbors wouldn't complain), "Oh Ea, Shamash, Asalluhi,
oh great gods, hear our prayers . . . "

As they continued, he allowed himself a little thrill
of pride: He had put these prayers together, painstak-
ingly copying them from books, then reordering them
as his inner voice told him was right and proper. He
watched, nodding approval, as the Children of Sumer

made offerings to the gods by burning some incense (only a little, again, so the neighbors wouldn't complain) and placing food at the foot of a stone statuette intended to represent Enlil: "God of Sumer," they chanted, "Lord of destinies, ruler of the world and the pantheon . . ."

A pantheon, Sedgwick mused, in which he didn't really believe, save for a few most potent beings. And for this one truth: The ancient gods of Sumer symbolized a pure, occult strength, a strength all but lost in these shallow modern days. Sedgwick meant to recover that strength, as did the other Children of Sumer.

But I alone shall succeed. Only I have the proper will, the proper blood. And only I will know the true goal: not merely Power but immortality.

The latter had been known in Sumer once, surely. Why else would it be such a central point of the Tale of Gilgamesh? An allegory, surely, of the true search.

The ceremony continued, following the prayers Sedgwick had drawn from his ancient, royal, racial memories. As they chanted, the Children of Sumer reverently unveiled a statuette: Lamashtu, the terrible lion-headed queen of demons. And at the sight of her, Sedgwick felt a stronger stirring of pride. That the scholars claimed she was Assyrian or Babylonian, not Sumerian at all—bah, they knew nothing! *He* knew, where it mattered, not on dry paper but in his heart, his mind.

And ah, the glory of this image! Unlike the crudely carved Enlil, which had been made by modern hands, this statuette was a genuine antiquity, so intricately worked that one could believe Lamashtu would unfurl her wings or clench her taloned feet. Sedgwick, his mundane, workaday self, had gone through a terrifying time during and after stealing the statue from an incoming shipment at the office—the one blatantly criminal act he had ever performed in his life—sure that he would be found out and arrested.

But Lamashtu had protected him, of course she had, she, the being in whom he truly believed.

Yes, he thought, thrilled, *Lamashtu, and the darker force behind her,* Minma lemnu, *"All that is Evil": No one can deny the true, eternal, ageless power of the Darkness.*

They made the same offerings of incense to Lamashtu that they had to Enlil, adding to it a small jar of oil and one of beer, and chanting in her praise, "She is fierce, she is mighty."

Was that enough, though? Was that proper? Sedgwick suspected, as he always did, that such a one as Lamashtu would have preferred a different offering, one more befitting her nature: something stronger, richer. He had sometimes thought about sacrificing a chicken to her, since live poultry was simple enough to find. But . . . a chicken? He knew, at the darkest edges of his mind, he knew what the proper offering should be, more, much more than any bird or beast—

Someday, Sedgwick told himself, *she will tell me what she wishes. Then I will act, then.*

"Come," he intoned, woolen fringes rippling as he raised his arms. "Let us begin our meeting. Let us begin the ritual of anathema."

Goaded by him, the Children of Sumer lifted their scrolls, reading aloud, cursing the name of the American Museum of Art in general and Denise Sheridan in specific:

"Let them be ensnared like the birds in a net,
    Let them be crushed like the ant beneath the foot,
    Let them be swept away,
    Let them be cast away."

"She and the museum both," Sedgwick hissed, cutting across their droning voices, "they have both failed to show respect for the past. For my own glorious ancestors! Look at those exhibits! All gaudy and profane displays. And those throngs of gawkers encouraged to come, sneering at the—the 'funny-looking stuff'—not one of them shows the slightest respect for the past! Hear, oh Lamashtu, hear oh fierce one, hear and heed! Let them be cursed!"

Something, Sedgwick realized with a shock so sudden it jerked his head up, was listening. He knew it, felt it, sure as he'd known his Sumerian name and nobility! Sedgwick glanced quickly about at the others, but they showed nothing, nothing, only went on with their droning chants—yet, for the first time, *Someone* was stirring.

Oh God, oh God, oh God.

No! Such fear was unworthy of him, of his blood, of—of Whatever was listening! Elated, terrified, heart racing so wildly he trembled, Sedgwick whispered, "Power will be mine. Power will at last be mine."

Ilaron was asleep and dreaming of his homeland. The realm had no sun and was swathed in perpetual gloom, but to him the near darkness was a normal thing. Only tall, graceful, magical trees that needed no sunlight grew there, and eerie blossoms glowed like so many white fires, but to him that eeriness was normal, too.

But this was not a pleasant dream. There in the endless darkness, under that sunless sky, he was about to put a desperate plan into action and escape that realm forever. In the dream, his motives weren't clear; he knew only a dreamer's overwhelming urgency. Urgency made his dream-hands clumsy as he struggled with the magic-guarded chest. Within were the gems collected during age after age of his family's long history, and they would be his if only he could get the chest open.

And, since this was a dream, time was skewed. He barely did get the chest open (sharp glint of gems within) before a voice said coolly:

"Ilaron."

He twisted sharply about, looking up over his shoulder to see Sestharalon. His cousin was a handbreadth taller than he, slender, elegant, as coldly beautiful as the realm: sleek black hair, narrow white face, glowing dark eyes.

Fitting, that regal beauty, that elegance, for Sestharalon was ruler here, and (his people whispered in terror and admiration) cruel even for one of these folk. Ilaron was his closest kin, various murders and sorcerous mishaps having taken care of everyone else, though there was no love between them; love was a weakness unknown in this realm.

"Clever Ilaron." Sestharalon's voice was smooth with mockery. "But not clever enough. I know your plan, cousin, or rather, your *supposed* plan—and I believe not a word of it. Self-imposed exile?" A wave of an elegant hand dismissed that as an impossibility. "What, one of our noble blood flee like a coward?"

"Think what you will, cousin. It is, nevertheless, the truth."

"No games, Ilaron. I know there lies a plan behind the plan. There must!" Sestharalon flung back the folds of his sleek black cloak to free his sword hilt. "This foolishness can only be part of something greater, we both know that: some devious and regicidal plot."

The idea of regicide wasn't shocking to either of them: If a ruler wasn't strong enough to ward off assassins, then he was not strong enough to rule. Or live.

"I'm not interested in your life, your throne, or anything else about your rule," Ilaron said as calmly as he could. "I wish only this, no more than this: to leave this realm and . . . " *And all that has come to disgust me.*

"And instead dupe some underling into slaying me?" Sestharalon gave a sharp, humorless bark of a laugh. "Oh, I think not, cousin."

"I am no liar!"

"This nonsense begins to bore me. No more devious plots, Ilaron. No more unbelievable stories. Fight me, simply as that." Sestharalon's sword gleamed free. "Fight me, here, now. Settle this quickly, cousin, or die."

Ilaron uncoiled to his feet, resigned, sword drawn. He and Sestharalon circled, graceful as dancers; closed, vicious as predators. No time for anything elaborate. Ilaron knew he must end this now, quickly, before anyone else intervened.

Sestharalon lunged, sword, body all one clean, deadly whole. No time to parry. Ilaron dropped, weight on one hand, pushed off, lunging up under his cousin's guard and felt flesh yield, felt Sestharalon's shock and disbelief. Ilaron scrambled to his feet as his cousin fell, dragging the sword hilt from Ilaron's hand. Sestharalon surged halfway to his feet again, eyes savage, mouth open as though to hiss out a curse. But blood surged forth instead. He convulsed, crumpled around the sword, then fell back, dead.

Ilaron, breathless and shaking, dragged his sword free, staring down at the limp body, not sure what he felt. Relief? Despair? Sestharalon was dead, and now he was, like it or not, ruler, and he—

Woke with a jolt, finding himself, to his unutterable relief, in the human realm, lying half-sprawled across his desk. Sunlight blazed through a curtain he hadn't quite closed, stabbing him in the eye. He fumbled frantically for his sunglasses, settling them in place with a grateful sigh, then sank back across the desk for a moment.

Sunlight. Yes, sunlight was always going to be a hazard in this realm. But right now he almost welcomed the alien brightness.

I am here, not back there. I am here, and my own free self.

The sunny openness of the penthouse was yet another reason he'd chosen it: His people were hardly likely even to consider seeking him in a place that was the very antithesis of their realm.

Unless Reschet tells them?

Useless to worry about that. Reschet was already gone from this realm, that much he'd learned from the evening's spells.

Ilaron straightened, then struggled to his feet, stiff and weary from having slept in such an awkward position; last night's . . . adventures had taken more out of him than he liked, and the dream had been far too close to reality, its shadow still hanging about him like so much psychic mist.

Nonsense. Human nonsense, to fear What Was, What Might Be.

Besides, his spells had also shown that Reschet's tiny breach in the Wall between realms had already healed itself. There was absolutely no evidence that the others had found him, let alone that they could reach him.

And yet Ilaron felt his face set in a grim mask as he considered, as he must from time to time, that this safe world, this bright new persona he had created, was almost surely a finite thing. They would not forget him, ah no, or forgive. Sooner or later, the challenge would come.

A silvery sword hung on one wall, as though no more than another elegant art object. But it was very much a using weapon, one of the few things that

Ilaron had brought from his homeland—the blade on which Sestharalon had died.

And any thief attempting to steal it is in for a lethal surprise.

A human would be instantly electrocuted, a nonhuman almost as swiftly drained of life. Ilaron snatched it off the wall and began a fiery, inhumanly swift series of swordplay exercises, a daily ritual intended today as much to work himself out of self-pity as to keep himself fit.

Breathless at last and feeling, if not restored, at least less hopeless, he set about the mundane tasks of bathing, coating his fair skin in sunblock, dressing, and brewing coffee. A brilliant human discovery, that last.

Wincing, Ilaron swallowed his daily iron supplement. Before he had worked out a safe dosage, he had nearly killed himself, lying dazed and delirious in an alley, praying with what was left of his consciousness that no human, no predator, would come across him. But since those dark early days, carefully calibrated amounts of the iron supplements had built up a fair immunity to the "poisonous" metal.

Ilaron replaced his sunglasses, the last weapon in dealing with this hostile environment, and headed for the gallery. Something was still nagging at his mind, nothing to do with his homeland, but about the seemingly harmless Children of Sumer . . . phaugh, the lack of sleep was fogging his thoughts.

The day was still milder than the norm for April, as only unpredictable New York springtime could be, too soft for the walk to be invigorating. The time was still relatively early, an hour or so before the gallery's daily opening, but his staff was already there.

"Good morning, Mr. Highborn!"

"A beautiful morning, isn't it?"

"Good morning, sir!"

Disgusting cheerfulness at this unseemly hour. But

then, humans actually *liked* sunlight. And these three, he assumed, had actually had a full night's rest. His kind didn't need much sleep, but there *were* limits.

He managed a nod and a muttered greeting.

Someone had left a *Daily News* lying across one desk. Ilaron glanced at it disapprovingly—a newspaper did *not* belong in this gallery—then looked again.

"East Side Rapist Found Dead!" the headline screamed, and Ilaron, after a quick glance at the police artist's sketch there on the front page, continued to his office with a grim little smile.

Last night's hunt really had been a slap in the figurative face of the Darkness.

The tranquillity of the office was restoring. Ilaron spent a few peaceful moments sipping a second cup of coffee and looking over the latest Sotheby's art catalogue, newly arrived from that prestigious auction house. Mm. Another estate sale, this one including various antiquities. Anything interesting?

Like his human colleagues, Ilaron had agents who went on international art searches for him, and trustworthy contacts who from time to time brought him items for the gallery. But that didn't mean he, again like those human colleagues, could afford to ignore the art auctions here in New York. Leafing through the glossy pages, Ilaron saw some nice but not spectacular Luristan bronzes, some agreeable but equally unspectacular Greek vases.

Nothing worth actually visiting.

Putting the catalogue aside, he casually checked a few sales figures left for him by his accountant—who was, naturally, quite honest; a stare into the human's eyes and mind at hiring time had assured that.

Ah, satisfying. Quite a nice profit, in fact.

His mouth quirked up in a sudden wry little smile at the thought. Humans, he suspected, might find the mundane details of running a business rather boring, but it was all still intriguingly alien to him. And after . . . last night . . . he was finding the routine surprisingly soothing.

But . . . the Children of Sumer.

With a sigh, Ilaron reached over and switched on his computer (*another* fascinating human invention), modem, and printer, logging on, then searching the Web. But as he hunted, he was bracing himself for an effort . . . now.

One quick burst of magic drew fuel from the gallery's electricity, pulled information out of the ether, filtered it through his computer and downloaded it neatly onto his printer. All around him, Ilaron heard the staff's startled "heys!" as the lights dimmed, then brightened.

No harm done. He had, Ilaron thought with a touch of justifiable pride, precisely refined the technique that he had invented; it now took only a few seconds to gather what he wanted from the ether, not long enough for the magic to be traceable, not long enough for the power drain to do any damage to the gallery's wiring, either. Unfortunately, human technology only worked on human subjects; he could not trace any Other who might be computer literate. But were any human foolish enough to commit anything to a computer . . .

Fortunate, Ilaron thought drily, *that I am not at all interested in espionage. Or vandalism.*

But what he saw on the printout made him frown and reach for the telephone.

"Ah, good morning." Denise Sheridan didn't sound too surprised to hear Ilaron's voice. Of course not: "I was expecting to hear from you sooner or later. About that cylinder seal—"

"A moment, please. We must meet for lunch, today."

"What—"

"Today."

"Can't you—"

"Not over the telephone. I will meet you in your office. Agreed?"

"Well . . . I . . . " Bewilderment in her voice, she finally said, "All right. Noon?"

"Indeed."

"See you here, then."

She hung up, still clearly bewildered, leaving Ilaron with a new problem.

How can I tell her what I have learned? The data is hardly something that would have been left on the Web for anyone to see, yet I doubt I can convince her I have suddenly become a a Hacker Extraordinaire!

And . . . since when *had* he become so concerned about others? Maybe he really was changing after all?

No. Not enough. Last night had proved that the Darkness was still very much part of him.

After an instant, Ilaron shrugged with fatalistic acceptance, straightening the line of his stylish Armani jacket.

"If you must be doomed," he quoted with heavy irony, "at least be beautiful."

FIVE

A Little Night Music

The realm was far from the human world, a land of smooth, pale grass, black-trunked trees and eerie white flowers, beautiful in a dark, chill way. The air was cool and still, clear of all scents. The heavy, velvet silence was broken only by the occasional soft burst of music or a thin, high wail of anguish.

This was the land Ilaron had fled, his once-homeland, the realm that the humans knew as the Unseelie Court, the evil side of Faerie. No sun ever brightened the utterly black sky, and the only light, cold and bleak, came filtering down through the gloom from sharp, unglittering stars.

Reschet chittered and grumbled to himself. He was only newly returned to his homeland, stealing quickly through the comforting darkness, still fuming over the rough treatment he'd received at Ilaron's hands, now and again stopping to rub a bruised shoulder.

Bad enough to be in that noisome realm at all, with its garishness, gaudiness, nasty sun, and iron. But to be attacked! To be grabbed and shaken like mere prey! Who would ever have expected one of the High Nobility to act like that? So crudely, so brutally—like one of those animalistic humans, yes, yes! Well, revenge for that crudeness would be taken, yes it would!

For a moment Reschet paused, head cocked thoughtfully, considering a revenge taken by . . . simply doing nothing at all. Surely leaving Ilaron alone in that human realm to slide slowly down and down into utter degradation was bad enough!

No. That was no fun, none at all. Much more pleasant to hear screams, see anguish, best of all to watch knowing that you were the cause of the suffering. Grinning, Reschet went in search of Kerezar.

Ah, Kerezar! A ruler, truly!

Sestharalon was dead, Ilaron fled. Reschet paused again, savoring the unintended rhyme. Dead, fled, fled, dead. Yes, yes, Sestharalon was most certainly dead. And Ilaron, who was his legitimate successor by right of bloodshed, had indeed fled.

And so the realm had seen a time of chaos and of terrible magics, what with every member of the High Nobility seeing his or her chance at the throne.

Not me, not me! Thrones are silly things.

Kerezar hadn't thought like that. No, no, ambitious Kerezar had fought and plotted, made judicious use of both violence and secret pact. And now he was the winner. Now Kerezar ruled.

Reschet's teeth flashed in a sharp, approving grin. No weakness for *this* ruler, ah no! Of course he must forever be watching his back, but that was the normal state of affairs for rulers, was it not?

Not my problem, heh, no, never that.

Kerezar was, as were all the High Nobility, strikingly handsome. *(I alone know the secret of that,* Reschet thought, *though I will never, ever be foolish enough to tell, I alone know that any who are stupid enough to be born ugly or deformed are . . . eliminated.)* Kerezar's straight fall of silver hair and his pale complexion made him seem almost delicate at first glance—an illusion that was swiftly shattered by the cool, almost scientific cruelty in his slanted black eyes. He was, Reschet thought with a happy little wriggle, the sort who enjoyed plots for their own intricate selves—yes, yes, Reschet could understand that!—and no one really knew just how many Kerezar might have in motion at any given time.

That Kerezar was safe on the throne at all (for now) meant that he was keeping (again, Reschet thought, for now) each faction at each other's throats and away from his.

Yes, a proper ruler, yes, yes, better than ever Ilaron might have proved!

And oh, he will be so delighted, indeed, delighted to learn what I will tell him!

A figure stepped smoothly out of deepest shadow to block his path. "Reschet." It was a warning.

Taller than many, almost willowy-thin, blue-black hair: "My lord Ahligar," Reschet recognized with a grin and a deep bow that hid a subtle sideways glance. No. The way was not clear to that side: an unfortunate stand of trees. The other side—

But before Reschet could dart that way, a second figure stepped out of hiding, blocking that route as well, a figure a touch more solid, almost stocky for that slender race: "Ah, and my lord Lehaiat," Reschet cried. "So, my lords, so! Strange to see you here, together—just chance, yes, of course yes. I see nothing but chance that you have come this way, to this precise spot, at the same time." *No sign that you work together, no sign that you plot, of course not, never.* But he was not afraid, merely wary. "What would you, my lords?"

Ah, but now there was a prickle of alarm, now a third figure had come up behind Reschet; the being didn't need to turn to know that. But a quick sideways glance, swift as a striking *tehtrel* told Reschet sleek hair, palest gold, narrow, narrow face: Arrainra. So, and so! This was interesting, it was! Three plotters, each of course never trusting the others, all three never trusting him.

No, they would not trust him. "Reschet." It was a purr from Lehaiat. "You have not been seen lately. Where have you been, Reschet?"

Reschet let his teeth flash in a sharp grin that was not quite a threat, never quite so obvious a thing as that. "Here, there, where the whim takes me. Yes, yes, around and back. Why, my lords? Why the interest, eh? I am no one, nothing."

"Are you?"

I have Kerezar's ear, sometimes, and that, that is what intrigues you, yes, I think that is the thing. "I am no one, I am owned by no one. No, no, never owned, not by you, not by our good liege lord."

"Really? And have you not just traveled here and beyond for our good liege lord?"

They know nothing. Else they would have chosen fact, firm words. "Have we not all? Are we not all loyal?"

"Loyal, indeed. We would be loyal to those who . . . sought out information. Or told us information now of what journey was taken, and where. We already know for whom."

Do you? You think I am Kerezar's toy? Ah, less than subtle, you three! Far less than subtle!

The three of them were slowly, ever so slowly, closing in on him. They might not know, but they suspected, oh yes, they did. They guessed he'd been hunting Ilaron. And they meant to find what did not exist: proof that the hunt had been at Kerezar's bidding. And too, they meant to learn just where he'd been—

No, no, my lords, no fun in that. Learn your own information, yes, as you will, but not from me!

Reschet waited, the very image of innocence, of total unawareness of the closing trap . . .

Then darted forward, straight at tall, lean Ahligar, who flinched reflexively. A duck, a dive, and Reschet was under tall Ahligar's guard and away, laughing. Magic quivered, struck, missed as the being dashed this way, that, but none could catch quick Reschet, none could strike quick Reschet down.

Safely out of reach, the being paused. So, and so, and so again. Three more would-be plotters. But Reschet could easily, easily avoid them. And Reschet would not warn Kerezar, oh no. If Kerezar was not strong and cunning enough to know of plotters on his own, then he did not deserve the throne.

Kerezar was engaged in tranquil research amid the glowing white flowers of his garden, standing over a slave stretched out and bound by magic to a marble table. His work was delicate, almost artistic, laying open skin and flesh with exquisite care, exposing nerves bit by meticulous bit; so that only the smallest traces of blood trickled down the smooth stone, and that, in elegant swirlings.

His face was calm. Kerezar rarely allowed himself the danger of showing his emotions, nor, he knew, was he sadistic for sadism's sake. In fact, he mused, pausing, needle-pointed implement in hand, he would never do anything for mere petty pleasure: Such excesses were both tasteless and foolish.

But that didn't mean he knew, or rather, wanted to know, more about mercy save that the concept existed . . . elsewhere. Nor, Kerezar thought, would he ever fail to take an interest in the slow, intricate, painful sacrifices to the Darkness.

A serene interest, he corrected. *One must never lose control. So unpleasant to do so. So perilous.*

And now, back to work.

Kerezar bent over his subject in renewed concentration, engrossed in testing this new means of torment, one that combined amplified despair with physical pain, watching the slow death of the slave with detached scientific interest, rating the number and intensity of the screams.

Part of his mind, though, was far from the experiment. Kerezar admitted without hesitation that he was hardly sorry that Ilaron's defection had paved his way to the throne. After all, he'd been in the midst of working out the details of his own plan to kill first Sestharalon, and then, when it became necessary, Ilaron. This way, his rise to power had been much more . . . efficient.

But for all his private satisfaction that things should have worked out so effectively, Kerezar shared a simmering anger with his people. The laws of the realm were—aside of course, from the Darkness—almost the only thing they all respected.

Our laws, Kerezar thought with only the faintest sarcasm, *are all that keep us from chaos.*

And Ilaron—ah, Ilaron was the foulest form of heretic. He had killed the ruler, which was a proper thing among the ambitious High Nobility—but he had done that slaying not for the logical, rightful reason of self-advancement, but out of mere self-defense, like some churlish underling.

Yes, and then, Kerezar reflected, then Ilaron had worsened that sin by actually *refusing the throne.*

Intriguing to see such perversion. Even, one might say, alarming.

Kerezar delicately readjusted an elegantly pointed tool, its handle filigreed silver set with the smallest of moonstones, along one of the slave's nerves, watching the experiment's eyes with care, since the slave had finally lost the ability to do more than moan.

Yes. There was still an excellently agonized response.

Ah, but Ilaron . . . the heretic had also, Kerezar mused, stolen his family's treasure. That the gems had rightfully belonged to Ilaron since the rest of that family was no longer alive was a minor point. It had been, Kerezar told himself, theft. Common, crass theft. Yet another sin.

More to the point, Kerezar thought, *there can be no greater insult to my reign than the knowledge that Ilaron has escaped and continues to escape both me and his punishment.*

There now, the slave had died, far too soon. Kerezar sighed ever so softly, his face showing only the faintest annoyance; this new method of torment clearly still needed work. He dipped a hand in the spilled blood, shook off drops onto the ground for the Darkness, tasted the blood himself to complete the ritual, then waved casually to another slave to clean up the mess.

Reschet suddenly appeared out of the shadows, as Reschet often did, narrowly escaping sudden death at a startled guard's hands—not at all unusual for the being, who one day, Kerezar mused, would miscalculate—and fairly bubbling with delight.

"Oh, most wondrous of rulers! I have news, news, wonderful news!"

"Ah?" Kerezar had turned from the marble table to seemingly absently let a long fingernail trace the petals of a glowing white blossom, watching the poisonous sap well up where he pierced a petal. He and Reschet both knew that there was nothing absentminded about it; Reschet shuddered ever so slightly, and Kerezar allowed himself the smallest quiver of perverse pleasure at knowing that had there been even the slightest cut on that finger, he would have just brought about his own death.

As he had, through a delicately poisoned garment, already brought about the soon to strike death of a certain would-be usurper, the former Lord Ahligar. In diluted form, the poison was subtle, stealing through the skin and into the system, working its fatal harm before Ahligar could have even the slightest of suspicions.

The death would be a clear message: no accident, this, no natural cause. And all would know who had been behind that death, and why.

Oh, not that the slightest treasonous act had been committed by Ahligar against him! Not yet. He had not taken and held the throne by meekly waiting for an attack. And as for the other two, Arrainra and Lehaiat? Kerezar had planted subtle hints. Each would think the other had been the betrayer who'd whispered their plans in Kerezar's ear; they would turn on each other and leave only one, or possibly none, alive.

Amusing.

With the faintest of smiles, Kerezar turned. "What news, Reschet?"

"The traitor, my ruler, the traitor!"

"Which?"

"*The* traitor! There is such a lovely, lovely chance of spoiling Ilaron's life."

Not by the slightest tensing of muscles did Kerezar betray himself. "Oh? How? Have you found him, then?"

"Yes, no, once, not now. My memory—you know my memory, ever-changing, swift, the wind."

Kerezar turned smoothly from the flowering bush. "In other words," he said over his shoulder, "you either won't or can't tell exactly where Ilaron is or how he can be reached." No use to threaten. It was quite possible that Reschet, being the unstable creature he was, simply didn't know, or rather, that his mind no longer held the information.

But Reschet was babbling on about other realms, strange places, planting enough hints, whether accidentally or deliberately, to intrigue Kerezar.

"Enough," Kerezar said shortly. As Reschet fell silent, Kerezar gestured to nervously watching slaves. "Fire," he commanded. "Water. Silver. The proper tools of scrying."

No need to tell them to make haste; they had all seen the slave die.

"Wait," Kerezar added to Reschet, who was showing signs of impatience. "Stay."

Reschet stayed.

"Now, Reschet, continue to tell me all that you know, that you can remember, of Ilaron and his hidden lair. . . . "

The words, vague though they were, would help him focus his concentration. As Reschet began his babblings once more, Kerezar began one, then another, then a long series of scrying experiments, each frustratingly brief, each offering the shortest, most tantalizing hints.

And then: one sharp, clear, startling bit of information. Kerezar kept his face coldly calm as ever, but he was genuinely shocked at what he'd just learned:

Ilaron had actually chosen to live among *humans*.

And in such a disgustingly perilous realm, too, where iron *is actually natural, and toxic* sunlight *as well.*

"It's true, it's true," Reschet babbled. "Ilaron has an immunity to iron!"

But Kerezar waved off that patent impossibility. No . . . Ilaron must be leading a miserable life, indeed, surrounded by the deadly metal and hiding from the deadly sun, and for a moment Kerezar, too, toyed with the idea of simply leaving the traitor to his fate.

No, he decided. *That is not enough. There must be a formal torment, here in this realm, for the sake of our laws. And,* he added with a touch of dark humor, *for the reputation of my reign.*

But what, exactly, was Ilaron *doing* in that realm? Reschet was hinting in his babblings something about Ilaron having turned into a . . . a dealer in human art, but Kerezar could hardly believe that, either. Buying and selling—had even so debased a member of the High Nobility sunk to becoming a *merchant*?

Surely not. There must be more to the picture than that, something deeper hiding behind the seeming innocence. Kerezar mulled over the scanty data, looking for plausible solutions. So now . . .

Could Ilaron have set up some dark, elaborate network? Possible.

If so, just how much power could he have already amassed? Unknowable. Yet.

This, Kerezar thought with the faintest of cool smiles, *begins to make the game only that much more interesting.*

Annoyingly, though, that while successive experiments utilizing the blood and life force of chosen slaves showed him a bit more about the human realm, useful moments of data, they failed to actually show him any way into that realm.

And after a long night of trial and failure, Kerezar knew he could try no more, at least not without rest. At a wave of a hand, a slave dropped to its knees, holding out a cool, restoring drink. Kerezar deigned to accept the cup, touching a magicked ring to it first, of course, to prove it free of poison.

Sipping, walking serenely about the garden, not allowing a trace of fatigue to show and never quite taking a predictable path an assassin might follow, Kerezar mused over what he'd learned, accepting with inhuman realism that Ilaron had covered his magical tracks far too well.

And Reschet, being Reschet, quite literally couldn't remember anything helpful.

An intriguing problem, this.

But one, Kerezar knew with calm certainty, that he would eventually solve.

Yes. When a problem seemed impossible from one

angle, the wise hunter turned to a different side. Returning to the now-clean marble table, Kerezar waved away all onlookers, then set Wards about himself lest some ambitious underling attempt murder while his attention was elsewhere. Taking a series of slow, steadying breaths, he set about his scrying once more. But this time he was concentrating with all his will not on Ilaron, but on humanity, on the human realm. . . .

Ah? What was this? The faintest of shadowy swirlings: Some foolish group, a human group, but brushed intriguingly with Darkness . . . Kerezar frowned faintly with concentration, ignoring the ever-increasing pounding in head and heart, tightening his focus . . . yes. Soon enough, he sensed them, the Children of Sumer, whatever that might be . . . lost them, sensed instead . . . what?

What, indeed? A strange sensation of stirring, waking Darkness, not quite like anything that he knew—though of course, Kerezar reminded himself, Darkness could take many forms. Some demonic force, though . . . yes . . . unmistakably that . . .

Lamashtu? Was that the entity's name?

So it would seem.

Lamashtu. Not the name of any demon he recognized. Not surprising, since the waking entity's aura was brushing upon . . . yes, he was sure of it . . . that frustratingly unreachable human realm in which Ilaron was hiding.

But this demonic awakening was not Ilaron's doing. That much was clear.

An instant web of plans flashed through Kerezar's mind, each plan in turn swiftly analyzed, dropped or revised till he had made his decision. He stopped the hunt for Ilaron completely; knowing that realm existed and harbored the traitor was sufficient for now. As for not being able to reach it—that, Kerezar mused, should only be a temporary setback.

With that, he set about reaching through the many layers of darker realms, hunting for the one demonic world in which a certain demon dwelt. He sought Lamashtu.

And, with a sudden burst of magical force, he found her.

SIX

Dangerous Liaisons

For a wary moment, Kerezar simply studied the demon, knowing he would *have* only that moment before she was aware of him. The winged, lion-headed woman-being, he mused, was beautiful in her own cruel, terrible way.

She is old, he thought, *at least as the humans measure time. Old and . . . what? Capricious? Most certainly bored.*

He could make use of that last.

"Hail, Lamashtu." The speech Kerezar used was nothing that depended on mere physical sound; it was the Unspoken Language by which his race communicated with demonkind.

And it was understood. "Newness." It was a delighted purr. "I know not your kind."

"Ah, but I know of you, great Lamashtu." Which was, Kerezar thought, quite true in its own vague way.

Lamashtu's great wings opened, furled, opened. "Do you, newness? Do you truly? Who am I, then?"

"A being of great age and strength," he hedged smoothly. "A being who receives not the worship she deserves."

"Do you truly know? I think not!" Her wings snapped open again, and her taloned fingers flexed. Her leonine eyes were yellow fog, swirling, deadly. "I am no petty little shard of Darkness! I am daughter to Anu, daughter to Heaven Itself! I did not fall, I was not banished—I *chose* to leave, I *chose* the Darkness!

"I am Fury, I am Rage, I am the Heart of Sorcery!

"I touch the water and it is poisoned, I touch a house and its walls are fouled.

"I seize an old man, and they call me Sudden Death.

"I seize a young man, and they call me Deadly Sunstroke.

"I seize a boy, and they call me Lamashtu!

"I seize a girl, and they call me Lamashtu!

"It is I whose touch destroys the unborn child, mine the touch that slays the boy, the girl, mine the touch that brings disease and death to all I see!

"And do you," she ended with a purr, "care to challenge me?"

A primal being. Dangerous. But . . . Kerezar smiled ever so slightly. "Mighty Lamashtu, do you think me a fool? I come with help, not challenge. You have," he hazarded, "been lost to humankind for far too long."

"Ahhh . . . it *has* been long, too long."

"Yes," he soothed. "Yes. They grow weak, foolish, the human beasts. They forget the proper ways."

"They do!" she snapped. "Once I had worshipers, those who feared me, honored me, pleaded with me. Now, now, the old ways are forgotten! For long, long ages no one has called upon me! No one has worshiped me!"

"I," Kerezar said sardonically, "offer you worship."

"I," Lamashtu retorted just as sardonically, "accept. For what good that does us both."

So, now! She might be old and bored, but she was *not* as stupid as the demonkind were wont to be.

A daughter of the heavens, yes. But a singularly bloodthirsty one. What, I wonder, went wrong in the heavens when you were engendered? For you hate the very thought of life, don't you, oh Lamashtu?

No matter. Her hatred was aimed only at the human realm. And that, Kerezar mused, could indeed prove useful.

"Someone else does call to you," he said. "I have sensed him."

"There is a genuine worshiper, yes, a worshiper of sorts." She shrugged, wings stirring. "A weak creature of little knowledge in a realm of softness."

"Will you answer his prayers?"

Lamashtu's sharp teeth flashed in what might have been a smile. "Only if my worshiper is wise. Only if he knows to give me blood, give me a life."

Kerezar smiled just as sharply. "The human shall do just that," he promised. "The way shall be opened for Lamashtu to return. But first . . . shall we bargain?"

"Shall we? Yes . . . that would be amusing. Let us bargain, indeed."

Lamashtu furled her wings tightly about herself as the strange not-human being spoke with her. No point in giving away any more of her emotions than she had already done: too easy to give in to the fiery rage that was so much a part of her. But no place for rage, not yet. This little being, whatever, whoever he was, this creature had a delicious aura of Darkness about him; he was clever, yes, nearly as cunning as she.

Nearly.

For though he was no young being, he was yet and again nowhere near her age. She, Lamashtu thought, who could remember the very beginning of things, the early days of mist and sunlight—

The days she would not see again.

No. No regrets, never that. Far, far better to be free, to do as she would, slay as she would . . . to know the ecstasy of pure, unfettered rage, the mad ecstasy of tearing a mortal life to shreds, seeing its promise lost for no greater reason than that she willed it, she, the slayer, the bringer of death whenever it so moved her—yes, far better the freedom, the rage, than any misty, gentle glory!

But this being who would bargain with her would not be impressed by rage. Clearly, he had long experience in dealing with demonkind; he knew to show neither fear nor overt contempt. Bemused, Lamashtu settled down to listen.

Ah yes, a cold, logical mind was here, as she'd suspected. And in that cold, logical way, she had to admit that the being was convincing her. Yes, ah yes, her hunting, her killing would be oh so much the richer, the more satisfying with his sophisticated aid. That he wished to enter the human realm to take revenge upon one of his own kind amused her; that he did not beg or demand appealed to her.

Yes, Lamashtu decided suddenly. This would cause redoubled chaos for humanity. This would cause redoubled misery. Yes, indeed. She would draw him to that realm.

But Lamashtu, devious as only one born of Light and willingly turned to Darkness could be, somehow failed to mention one small, small detail. She would, she decided but did not say, draw him to that realm—

But on her own terms. He would be transported, yes, but matters would not be *quite* as he expected. Too easy to send him to a realm with an army behind him! Oh, indeed, let the odds be more even. Then, Lamashtu thought with an inner shiver of delight, all the more misery could be unleashed.

Ah yes, I will enjoy myself! After so very long in idleness—I will enjoy myself!

Charles Sedgwick, High Priest of Sumer, stirred restlessly in his bed, coming suddenly awake, staring up at a still-dark ceiling, heart pounding fiercely.

He heard it. He still heard the voice. It would not let him be!

Throwing off the tangle of blankets, Sedgwick sat on the side of the bed, head in hands. He knew what it meant to hear voices no one else could hear, that was something that turned up in all the news stories of people who took guns or axes to other people: "He heard voices."

"Uncle Haddad. Crazy Uncle Haddad."

No! He was *not* crazy!

Then what was he?

High Priest of Sumer. Hanish. He should be honored, not afraid. Honored.

Sedgwick got to his feet, prowling nervously about the small confines of the apartment, pacing like a beast in a cage, shivering though the night was warm.

And all the while, the voice whispered. Whispered. *Whispered.*

What was happening? If he wasn't going nuts, who was calling him? Was it Lamashtu . . . ? Was it Lamashtu seeking him in his dreams and awakenings? Was it she sending this distant murmuring slipping through his brain?

It must be she. Sedgwick clung frantically to that thought. It must be Lamashtu, because the only other choice was—was the padded room somewhere. It must be Lamashtu—

No, no, it was! He could hear the voice clearly at last, telling him over and over, clear as words spoken aloud, what the demon wanted, needed, *demanded* before she would—before she could—manifest.

A life. Lamashtu wanted a life.

A human life.

God, no! Sedgwick threw his hands over his ears as though that physical act could shut out a mental voice, just then wishing with all his heart that he was nothing more than he seemed, common little Charles Sedgwick, the weird little guy at the corner desk, don't worry about him. This was what he had known all along, what he had feared, this sacrifice of—of—

No, I—I can't! That's—that would be murder!

But the whisper continued mercilessly, wearing down merely human resistance, the whisper of *Lamashtu, power, immortality, Lamashtu beside him, all power, endless, endless power and life, endless, endless life.*

And slowly Sedgwick's hands dropped to his sides. He wasn't a weird little no one, he was Hanish, born to great things. Here he stood on the verge of wonder, of greatness, needing only one step to reach the power for which he'd dreamed. Why was he being so so *small*? Was he not of the ancient blood? The pure blood?

And what if he *did* perform the . . . sacrifice? What of that? Was it anything less than the mighty priest-kings of his ancestry would have performed? Sedgwick stood with eyes shut, listening to the whisper with all his might, drinking in the words, the images of wonder.

His eyes snapped open. With a sudden flash of insight so sharp he staggered against the bed and nearly fell, Sedgwick knew exactly who the sacrifice must be.

Oh, perfect! Oh mighty Lamashtu, yes, yes, *perfect!*

Had she inspired him? Or had he used his own cunning, his own cleverness to extrapolate—

No matter. He need only wait a little, little longer. Then he could act. And after that, after that, mighty Lamashtu would reward him.

She would reward them all.

SEVEN

Theme and Variations

Ilaron stopped on the east side of Fifth Avenue, on the corner of Eighty-first Street, waiting impatiently for what seemed like a never-ending flood of taxis and buses to pass. With his swift reflexes, he had long ago mastered the New York art form known as "jay-walking," but it still would have taken more nerve than he cared to waste to cross too closely in front of all those hurtling boxes of iron.

The vast bulk of the museum loomed up before him on the west side of the avenue, stretching north and south for several blocks, its grey, sooty stone tinged with the faintest hint of reddish gold in the nearly midday sun—

Ah, the traffic light had finally changed. Ilaron hurried across the street, glaring at one motorist turning onto Fifth Avenue who did not seem to believe that pedestrians had the right of way. He navigated his way up the museum's outer stairs, weaving through the maze of ubiquitous Step Sitters—so, he knew, the museum staff called them—those museum visitors who had, as visitors did every day, picked the steps as *the* place to sit.

A stop at the Reception Desk inside the front entrance gained Ilaron a visitor's pass and well-meaning but unnecessary directions to the Department of Mesopotamian Art and Archaeology. He hurried on, weaving his way through the humans. And at last, after traveling through the seemingly endless halls, Ilaron arrived at Denise Sheridan's office, ever so slightly out of breath, just before the stroke of noon.

Denise's young assistant, Sarah, met him at the door. "Oh, Mr. Highborn." A hand went to her hair, absently twisting a blond lock, and Ilaron raised a brow.

"Please, don't worry, Sarah," he teased, somber-faced. "Your hair is charming just as it is."

Her hand dropped as though she'd been stung. "I—I'll just tell Dr. Sheridan you're here. Oh, ah, you can take a seat—oh, wait, I'll just move these books—it's not too elegant a chair, I'm afraid."

"Your touch," he told her, "makes it a throne."

She blushed, smiled, fled. Ilaron watched her scurry down the hall, and the good humor faded from his face. So charming, so young, so innocent. He would never tell her how nervous she made him—certainly not because he was afraid of her or attracted to her, but because that youthful innocence touched the Darkness within him, the Darkness that whispered, *innocence is merely something to be degraded*—

No. He would never give in to such utter depravity.

Even so, Ilaron was very glad when Denise came out to greet him. Her suit, since she could hardly have been planning to lunch with him, was an everyday outfit in practical dark blue, but she'd brightened it with a small gold pin and a colorful scarf, and he dipped his head in appreciation.

"Quite charming."

Denise was hardly Sarah, to be so easily flustered. "Ilaron, what was so very urgent—"

He shook his head, not wanting to risk having Sarah overhear. "Lunch first, questions after."

Denise hesitated, then shrugged slightly. "So be it. I've made a reservation for us in the Executive Dining Room. Shall we . . . ?"

They wove their way back out through the lunchtime crowds of visitors and staff alike, only to nearly run right into a tall, lean, clean-featured man in a nicely cut tweedy suit.

"Alan!" Denise gasped. "Ah, Alan Atherton, that is. Ilaron, this is—"

"Alan Atherton, Museum Director," Ilaron finished drily. "I've seen the photographs." *Of a smug, well-bred human, yes, with those twinkling blue eyes and those tasteful streaks of grey amid the nicely wavy blond hair.*

He'd seen the man, as well. They occasionally moved in the same art circles, attending the same social functions, but so far Ilaron had managed to avoid introductions.

More politic that way. No risk of letting slip any too-honest remarks.

No escape this time. Denise, who had quickly recovered her composure, was saying, "Alan, I'd like you to meet Ilaron Highborn."

Atherton was summing Ilaron up with so obviously mercenary a glance (costly shoes, suit: money here) that Ilaron nearly laughed in contempt. He had long ago summed Atherton up in one word: pretentious.

They exchanged the expected handshake; Ilaron knew about this human male test of strength disguised as a gesture of greeting and was prepared (inwardly sighing at this human childishness).

Then he saw his name register in Atherton's mind. The human smiled charmingly, eyes narrowing just a calculating bit. "Ah, you are *the* Highborn of the Highborn Gallery?" At Ilaron's wry nod, Atherton continued, "*So* nice finally to meet you. We never have seemed to come face-to-face at any social events, but Denise has often mentioned you in her reports; you've done a great deal to enrich her department.

Very kind of you. And a bit profitable for you, too, eh?"

That, Ilaron mused, was said with a rather remarkable combination of regard (for money) and condescension (for Denise's department and anyone involved in it). "I enjoy adding to human knowledge," he said without expression, and watched Atherton blink, trying to puzzle out his meaning. "It has been . . . interesting finally to meet you," Ilaron told him carefully. "Perhaps we shall meet again." *Not if I see you first.* "But now, if you will excuse us, I fear we do have a lunch reservation waiting."

And you are not *going to try to join us, are you?*

No. Atherton might be pretentious, but he wasn't stupid. He went his way after a parting shot, meant to be humorous, to both Ilaron and Denise, about "Socializing with the enemy, are we?"

Ilaron glanced drily at Denise, who was very carefully not meeting his glance. "My poor Dr. Sheridan." It was a fair imitation of Atherton's theatrically clipped British accent. "I now have more sympathy for you than ever before."

As she choked on a laugh, Ilaron just barely bit back an acerbic addition that in his realm Atherton would have been considered sporting material. "Why not," he added, trying to keep the conversation light, "give the man what you say he wants: a nice, splashy exhibit?"

"I've considered it. But . . ."

"Oh, come. The Assyrians, for one, were certainly a violent people. Can't you do something interesting with something as dramatic as that?"

She snorted. "Right. Something that will play to the public's love of horror and bring in a decent throng to please Atherton's avaricious soul. I didn't say that last."

"Of course not."

Suddenly Ilaron straightened, wondering, listening with more than physical attention—

Bah, no. Useless. In such a crowded place, filled with humanity of all kinds, there were simply too many interfering minds and auras for him to be sure he'd sensed anything genuinely odd.

"But . . . you know . . ." Denise was saying thoughtfully, unaware of his moment's inattention, "that's not a bad idea! 'The Assyrians: Civilized Killers,' or something like that. Not bad at all. Thank you!"

Are you still going to be so optimistic, he wondered, *when I tell you what I have learned?*

But he would say nothing of that. Not yet.

They hadn't noticed him. Neither *she* nor the man she was with had noticed him.

Charles Sedgwick, leader of the Children of Sumer, had come to the museum to brood, as he often did when he could steal away from work. And what if those who tried to lord it over him at his job complained? What if they even threatened to fire him? That was nothing, the mere mundane world, far removed from the sacred, the holy Sumerian artifacts that he came to secretly worship.

But today he had been watching Dr. Sheridan, watching for some time—from a wary distance, of course, not quite sure how to do what he wished.

What he must.

But the whisper was still in his brain, not letting him rest, reminding him that the Children of Sumer were meeting again this night. Reminding him that Lamashtu must be honored. Remembering that brief touch of Something listening, Sedgwick smiled thinly. This time action would at last be taken!

Denise glanced subtly about, trying with a touch of nerves to see the restaurant through Ilaron's eyes. It looked, she thought, very much like what it was: a small gallery that had been turned into a private dining room. Not really, she suspected, what Ilaron would consider elegant, though the peach-colored walls did at least give it an attractive warmth, and the framed floral prints lining those walls were charming.

Nothing of Ilaron's reaction could be read from that cold, quiet face. Scanning the menu, he murmured, "The choices look pleasant enough."

Aha. Rare that he was even momentarily distracted. Denise took advantage of the chance to study him.

Handsome, God, yes! Those clean, sharp, almost cruel features—Whatever ethnic group produced him did a terrific job.

The lighting was just bright enough in here for him to be justified in still wearing his sunglasses without looking bizarre or pretentious, and that added another layer of mystery . . .

Suddenly he glanced up over the menu. Embarrassed at having been caught staring, Denise heard herself mutter something about, "Your eyes truly are light-sensitive, aren't they?"

You idiot! That makes it sound as though you thought he'd been lying about it!

Taking many a woman's refuge, Denise fumbled frantically with her purse, not sure what she was hunting, hoping that she wasn't blushing too noticeably—only to have a forgotten paperback fall out of it. Ilaron, in one smooth, graceful movement, politely retrieved the book, and Denise caught a glimpse of the cover.

Oh God.

It was one of her "guilty pleasure" fantasy novels, not one of the intelligent ones, but classic Junk Food, complete with a garish cover depicting a grim-faced Dark Elf. Ilaron glanced at it, then handed it back to her.

"And do you," he asked, his voice so bland she was sure he was laughing at her, "believe in such beings?"

"No, of course I don't!"

"A pity," he murmured with an enigmatic little smile. "Ah, here is our waiter."

They placed their orders, ate and drank with nothing more than small talk about the Arts. But over coffee, Ilaron leaned forward slightly.

"Denise, the reason I asked for this lunch was that I wished to warn you. I have been investigating the Children of Sumer."

She hesitated. "And . . . ?"

"And I have learned some alarming things about them. The Children of Sumer have begun to worship the Darkness."

The melodramatic phrase startled her, particularly since it had been said in such a matter-of-fact voice. "B-but that doesn't mean anything!" Denise protested. "I mean, that's their problem, isn't it?"

"Ah?"

"Well, yes, the Children of Sumer make me nervous, I admit it. But there are who knows *how* many cults in this country, and most of them aren't hurting anyone but maybe themselves!"

"Most."

"Ilaron, cults are *known* for strange rituals. That doesn't mean that the Children of Sumer are ever going to turn actively dangerous. Unless," she added in sudden alarm, "you have some evidence?"

Ilaron hesitated, as though not sure how to word what he wanted to say. "Tonight they will meet again," he said at last. "And blood will be shed. Very possibly human blood."

Denise stared. "How . . . can you . . . possibly know this?"

"Let us just say that I hunted down the information

via the Internet. People are not wary of what they post there."

"Yes, but—"

"Please. Read this."

Denise numbly took the paper, which turned out to be a computer printout. Details of meetings . . . of a sacrifice . . . Her horror grew as she read too many details, too much specific description. Too many rational words—these weren't merely someone's psychotic rantings, and she looked up in shock.

"They really *do* mean to kill someone. My God, Ilaron, we can't just ignore this! We have to take it to the police."

But he shook his head. "We have no idea where in all this vast city the Children of Sumer will meet, who they are or even how many they number. What use is that to the officials?"

"But we can't just . . . Ilaron? What is it? You . . . don't think that *I'm* in danger, do you?"

"Perhaps not," he said after a disconcertingly long pause. "However, they *have* been writing to you. Circumstantial evidence, I admit, and it may mean nothing. All I can suggest is that you take extra security precautions just, as the saying goes, in case. Ah, here is the check. Permit me."

The sheer urbanity of that shocked her back to her senses. This was New York. Gentlemen did still sometimes pick up the check, and mad cultists only acted out their fantasies on television, or in some rural backwater.

Still . . . he *was* worried about her, or at least concerned, and that was, well, somewhat alarming. It was also, she admitted to herself, eyeing her handsome lunch date, not exactly unflattering.

All right, then, she'd give him some reassurance in return. "I'll tell you what," Denise told him. "I'll see if I can't pry an extra guard or two out of Security."

She suspected that it was not as much as Ilaron wished. But all he said was, "Excellent."

Sedgwick, knowing for the first time what was meant by an agony of nerves, lay in anxious, heart-rending-terrified wait for Denise Sheridan.

He prowled and lurked, there at the base of the museum's outer stairs, growing more and more nervous as the day faded and the night came on. Where was she? He'd had to give up on lingering inside the museum since the guards had begun to eye him suspiciously. Had Sheridan sneaked out some other way? Part of him wanted very much to believe that, to just go home and forget about—

No! Here she was! She must have been working late, but now here she came, hurrying down the outer stairs with practiced ease, never touching a railing, never noticing him. She cleared Fifth Avenue at Eighty-third Street, went north a block and turned east on Eighty-fourth Street, covering the ground with a New Yorker's determined stride. Sedgwick, never daring to pause, scurried across the avenue in front of a speeding taxi, ignoring the driver's shouted curse, then fell in behind her, his heart racing.

Damn, oh damn, these modern streetlights were too bright, eliminating shadows—that was the idea, of course, fight crime, he was all for fighting crime, but they just didn't leave any good hiding places! All he could do was keep following at a wary distance, past the pricey town houses and embassies, across Madison Avenue, heading to . . . where? Park Avenue, with all those expensive houses and wary doormen? Lexington Avenue, and the subway there? He had to catch her before she could vanish underground!

Wait, wait, they were passing a school, empty now that it was past the dinner hour and presenting a blank expanse of wall and yard.

Now, now, it has to be now!

Gathering up all his nerve, he attacked—

But Sheridan didn't faint or fall submissively into his arms. Sedgwick grunted in pain as she got him a good kick on the shin and, house keys clenched in her fist, raked his arm, his cheek, with fire. He clung to her with terrified strength, too wild with panic at his own daring and her unexpected ferocity to do the sensible thing and run off. One of them was going to get hurt badly, and he didn't know which—

Suddenly a tall, lean form lunged at him, tearing him from Sheridan with horrifying strength. Sedgwick fought back in utter terror, but this stranger was stronger than he, too strong, too quick, face coldly savage behind dark glasses—enjoying the fight, Sedgwick realized with a shock, welcoming a chance to kill—no, *no!*

With the sudden burst of strength of the truly desperate, he tore free, leaving a sleeve in his attacker's hand. One wildly flailing arm caught the stranger a glancing blow to the head, sending the dark glasses flying, but Sedgwick didn't wait to see what he'd revealed. He didn't want to know, he didn't want to see, he wanted only one thing, and that was just what he was doing, racing off in blind panic, his mind yelling a jumbled *runrunrun!*

Ilaron hunted frantically for his sunglasses, shaking, very much aware that the primitive grappling with Sedgwick had roused the Dark lust to kill. Fighting that inner battle not to slay his foe had slowed him just enough for the human prey to escape, and now it was—

Ha, there were the sunglasses! He snatched them up—

Too late. Denise had already seen his inhuman eyes,

their alien shape and coloring undeniable in the bright streetlights. "Who—what—"

No time for that now. Those in the surrounding town houses couldn't have failed to hear the struggle, and (rare for this city) someone was starting a fuss, threatening to call the police. Slamming his sunglasses back onto his face, Ilaron took Denise by the arm and hurried her away.

But of course Denise wasn't going to so easily forget what she'd just seen. As soon as they were safely out on the wide expanse of Park Avenue, she asked Ilaron bluntly, "Who are you? And—what?"

Could he fend her off with some smooth words about mutations? Humans did seem to be enthralled by genetics. . . .

No. She was not going to be fobbed off so easily.

"Do you remember the book that fell from your purse?" Ilaron asked warily. "The fantasy novel?"

She, naturally, exploded. "You're *not* going to tell me you're a Dark Elf."

"Not . . . exactly."

Ilaron started forward again, and Denise, after a moment, followed, insisting, "Where are we going?"

"Back to my gallery. We both," he added, with a glance her way, "need a chance to recover."

The gallery window was barred shut, of course, and the night guard, Harry, a stolid former policeman, was on duty—and rather surprised to see his employer at this hour.

"Mr. Highborn! Is anything wrong, sir?"

"Nothing. Let us in, if you would."

Harry obligingly shut off the alarms and unlocked the door and security gate, standing aside to let them pass. What he was thinking, Ilaron couldn't guess, but Harry said not another word, only locked up again once they were inside, reset the alarms, then calmly continued his patrol.

Good man.

Ilaron ushered Denise through the dimly lit gallery, steering her safely past the various pedestals into his private office, and shut the door.

Just in time. As he'd suspected, the woman was beginning to shake, belatedly reacting to the battle. Ilaron kept a bottle of good brandy in his office cabinet, since that seemed to be part of human sociability, and he had noted that a small amount of brandy seemed to have a calming effect on human nerves.

So it proved now.

"Nice," Denise said tersely after a few sips.

Ilaron nodded but said nothing, giving her time to sit and recover, giving himself time as well, waiting with inhuman patience for the questions he knew must come.

And, hopefully, would be able to answer.

EIGHT

Twilight Time

The brandy spread through her body like liquid warmth, melting away the chill of shock. Denise came to herself with a jolt, realizing with embarrassment that for who knew how long she'd been just . . . sitting here in Ilaron's office, clutching the now-empty little glass as blankly as someone lost in a trance.

Dammit, this was ridiculous! She wasn't hurt, she'd done all right against that attacker, hadn't panicked or frozen up or any of the other stupid things women were said to do in an attack. She had even drawn blood!

Blood, nothing. I would have killed that bastard if I could.

Now there was a chilling bit of self-realization.

Maybe not so chilling at that. Downright useful in the "big city." Survival mechanism and all that. And if she'd just had one hell of a shock, well, now was her chance to start recovering by getting some good, solid data.

And aren't we the tough girl? Denise jibed at herself, then realized that if she could still be sarcastic, she was pretty much recovered after all.

"Yes," she assured the wary Ilaron, leaning forward in her chair to put the glass down on his desk. "It's all right. *I'm* all right. But—"

"But you have questions. Quite understandable. Ask what you would."

You bet I will. "First," gesturing to the sunglasses. "If you don't mind?"

Ilaron obligingly removed them, sitting absolutely still and letting Denise look at his eyes as closely as she wished. She only just kept from drawing in a sharp breath in shock. Seen up close, yes, and in better light, there could be no doubt about it:

Alien.

Slanted—well, some human eyes were that. But . . . night black irises, larger than the human norm. Yes, and as if she needed further proof, those eerie, gold-rimmed pupils were narrowing slightly, contracting against the light. Denise felt a little shiver run up her spine, a chill weight settle in her stomach despite the brandy. Why shouldn't she be stunned? The world had just changed, no, no, it was all of reality that had just altered itself around her. To her amazement, she heard herself saying in what sounded like an amazingly controlled voice nothing more than a reasonable, "No contact lenses. No tricks. They *are* your natural eyes."

"Indeed."

I don't believe this, I don't believe this, I don't—
Stop that.

But what else was going to happen, what else was going to change, what else—

Denise took a deep breath. "I'm trained as a scholar, used to scholarly research, so I—I'll try to be as concise and logical as possible." *Which may not be very possible.*

She took another deep breath, trying to steady herself, then snapped at herself, *All right, woman, before you start hyperventilating, say something!* "To put it bluntly: extraterrestrial or extradimensional?"

I don't believe I said that, he's going to deny everything, call me insane . . .

Ilaron blinked, clearly trying to follow her admittedly frenzied train of thought. "Extradimensional, I would think," he said after a moment, "if I judge the word correctly. For I am originally of another realm than this."

Oh God. "Which?"

The faintest of smiles touched the corners of his mouth. "You are a reader of fantasy fiction. Therefore, I suspect you have at least a passing acquaintance with aspects of what your people call Faerie."

Oh God. "Go on."

"And you have, I am guessing, heard of the Unseelie Court, the humans' rather inaccurate but wonderfully descriptive name for my people?"

"The—evil side of Faerie. Yes." Denise eyed him warily. "You . . . aren't going to tell me you really are a Dark Elf, are you?"

The faintest of smiles, quickly there and gone again, flicked at the corners of his mouth. "Hardly anything as clichéd. Or, for that matter, as perversely romantic. Denise, I come from a realm where there is no such thing as your human sense of romance, no such things as trust or hope or sunlight."

"I . . . don't . . ."

"Hear me out. You would need to learn this sooner or later."

Quietly and unemotionally, Ilaron began to describe life in his native realm, for the High Nobility, for the lesser kind, for the slaves. Denise, stunned, listened to details of a world of everlasting night, of endless maneuverings for power, of an utter lack of love or joy, a realm of casual evil, offhanded cruelties, slow, deliberate torments—

"T-that's enough," she said hastily. "Almost enough. To convince me, I mean, that you are who and what you claim. Rather than just some very imaginative psychopath."

He never flinched. "Do psychopaths—yes, I am acquainted with the term—do they have eyes like these?"

"Of course not, but—"

"But it's all rather fantastic for you. And it could all still be a trick. I understand. Watch, then."

She wasn't quite sure what he was doing. Those amazing eyes closed. His face grew very still. Then she heard him murmur something very alien in sound, felt sudden static prickle through her hair and along her arms, saw the lights flicker for a moment—and found herself facing:

"Asurbanipal!" Denise breathed. "That's the Assyrian King Asurbanipal."

She wasn't foolish enough to think he'd conjured the real man. But this was a perfect three-dimensional image of the face and figure she'd seen on so many wall reliefs, an image sharp as a hologram, though she'd never heard of any holograms the size of a man—

"Illusion!" she cried in sudden comprehension.

And it was gone. Denise stared at Ilaron in new wonder. He was breathing a touch more heavily, and she caught momentary weariness in those eerie eyes.

"That wasn't a trick," she told him, almost accusingly. "You worked a spell. That was actually an honest-to-God magic spell."

"A small one, yes." His voice wasn't quite steady yet. "Convinced?"

"Y-yes. Yes. Magic. Magic's real, can't deny that. And you—can't deny you, either. And that means— Oh my God!" It came out as a burst of near-hysterical laughter. "You—you're an illegal alien!"

"I beg your—"

"No, never mind, I'm not going over the edge, honest. J-just give me a moment."

It took more than a moment. *No wonder I couldn't*

figure out his accent! No wonder I couldn't guess where he was from!

But there were more questions that needed to be asked, and at last Denise managed to continue, "All right, all right, I have to know this. If you're from such a . . . dark place as you claim, what are you doing here in the human world?"

What if he says that he's a scout? An advance guard for an invasion? Lord, no, that's too fantastic!

Oh, right. And all the rest of this isn't?

"I am," Ilaron told her, "a heretic."

It was the last thing she'd been expecting. "What . . . ?"

Was there all at once the faintest sag to that proud carriage? "As I've tried to make you see, my people's existence is endlessly cold, endlessly evil—and I came to find it endlessly sterile. I d-dared to question it."

"And that was all it took?"

"That was all it took."

To her astonishment, she saw that he was trembling. But with what was clearly a great effort, Ilaron forced himself back under control, sitting rigidly straight-backed.

"Once begun," he continued steadily, "the questions could not be stopped. I came to understand that if there is evil, there must be corresponding good, and vitality in place of emptiness. But there was no hope of changing my society, or of changing my life in my native realm.

"And so, for quite some time I hunted for an escape, secretly since not even my rank would have protected me were my . . . heresies found out. I discovered this human realm by chance, and I . . . came to like what I saw."

Denise caught the faintest flash on his face of— what? A memory? A startled, wonder-struck memory of realizing that what he had longed for actually did exist?

"I studied your realm," Ilaron said, small, banal words for the intense emotion Denise suspected he was feeling—though the coldly beautiful face still gave almost nothing away—"studied everything I could as thoroughly as I could, till I knew I could hope to survive here. The human world . . ."

And here at last the warmth broke free beyond his controlling, flooding his voice. "For all its faults, the human world is full of life and the joy, the sheer wonder, of laughter untainted by malice."

Wait a minute, Denise thought with a sudden jolt. *There's got to be something he's not telling me. He may have physically escaped the, ah, the Darkness— but how much of that Darkness is still with him? How much is still a part of him?*

Did it matter, so long as he kept it repressed? Most humans had a darker side, after all, and few of them revealed it.

Oh, right. But few humans could work magic—

Yes, but humans had enough weapons of destruction within easy reach, yet despite the headlines, few people actually did, well, turn to the dark side. Besides, that flash of startled joy on his face, the sudden warmth in his voice . . . nothing of Darkness there.

He's not human, she reminded herself. *And he can't exactly sever what he was from what he is. There has to be* some *residue.* And if he had—no, *since* he had turned his back on the past . . . *God, what a struggle, going against everything you've been raised to believe, going against your very instincts!*

She couldn't say any of that. "B-but why, of all the unlikely things in the world, become an *art dealer?*"

Ilaron frowned at her in indignation. "I have to do *something* for a living! I brought a goodly number of gems with me from my home realm, gems that I've learned, much to my delight, have an even greater value here. But while they . . . ah, what's the phrase? . . . while they certainly have 'bankrolled my enterprise' and continue to fund my investments, they are hardly going to last forever.

"Besides," he added softly, with what Denise thought could only be perfect sincerity, "human art in all its myriad expressions, the music, the paintings, the dance—all of it is so fascinating, so wonderfully vital. You cannot know, you who take such things for granted. It is a new world to me, an ever-changing, everlasting world, a joy of which I will never weary."

For the barest instant his icy control slipped, for that barest instant he smiled, truly, openly, transforming his cold face into something almost gentle—

Only in the next heartbeat to have the mask descend once more.

He doesn't know how to smile! Denise realized with a sharp little shock. *Not an open, innocent smile— nothing innocent in his native world. Social conditioning, I guess: dangerous to reveal any gentleness in that realm.*

I was right. He hates what he was.

For some time after Ilaron had finished, Denise was silent, too overwhelmed by what he'd revealed and by her own thoughts for speech. But then she straightened, feeling like a diver about to take a dizzying plunge.

"I may be making the biggest mistake of my life," she began, "and if I have, that life's going to be awfully short. But no matter what your background—no matter how downright bizarre—I cannot believe that you're evil.

"And I'm not being a romantic idiot, either!" she added more sharply at his raised eyebrow. "Look, Ilaron, there is no reason for you to have treated me and the museum with that unblemished honesty. You could have been cheating us six ways to Sunday, magicking us into doing whatever you wanted—yet you've never once been anything but honest.

"Besides, the warmth in your voice just now, when you spoke about this realm, was hardly feigned." Denise gave him a quick, mischievous grin. "And I really like your smile."

He frowned, clearly puzzled. "I don't see what that should have to do with—"

"Oh, and there's that little matter of you saving me from the attacker! Why *did* you?"

Ilaron hesitated. "I like you," he said at last, as though making a surprising—and surprised—confession. "It is a pleasure talking to someone with wit and intelligence."

"I suppose I'll take that as a compliment," Denise said drily.

But something of her conflicting thoughts about him, his realm and its customs, must have shown on her face, because Ilaron frowned and asked uncertainly, "Denise?"

Damn, she could feel herself starting to blush. But now she couldn't very well not say it, so Denise began awkwardly, "It's none of my business, but . . . well . . . I was suddenly realizing how . . . lonely you must be."

"I hadn't really considered it." His voice was flat. "In my native realm, there is always an undertone of danger to being in another's company. I'm . . . not used to being the object of non-malicious concern."

"God. No wonder you wanted to escape." But then her voice sharpened. "What about the others? Are they going to come after you?"

"If they can."

"Is *my* realm in danger?"

This stopped Ilaron short; apparently he had never really considered it. "This is," he said carefully, "a very perilous place for those of my kind, what with its sunlight and its heavy use of iron."

At her questioning eyebrows, he quickly sketched in his means of adapting.

"I applaud your cleverness," Denise drawled when he was done. "But, you know, I'm not exactly reassured. If you can manage, so could others."

"There is," Ilaron countered, "a sizable difference between invading and inhabiting a realm."

Before they could get any further, a sudden sharp *beep* made Denise jump and look wildly around. "What—"

Her stare zeroed in on Ilaron's computer. Which was, she saw, booting up all by itself.

Oh God, now what? "Ilaron . . . ?"

"I've programmed it—not, let us say, by normal means—to alert me when there is any message . . . ah . . . radiating is the closest word . . . radiating with the *feel* of magic."

"Oh, is that all?" It was a very small voice.

But Ilaron ignored her for the moment, studying the screen. Sure enough, a message was forming, scrolling itself slowly and smoothly up without his needing to touch the mouse.

"So-o . . ." he murmured.

"What? Ilaron, what?"

"The Children of Sumer are meeting tonight," he read aloud. "Just as I told you. And," Ilaron added, glancing back over his shoulder at her, "I was right about this as well:

"This night there will indeed be a blood sacrifice."

NINE

In the Still of the Night

For a heartbeat, Denise stared at Ilaron without comprehension. Too many shocks in too short a time, far too many. A blood sacrifice? A human sacrifice? Here, now, in twentieth-century New York City?

Hell, why not? she thought darkly. *A city this size— who can say what happens behind the scenes? So many homeless, so many runaway kids, so many perfect victims—*

But then Denise stiffened in realization. "That wasn't a random attack, was it? The man who tried attacking me—he was one of the Children of Sumer, wasn't he?"

Ilaron nodded, not adding the obvious: It was she who'd been intended for the sacrifice.

To her amazement, her first reaction to that horrifying idea wasn't shock or fear. It was fury, pure, hot, primal fury. "How *dare they!*"

Ilaron turned all the way around in the chair to stare at her, astonished.

Denise glared right back at him. "You don't get it, do you? This isn't some Third World country, somewhere without human rights, this is *America,* dammit! This is *New York!* And I'm not some poor little nameless runaway kid or some homeless addict without the sense to—I'm a curator, curse them all, every last cultist, I'm a scholar, head of a department in one of the world's greatest museums! How *dare* some fanatical idiot try to turn me into a—a mindless, soulless piece of—of—"

Ilaron raised an eyebrow. "Fortunate for him, I think, that he's not here right now."

"Very! Not," she added, deflating slightly under the calm stare of those alien eyes, "that I'd tear him apart here. Wouldn't want to get blood all over that nice carpeting." The first wild flush of rage was fading. "We . . . really don't know who or where that idiot is, do we?"

"We might." Ilaron held up a scrap of fabric. "I accidentally tore this from the attacker's sleeve during our struggle." He glanced at it speculatively. "Enough residue, I believe. I should be able to locate him through it."

Just a short time ago—a remarkably short time ago—she would have thought him insane. Impatiently brushing that thought aside, Denise asked, "Well? What do you need—"

"No. Not here. I will not work magic twice in one day in the same place."

"I don't . . ."

"That would create too clear a sign for any watcher."

He plainly didn't mean a watcher on any merely physical level. "Oh. Of . . . course." *And here I thought I had problems—at least the guy who attacked me was human! Lord, what a weird life he leads. Weird and perilous.*

"All right, then," she said, determinedly rallying, "where *are* we going? Oh, and don't look at me like that! You can hardly deny that by now I'm thoroughly involved."

"Yes, but—"

"But what?" Denise snapped in renewed rage. "I can't exactly tell the police that some nameless man working from I don't know where tried to attack me, wanting a blood sacrifice, only to be chased off by someone who—who's not even human! And I'm sure as hell not going to go home and just sit there waiting for something to get me!

"Besides," she finished in out-and-out fury, "if my department's in danger, I damned well want to know more about it!"

"Ah. Excellent points."

A human male, Denise thought, a little unnerved, might have argued those points further, been more, well, protective. Ilaron continued, without the slightest uncertainty, "So be it. We are headed for a nearby place that's at least a token closer to nature, which will make spellcasting easier."

Closer to nature? "Central Park?" Denise exploded. "We're going to Central Park? *Now*?"

Ilaron . . . looked at her. Merely looked. For an instant, those alien eyes were cold and indescribably cruel, and Denise felt herself shrink back against her chair.

He's the good guy, she reminded herself, *your own arguments proved it. The good guy. There, see, he's gotten himself back under control. Just another nonhuman having a momentary slip. Nothing alarming. Oh, right.*

And to think that she had started the morning in such a mundane way, to think that just a few short hours back she had believed with everyone else, everyone human, that the world was still a solid, stolid place.

But damned if she was going to back down now!

Besides, Denise thought, only partly in jest, *the plot's got me hooked. I want to know how this story's going to end!*

Cute. Much too cute. Gritting her teeth, Denise followed Ilaron out into the night.

*   *   *

The park north of the museum and the Eighty-sixth Street Transverse was hardly dark even now, but despite the intense modern lighting, shadowy corners remained, enough to remind Denise of every lurid Central Park crime story she'd ever read. Hidden from casual sight behind a row of bushes, the sound of traffic out on Fifth Avenue reduced to a dull mutter, she crouched on what she hoped were only dead leaves, shivering a little as the dank chill of the earth stole up into her. Ilaron, there beside her, showed not the slightest hint of discomfort.

This is insane. My shoes are never going to be the same, or my stockings. And if anyone sees us—right, I can just see myself explaining to a cop, "We were just, well, necking, officer, like a couple of kids. What else would two adults in business suits be doing kneeling on the ground in Central Park at night?"

And what *was* Ilaron doing? No light—but then, he hardly would need any. She would have welcomed a nice, comforting little fire, though. He was murmuring something eerie, and sure enough, she felt static prickling up her arms and through her hair—the feel of magic, no doubt about it. Exciting, she had to admit it, even though she was terrified at the same time. The nearest streetlight dimmed and went out with a "pock!" that made her start, but Ilaron never moved.

Just when Denise was wondering what she was going to do if he never moved again, Ilaron murmured, "I see a house, three stories . . . old . . . brick, faded red brick . . . a house facing no true direction."

Frowning, he came back to himself, rubbing a hand over his eyes. "That made scarce sense to me. What about you?"

"Mm. I'd guess that you were talking about a town house, one older than the standard Victorian brownstone. Well, that's not impossible; there are still a fair number of houses in the city dating from the early nineteenth century. Even some from the late eighteenth century."

"Well and good, but what do you make of 'facing no true direction'?"

Denise pursed her lips. "That, I don't know. 'No true direction . . . ' It sounds like something out of your world, not mine . . . "

"It's not," flatly.

"No . . . but . . . Ha, wait, I've got it—the Village, you had to be talking about the West Village! The streets there are so twisted some houses really don't seem to face any true direction! But . . . there have got to be at least a dozen likely candidates. Can you narrow it to a specific street, maybe even a specific address?"

Ilaron got lithely to his feet, pulling her easily up with him, impressing her by that touch of casual strength. *And he's so blasted* graceful, *too. And clean, not a leaf sticking to him.*

"I can," he said, "though I'll have to actually see the street and house to be able to identify it. And," Ilaron added with sudden sharpness, "we must hurry."

"Not before we call the police."

"We can't—"

"We can! Ilaron, we're not the stars of some stupid detective show on TV! For all we know, the cultists have guns or munitions—I *am* calling the police."

After a moment's hesitation, he dipped his head in surrender. "When we're closer to the site, yes. I'm not vain enough to think I can take on the whole cult. Even if I could, that would mean using enough magic to blaze like a beacon across the realms. Besides," he finished with a sharp grin, "there's a certain satisfaction in having the Children of Sumer most mundanely arrested."

Hurrying back out onto Fifth Avenue, brushing off her skirt and stockings as best she could as she went,

Denise flagged down a taxi by sheer force of will, practically flinging herself in front of it, arm raised commandingly. With a glance at Ilaron, she told the driver to head down to the West Village.

"Big area, lady. *Where* in the West Village? Or you just want me to cruise?"

"Just head on down, oh, Seventh Avenue, I guess." *And doesn't that make me sound ditzy.* With another glance at Ilaron, who nodded grimly, she added, "We'll let you know when to stop."

Ilaron contributed a flat, "Just hurry."

With a shrug that said weird passengers were all part of a day's work, the driver wove his way down Fifth Avenue, cut across the park at Sixty-sixth Street, and eventually went barreling down Seventh Avenue.

As they entered the maze of the West Village, Ilaron snapped suddenly, "Here!"

The startled driver hit the brakes so suddenly the taxi nearly slewed sideways. Ilaron and Denise scrambled out, Ilaron tossing money at the man.

Where are we? Denise wondered. *Barrow? Commerce? Somewhere around there, I guess. Haven't been down this way for a while.*

She glanced quickly about, noting with a New Yorker's automatic absorption of surroundings that on one corner of Seventh stood a record store—or whatever they called them in these days of CDs and laser discs—one of those stores, window covered by layers of rock posters, that stayed open till all hours.

And, wonder of wonders, there was a pay phone, a *working* pay phone, in front of it.

"Ilaron—hey, wait!"

Ilaron, ignoring everything but the hunt, was prowling down one of the narrow, weirdly angled side streets. Denise hurried after him, not quite having the nerve to grab his arm.

He stopped dead without warning, and Denise nearly crashed into him.

Ilaron never noticed. "There," he said intently. "That is the house."

Narrow, worn, and unprepossessing, it was so oddly placed on the oddly bending street that Denise thought, *It really doesn't seem to face any known direction!*

"Ilaron? Ilaron!" Now she did dare to catch his arm, alarmed at the savage tension in it. *Like grabbing the limb of a predator on the hunt.* "Listen to me. Listen! You can't attack on your own, we already established that."

Had he heard her?

Yes. Reluctantly, Ilaron turned from his prey, following Denise back to Seventh Avenue, where she made an anonymous call to the police:

"Cultists. That's right. No, I don't know if they're armed, but they might be. I don't think they have any hostages. But one of them already tried to kidnap a woman."

With that, Denise hung up, not because she was trying to be mysterious but because she was afraid Ilaron was going to slip away. She'd had to practically hold him there by force during the phone call, literally, with a hand clenched on his arm, very much aware that he wasn't human: He fairly burned with the effort not to hunt.

And, she thought uneasily, *maybe kill.*

Sedgwick's heart was still pounding so fiercely he was sure that he was headed for a heart attack. His mother had always said—

No, no, never mind that!

But he could still see that moment when he'd grabbed the woman. Who would have expected her to fight back? Yes, and then that—that stranger had attacked *him*! Sedgwick had fled in blind terror, finding himself down here without any memory of the trip, still not sure if he was more afraid of having not carried off the woman or of having tried to do it at all.

I've never done anything like that before, never!

But Lamashtu had been whispering in his mind all the while, prodding him to the attack, and here she was in his mind again, telling him that *she wanted blood, she wanted a life,* and if he craved her powers, if he craved his own survival, he had better provide both.

A victim, Sedgwick thought, and tried not to shudder. *We must have a victim.*

Wait, wait, look at that. Wandering out there near the end of the block was—thank you Whoever, Whatever, just what he needed: some nameless, near-mindless drunk. No one would miss the sorry creature; no one would notice the drunk's disappearance.

Why, I'll even be doing the neighborhood a favor, ridding it of such scum!

"Come on!" Sedgwick hissed to the others with him. "There's our hope!"

He and they warily circled the drunk, who blinked at them blearily, unaware of danger. It was almost too easy to grab their prey. Together, they dragged the filthy, feebly struggling creature down into the basement, frantically whispering "shhh" at each other.

"Tie him!" Sedgwick commanded.

But the drunk, vaguely growing aware of his peril, had begun to flail about wildly. Someone yelped in pain.

"My node! He hit me in de node!"

"The altar! Watch the altar!"

A crash, a scramble—

"Hang on to him!"

"I can't—watch out!"

With a furious sigh, Sedgwick waded into the struggle. Idiots! After several abortive tries, he finally got their captive properly tied, arms and legs, then backed off, wishing the ventilation was better.

"Straighten the altar. I don't care if your nose is bleeding—just do it!"

Oh, that he should have to endure such underlings! And it was petty of him to be bothered by the reek. Mere stench didn't matter. The creature wouldn't be around much longer.

Sedgwick glanced about at the others, frowning, thinking scornfully, *The Children of Sumer!* They had all agreed to a sacrifice—but those had been easy words. Now, faced with the reality of a living, breathing human being, no matter how disgusting, they were all standing frozen, suddenly plainly too frightened to move.

But Sedgwick felt Lamashtu pulling at him, telling him *she needed the blood, the life.* "It's too late for you idiots to back out now!" he snapped. "You can't!"

Before any of them could muster an argument, Sedgwick continued savagely, "Which one of you wants word to get out about your secret activities? You?" His finger stabbed out like a knife. "You? How about you? Anyone? Right! You're all as deeply involved in this as me—and if you don't agree, if you don't obey, well, wait till your employers, yes, and the media, learn about this!

"Besides," Sedgwick added, his voice suddenly cajoling, "the rewards for obedience to the Old Gods will be wondrous. Power. Wealth. Even . . . think of this . . . even immortality."

The words pouring smoothly from his lips, Sedgwick told them, "And what is this one useless creature compared to that? Hardly human, this one. Look at him! Filthy, barely able to stand, let alone think. And who knows what crimes he might commit, might have already committed, to feed his addiction? Crimes we can stop right now! Do you hear me?"

"Yes!" It was a dazed shout.

"Are you with me?"

"Yes!"

"All glory to us, then! All glory! This shall be a deed of worth, a deed of strength, a deed of justice! With our act this night we better all the human race! Hear this, hear me, obey, obey, obey!

"All hail Lamashtu, *ga e Lamashtu, ga e Lamashtu!*"

"All hail!" they shrieked, all restraint gone. "All hail! All hail Lamashtu!"

"Yes," he screamed, head thrown back in ecstasy, "*ga e Lamashtu, Lamashtu, Lamashtu!*"

Sedgwick was only vaguely aware that the words streaming from him weren't his. But it didn't matter. It didn't matter at all.

"All hail Lamashtu!" he shrilled, and raised the knife.

Ilaron, Denise closely trailing him, hurried back down the narrow street, only to stop short once more, staring, just barely keeping himself from pacing restlessly—or from charging the house in which he sensed, he *knew,* a clumsy, deadly ritual was continuing. There was a terrifying, alluring sense of Darkness rising, growing . . .

Where are the police? If they don't arrive now, if they arrive too late or not at all—

Yes! The police were there, at last they were there, but almost too late. The ritual, Ilaron knew without needing to see it, was almost at its peak, the knife, the knife was being drawn across the victim's throat . . .

. . . *the blood spurts out, the rich red blood, and the Darkness is there, rising, rising—*

"No!" Ilaron screamed in sudden realization. Without another word, he grabbed Denise's arm, dragging her away with him, half carrying her in his panic.

"Ilaron! What—"

Behind them, the world suddenly exploded into fury. And an invisible hand seemed to pick them up and hurl them to the ground, glass shattering around them.

TEN

Ode to Joy

Denise and Ilaron struggled back to their feet, unhurt save for bruises and scratches, but breathless and disheveled. Ears still ringing from the noise, Denise looked back over her shoulder in disbelief at the smoldering wreckage of what had been a town house. Miraculously, the surrounding houses hadn't come down with it.

"A bomb!" It came out as a gasp. "That's it, they *did* have munitions!"

"More than that." Ilaron's voice was choked. "Much more. Worse." As Denise stared at him, he tried in desperate, broken words to describe what was happening: "Darkness. Demon. Terrible being . . . hole torn in—in reality. Too sudden— Knows me, what I am . . . calling me, Darkness pulling at me . . . and I—I—I cannot fight the lure!"

God, the torment on his face! In that moment, any doubts she'd had about him were gone. "I can," Denise said shortly, and grabbed his arm—

And in that moment of contact knew, *felt* the Darkness out there, felt it, mercifully, not with the full force Ilaron must be experiencing, but enough to realize that she had to get him, them, out of there *fast*!

All around them, people were rushing out of surrounding houses in a panicky need to know what just happened to their world. But Denise, with the strength of a truly desperate woman, fought her way through the mobs, pulling Ilaron with her, away from the chaos.

But where could she go? Where could she get him away from—from whatever was back there?

Ha, yes! Suddenly inspired, she half dragged Ilaron out onto the mercifully more normal width of Seventh Avenue, looking fiercely about. Nothing but ordinary traffic here so far, and the record store, where was the—

Ha, yes again, there it was, and yes, it was still open!

The startled clerk, a scrawny teenager engrossed in a *Rolling Stone,* looked up in alarm as a wild-eyed, disheveled woman dragged a wild-faced disheveled man to the earphones used to let customers sample CDs.

"Classical CDs!" she shouted. Wordless, mouth open, he pointed.

A small section, too small, but they should have, they must have . . . Denise leafed frantically through the CDs, cried out in triumph and pulled one out. Wrestling with the CD's nearly impervious packaging—dammit, dammit, why did they use plastic you needed a blowtorch to open, what was this, safe recording or something—she finally tore it apart by brute force, all the while terrified that Ilaron, who was standing beside her far too tensely, was going to break and rush outside. Dropping the CD in the machine, quickly adjusting the volume so she wouldn't deafen him, Denise jammed the earphones over Ilaron's ears and pressed "Play."

Then she stood, watching, panting, thinking that she was going to have a good, old-fashioned case of hysterics when this was all over, but not now, not here, as Ilaron listened to Beethoven, to the Ninth Symphony, to the glorious fourth movement, the "Ode to Joy," listened to the music that was all joy, all hope, all Light.

Oh God, let this work, please, please, let this work!

And slowly, to Denise's breathless relief, she saw the torment slide away from Ilaron's face. The wildly joyous music was, as she prayed, helping him, giving him a wall to shut out the Darkness.

Wherever it is, whatever it is. At least it doesn't seem to know about me, God, I hope it doesn't know about me . . .

The clerk, meanwhile, had recovered enough to stammer out indignant, confused words. "Who— what—what the hell—"

Denise turned to him. "Flashback," she said succinctly. "Gulf War."

Oh. He nodded knowingly.

"The explosion," she continued. "Didn't you hear it?"

"Well, sure, I heard something. Thought it was a truck backfiring or something. You know."

But at the sudden wail of sirens, the teen dropped his magazine and hurried to the door. "Jesus, there really is something happening out there. Cop cars— ambulances—what was it, a bomb?"

"I guess so," Denise said in weary, wary understatement. "Something like that."

Ilaron, vaguely aware of Denise and the outside world, was doing more than merely listening to the glorious music. He was using it to fuel his will, sending the power and joy of it out and out with all his strength, throwing off the Darkness, sending the Darkness flying away as though it had struck against a smooth wall: *no one here, nothing here.*

At last he dared to take the earphones from his head, listening with more than physical hearing . . .

Nothing. Nothing but the psychic echoes of pain and death. The demon was gone, though where and for how long, he could not say.

Denise was watching him warily. "Are you all right?"

He nodded, suddenly aware how he and she both were scratched and bruised from the blast that had hurled them to the ground—till this moment, he'd felt nothing physical at all. And suddenly he was aware, as well, of being unutterably weary, more weary than ever he could recall having been in this realm.

The demon . . . the Darkness . . . took strength . . . too much strength . . . warding off the Darkness . . .

Oh, how he ached to sleep . . . just go home during this temporary lull and sleep. Denise, he knew from a glance at her drawn face, felt the same.

"We're safe now," he reassured her. "Reasonably safe." The words felt as though they were being forced through a thick veil of fog. "Just the same . . . just the same, I intend to see you home."

Reasonably safe? Denise, aware that Ilaron wasn't the sort to be merely, humanly, chivalrous, wasn't so sure about their being safe at all. But he was clearly in no condition for an argument.

And I have to admit I'm glad of the escort.

For what it was worth. During the ride in the taxi they had miraculously managed to snag amid the confusion outside, Ilaron sat blank-faced and silent, as close, Denise thought, to being unconscious as was possible for someone still sitting bolt upright. Her subtle touch of his hand, as though she'd brushed it by accident, brought no weird sense of *Darkness out there*. He was merely . . . weary. Fighting off the Darkness, resisting its lure, must have taken everything out of him. It was Denise who had to pay the bemused driver, Denise who had to maneuver Ilaron into the building, onto and then off the elevator.

And by the time they had reached the door to her one-bedroom apartment, Denise knew without a doubt that her escort wasn't going to make it to his own home.

I always thought it was a cliché, describing someone as "out on his feet." But he certainly is that.

Sure enough, as soon as she'd let them into her bookcase-lined living room, murmuring something about, "Trite line, but I really do have a perfectly comfortable couch," Ilaron collapsed full length onto the fortunately carpeted floor.

For one heart-stopping moment, Denise was sure he was dead. Dropping to her knees at his side, she seized a wrist, fumbling for a pulse—

To her unutterable relief, she found one. A steady one, too. Though he lay exactly as he had fallen, not moving in the slightest, Ilaron was merely lost in totally exhausted sleep.

But this is a ridiculous way for him to spend the night.

"Ilaron . . . ? Ilaron?"

Nothing. Denise gingerly shook the hand she was holding. Still nothing. She released his hand and shook him more firmly by the shoulder, trying to rouse him enough to get him onto the more comfortable couch. But Ilaron didn't stir or even make a sound.

At last Denise got to her feet in surrender, hands on hips, looking down at him.

Wonderful. Just wonderful. She'd been attacked by a cultist, taken part in conjurings in Central Park, nearly gotten blown up, and now she had a—a Dark Elf or whatever he was asleep on her rug.

Just another day in New York.

Not knowing what else to do, Denise threw a blanket over him, then tiptoed into her bedroom. She returned after a moment, marking pen in hand, and penned Sumerian and Babylonian cuneiform charms against evil over all the windows and doors.

Feeling a little foolish, she paused, looking down

again at her unexpected guest. Not every day that she had a strikingly handsome man asleep in her apartment.

A pity he's so exhausted, Denise thought wickedly, then added, *and not human.*

Ah well. Life went on, and handsome men on her floor, lurking Children of Sumer, and whatever else might be out there notwithstanding, she still had to go to work in the morning.

But of course, Denise thought much later, lying in bed, eyes wide-open, she was by now both far too tired and wired to sleep. Here she was, as awake as ever, trying to block the memory of that terrible explosion from her mind.

More than an explosion. Ilaron had said that something of Darkness had been released . . . yes, by the Children of Sumer . . . something presumably very powerful if it had had such an effect on him—powerful enough that she had felt the echo of it just from holding Ilaron's arm.

Why am I not hysterical? I should be hysterical. I mean, I've earned the right to a full-fledged nervous breakdown: magic, demons, cultists—the whole world turned upside down. I should be screaming or sobbing or something nice and dramatic. I should definitely not be feeling . . . God, I can't be enjoying myself, that doesn't make sense! Have I had that breakdown and not yet realized it? Is that possible? Or am I just now going merrily over the edge?

No. Ilaron was undeniably real, undeniably lying out there totally zoned, or whatever the current slang might be, on her rug. And if she could accept him and his magic and all the rest of that, she could accept that demons were real, too.

Of course. No problem.

Hell, considering the headlines, seeing what good old

human beings can do to each other, something as old-fashioned as a demon shouldn't be so alarming.

What had it been, though? Or maybe, who?

Come on, woman, think. Logic beats hysteria.

All right. A bunch of cultists. No magic to them, just lots of fervor. What would they, *could* they, have released? Nothing of good old medieval demonology, that was certain, not with a cult name like the Children of Sumer. What, then . . . ?

Gradually, the scholar in her took over. Giving up on sleep altogether, Denise threw on a robe (good and concealing, just in case, since she wasn't sure what she might find—or do—were Ilaron to wake), grabbed a pocket flashlight, and tiptoed back out to the living room.

Her guest was still very much asleep.

Disappointed, are we?

Don't be a fool.

There wasn't a sound from Ilaron save soft, regular breathing; his kind apparently didn't snore.

One point in their favor.

No time for silliness. Denise went hunting for the books she wanted by the flashlight's little beam, glad that she'd been scholarly or bored enough one grey winter's day to have alphabetized everything. It wasn't easy managing an armful of books and a flashlight without dropping anything or banging into anything, but she did it.

Safely back in her bedroom, wondering if she was being foolish or a realist, Denise searched down the various lists of Mesopotamian demons. Tiny print, some of it blurry. A good many unnamed evil beings from Sumer, Assyria, Babylonia, a few more with definite "personalities": *Asakku,* a sort of demonic Gang of Seven—no, from what Ilaron had said, there was only one demon, not a gang. *Bel Uri* was Lord of the Roof, whatever that meant—unless the cultists were into architecture, no, again. *Bennu* seemed to be a minor demon who caused fits. Definitely not that one! *Lamashtu* . . . well, there was a major demon, all right, demon of disease, but . . .

Denise sighed, yawned. Too many of the evil critters, far too many. Paranoid types, those ancient Mesopotamians, or maybe a few anal-compulsive scholars of the day with far too much free time.

Shredding a tissue for want of better bookmarks, Denise marked pertinent pages. Too many of those, too.

Ah well. No way to come to any clear conclusions, not this night. She finally gave up the search when she was caught by surprise by a yawn so mighty she nearly dislocated her jaw. In the middle of closing the books, letting them slide to the floor as softly as possible, Denise slid off as well, into an exhausted well of sleep.

Sedgwick had been wandering about in the night for some time, too dazed to quite understand what had happened. He still wasn't sure where he was . . . he wasn't really sure of anything. The last clear memory he had was of . . . was of cutting the throat of the sacrifice, yes, and of his horror and that perverse feeling of power at the gush of blood and the knowledge that he, *he,* had taken a life.

Then there had been the eruption of—of . . . the explosion of . . .

He wasn't sure. As far as he could guess, he alone had survived the—the blast. Yes . . . and so far no one had even noticed his absence.

Foolish little human. I notice. But you know nothing, nothing.

She was shielding him, inhabiting him, she, the demon Lamashtu, a part of him for the moment and, ah, yes, yes, she was so wonderfully, so savagely delighted at being back in the flesh-and-blood world!

After so long, so long: yes and yes and yes!

Lamashtu could sense the teeming life all around her, and she laughed through Sedgwick, feeling the old, fierce flame of rage sweet as joy stirring within her, welcoming it.

Oh, but this new realm was going to be good hunting for her! Demon of disease and death that she was, it was going to be wondrous hunting!

Lamashtu reached out with Sedgwick's hand to shove a startled passerby, who snapped an angry remark, then staggered a few steps and fell, choking, fighting for air, already dying, blood oozing from the pores of his skin.

Ah yes, she thought, *this realm will make good hunting, wondrous hunting, indeed!*

ELEVEN

Stranger in a Strange Land

Kerezar fell helplessly to his knees, frantically stifling a scream. Nothing had prepared him for this! Nothing *could* have prepared him for this, for the sudden onslaught on all his senses as Lamashtu tore him from his realm, pulled him into the human realm after her—

And then dropped him into this wild blaze of sight, sound, stench, the harsh artificial light, the iron, the deadly iron all around him. Gasping, he flung a hand over his eyes, forcing himself with every scrap of will not to cry out, not to fall flat in horror.

Instantly he was aware of how the demon had tricked him, played him false—for he was in this human realm *alone,* with none of his guards behind him.

But right then, stunned, alone, amid all the gaudy sound and light and iron, he could think of nothing but struggling to his feet and madly, frantically, hunting for shelter.

There! That shed was wood, only that, blessedly free from iron. Crawling inside his temporary sanctuary, trying not to notice the foul odors, Kerezar huddled for a time, helpless as a slave, waiting for his senses to adjust.

They will adjust. They will. He repeated that like a calming discipline. *Ilaron survives here. My senses will adjust.*

As they gradually did. Panic lessened. His mind

started thinking clearly once more; his dazzled vision began to return to normal, even with all that abrasive artificial light blazing outside the shed.

Logic. Organization. Calmness. Separate the chaotic mass into manageable items. Question, then answer, till chaos was gone.

Point: He was alone here. The demon had betrayed him.

Answer: A nuisance, not a true problem. He was, Kerezar knew, quite competent to take Ilaron by himself. Granted, it must be done swiftly, before those left behind in his realm spread too many awkward rumors. But that, too, should not prove a true problem. Should tools be needed, there were certain to be suitable humans.

Point: This was a very foreign realm.

Answer: Again, a nuisance, a minor peril. It was, after all, no more than a human realm, one of the many inhabited by those creatures. Thanks to his studies, he was wearing a reasonable imitation of human garb, and knew the language spoken in this city, as well as some of its customs. That should serve. He could swiftly learn anything else he needed to know.

Could he? *Ah, the iron, the light, the blinding, blazing—*

No. Logic. Control.

Point: He had no idea where to find Ilaron, or where, for that matter, he was.

Answer: A human would easily, willing or not, serve as guide. And this was a literate society; they would have maps, data from which he could make deductions.

Point: He needed shelter, funding.

Answer: Funding could be easily taken. Shelter could, with a little careful questioning, be found.

So be it. The cold logic of the equations was helping. As was the knowledge that he was, even in these surroundings, still himself.

He would not panic again.

At last, looking around at his foul sanctuary with disgust, Kerezar felt confident enough to step out of hiding, brushing off his clothing and, despite his self-control, fuming a bit at the humiliation—

"Well, guys, look at this!"

"Aw, pretty thing, ain't it?"

Kerezar stiffened, looking up to find himself suddenly face-to-face with a group of humans. Young males, he guessed. Yes, and ugly creatures as well, their heads shaven, their clothing bizarrely torn and pierced in what seemed a deliberate fashion.

And in their eyes flickered unmistakable bloodlust. Kerezar saw them register his long, silky, silvery hair and elegant features, and saw the bloodlust brighten. He had no idea what "Fag!" or "Gay bastard!" meant, but these fools had obviously just mistaken him for prey.

I am in no mood for human stupidity!

No need to waste magic on such scum. His sword was drawn in one smooth blur. A quick, efficient thrust sent one human gasping out his life on the pavement. The others—

The others were suitably impressed, as well they might be, hovering on the edge of attack or flight, too stunned by the swiftness of death to act. For an instant, Kerezar toyed with making a proper sacrifice to the Darkness out of them all, and took one smooth step forward.

But then he stopped, senses alert, drinking in the evil surrounding them. True, it was petty, nasty, ridiculous compared to the grandeur of true Darkness, but it was . . . valuable, perhaps? Might these ugly young things possibly prove useful?

Perhaps. Time to impress them before the young

fools did run or, more stupidly, tried another attack. Kerezar delicately wiped the slight bloodstain from his blade, flicked a token drop to the pavement, tasted a second, making sure they'd seen, then gave the teens their first chance to see his eyes clearly, holding them with his stare, willing them into submission. As he silently ordered, the slain human was forgotten—

But to his surprise the humans' submission came in the form not of fawning or pleading, but of much excited whispering and unfeigned, unforced, admiring glances.

What are *they nattering about? Hellraiser? Candyman? Ah . . . some horrific form of entertainment, I would guess.*

Whatever type it had been, they must have had a steady diet of it. And that entertainment had evidently taught them a perverse lesson. For they were staring at him not in fear, or rather not in fear alone but with awe as well, true, dazed religious awe.

"Satan!"

"Prince of Darkness!"

After a second's confusion, he realized, *They think I'm their force of Ultimate Evil! How charming. And how kind of me: I have given them faith where they had none. Oh, and how very fortuitous.*

He granted them all his coldest, cruelest smile and the slightest, most condescending dip of his head. "Perhaps." It was a purr. "And if I were he of whom you speak? If that were so, why, I might be truly . . . grateful to those who aided me."

Their fallen comrade was by now completely forgotten, erased from their minds as much by their own terrified, fascinated eagerness as by his will. Delicately, Kerezar played to their weaknesses, hinting at pleasures beyond human understanding for those who followed him, hiding his utter contempt at the simplicity of their desires. Endless carnality seemed the lot of it, that, and equally endless piles of shiny coins.

Oafs.

Ah, and they were still so charmingly afraid! He could scent the terror beneath the lust, savor it, forcing himself to remember that one did not slay one's hunting hounds, or soil one's hands on the unworthy.

And yes, underneath the fear, the lust, there was still that undercurrent of pure wonder at their own fortune.

How delightful, Kerezar thought flatly. *I definitely do seem to have given them religion. Listen to the little things whisper, thinking I cannot hear.*

". . . coolest thing that ever happened, *ever.*"

"Satan himself—"

"Telling us we're his men. Damn' straight!"

"We were already gonna burn, right? Hell, might as well have some fun first."

"And fun," Kerezar said sardonically, cutting into their not-quite hysteria, "you will have."

Now, to see if the tools would, indeed, serve their purpose. If not, they would, of course, be broken.

Sword drawn, he circled them. Each in turn received the slightest slash of the blade, deliberately minor, deliberately, since he was teaching a lesson, painful, coldly amused to see each in turn try not to flinch or cry out.

And with each, Kerezar paused to let them all see him deliberately, delicately, taste that boy's blood (hoping wryly as he did so that the process wouldn't poison him since there was the slight hint of some iron compound in that blood). It was more than mere melodrama: Blood had its magic, and by tasting this, he was establishing a link with his human tools.

Finished with his improvised ritual, Kerezar backed off, staring at them all. "You are mine now, body, blood, soul. And now you will do my bidding."

His cold face showing not a hint of his disgust, Kerezar told them, "I have come here hunting my prey. Tall, dark-haired, fair-skinned . . . "

He continued with his description of Ilaron till there could be no mistake. "I wish him found." It was the crack of a whip. "Do you understand me?"

"Yeah!"

"Damn' straight!"

"We'll find him."

"Only, you gonna let us watch, okay? Let us watch that fucker get dragged down to Hell?"

Hell? They had mentioned it frequently. What was it? Ah, yes . . . some fanciful human place of eternal punishment. One in which, Kerezar suspected, most of them hadn't believed. Till now.

"Perhaps," was all he said.

Understatement was *so* effective. By now they were fairly bursting with pride and vicious anticipation.

"We'll find the bastard for His Satanic Majesty!"

"You bet we'll find him, no sweat!"

Kerezar held up a hand. "You are not," he warned, eyes chill, "to harm him. Merely to point the way."

Odd, ugly, uncouth helpers. But one never rejected a tool merely because it wasn't aesthetically pleasing. These creatures, scum though they were, were immune to sunlight and iron; they could be his eyes and ears during this realm's garish, deadly day.

And their petty evil did amuse him.

But one human pointed out uneasily, terrified of offending Satan, "We . . . uh . . . could use a little help, begging His Satanic Majesty's pardon. Give us a clue or something, maybe? It's not that we don't know where to look, you understand. Just that, you know, there are a *lot* of people in this city, something like, what, eight million?"

That staggered Kerezar. The thought of so many people, albeit only humans, deliberately living in such close quarters—like a swarm of insects! He was not going to be able to single out Ilaron's aura, not with so much interference.

Nor, though, can he find mine.

Kerezar quickly seized on his only clue, the one given to him by Reschet: art. Yes . . . even in a city of this amazing size, the buying and selling of human art could not be the most common of activities.

Once again, though, he had to wonder what game Ilaron was playing, what dark secret lay behind the obvious facade—no matter. He would learn the truth eventually.

"Art," Kerezar told the humans. "Seek him where art is bought and sold. You will not give up, and you will not fail me." In his voice now was the hint of potential torments beyond bearing. "More," he added severely, scenting their heightened fear. "You are *not* to get yourselves into any trouble. You are merely to look and learn, then report back to me here. Is that clear to you?"

They agreed, wild with terrified excitement. This was a helluva lot more fun than beating up some stupid gay! They were now full-fledged Agents of Hell.

Yes, Kerezar thought cynically, *and with visions of money, power, women filling your ugly little minds.*

"Now, *go!*"

He watched them leave with the faintest of cold smiles on his lips, then spat, trying to cleanse his mouth of the foul, coppery taste of their blood and the slight but burning hint of iron.

Useful tools, yes, most fortuitously come upon. Short-lived tools, naturally, since of course they wouldn't survive once he no longer needed them. But for now, decidedly useful.

He could not remain here. Eventually someone must stumble across the body and ask awkward questions. The first step had been taken, though. Now the next matter facing him was shelter.

More than shelter. He must, Kerezar thought with the smallest wince of distaste, find someplace *decent* to stay.

As decent as can be found in this human city.

Which brought up the matter of funding. Kerezar already knew from his studies that these humans used a simple system of currency. Therefore, it was logical to assume that most, if not all, of them would be carrying at least some such coinage. So, and so . . .

It was an easy matter to find a man walking alone, slip up behind him without a sound, and slay him—again, a quick, neat, efficient thrust of the sword up through the heart and out again, coolly enjoying the feel of death overwhelming a life, letting the body fall so that not a drop of blood stained Kerezar's clothing.

He hesitated only a moment. It was, perhaps, a touch debasing to turn common thief . . .

But then again, he was only committing such thievery in order to fund his hunting. Even theft was an honorable enough action when one was stalking a traitor.

Kerezar found his prey's money in a leather holder. The rest of the wallet's contents, he left, suspecting that those thin rectangles of artificial material were part of a technology he could not tap.

Yet.

Had he enough currency? If not, no matter; a city this size would teem with potential victims.

The thought of victims reminded Kerezar of the demon he'd loosed in the city. *Lamashtu,* he thought almost amicably. *She will find good hunting here.*

Let her have her freedom for now. He knew the shape and feel of her aura; thanks to that, he could surely always rein her in should he have need of her. As for her trickery—oh, he could feel no animosity toward her for that; deceit was, after all, merely a part of demonic nature.

Kerezar smiled thinly, not at all displeased with the pattern of events. This game, for all its inconveniences, promised to be . . . most intriguing.

Much later, Kerezar was footsore but oddly satisfied. He had been walking steadily north and north again, following the faint psychic trail that told him where a greater collection of human auras were gathered, casually turning his head aside whenever he passed someone to hide his eyes. He had passed many a store by now, many a gathering of human diners, felt human auras inhabiting almost every room in almost every building.

But there had been nothing useful, not yet. He needed a more complete disguise, something to hide his alien eyes, before he could safely mingle with humans. And there must be that greater concentration of humanity. The more of them, the less likely one alien aura was to be detected.

So far, at least, he hadn't found the noise or stink too unbearable. That was surprising. As for the vast amount of iron . . . one endured what one must.

So, now. Look. This noisy city never did seem to settle down for rest. Vendors were still selling their wares on . . . what was this broad cross street? Kerezar had quickly seen that these humans marked their intersections, and read off the sign the numerals that translated to Fourteenth Street. He glanced about in faintly scornful summary. Not a fashionable place, really, not one where he might find a decent lodging.

But all those merchants with all those goods spilling out onto the walks . . . useful. A quick, casual swirling of will and he'd gained himself a pair of sunglasses from one merchant and a small suitcase to simulate luggage from another.

Now, Kerezar told himself, *I am a reputable human. A man of business from a foreign realm. One who has gotten himself slightly lost in this vast city, a not-unlikely situation, surely.*

It should not be at all difficult to throw himself on the mercy of someone reputable, one of the officers of the law, perhaps, who he'd seen patrolling in their easily recognizable uniforms, and ask him for advice regarding lodging.

And then . . . guard yourself, Ilaron. Guard yourself as well as you can.

Eric Lansdowne, actor, dancer and right now desk clerk, leaned on the marble countertop and tried not to yawn. If he had to work other than on the stage—he and who knew how many more like him—the young man told himself that he could have done a lot worse than finding a job here. The Marriott Marquis was large, the employee benefits were nice, and it was right in the middle of the theater district, perfect for catching those sudden auditions and (*Oh God, please*) callbacks.

Of course, the job also meant drawing the occasional night shift. But hey, it was only temporary. And—

Whoa, attention. Here came someone now . . . foreigner from the looks of him, odd cut to that suit, and only the one bag—well, businessmen traveled light these days, nothing odd about that. Tall, slender, geez, gorgeous face, like something out of a dream, all clean lines, yes, and that long, straight hair, true silver. Too bad the guy's eyes were hidden by those sunglasses—

Suddenly aware that he was staring, Eric put on his best "I'm at your service!" smile. "Yes, sir? Can I help you?"

"A room." The voice was heavily accented. A pause. "Please."

"Of course, sir. We do have a vacancy for tonight into tomorrow—"

"Longer, I believe. Forgive me. I do not yet know for how much longer." He waved a graceful, deprecating hand. "Business. You understand."

"Of course," Eric repeated. *Damn, what accent is that? Not Italian or Russian or anything like that, and that fair skin and those feature . . . what* is *he?* "Not a problem."

"Excellent."

The stranger's smile should have been charming, and yet . . . *Something behind it,* Eric thought uneasily, *something cold. I don't think I want to know what business he's in.*

They did a quick back-and-forth as to the rate, and then the stranger further startled Eric by saying, "I am, as you see, very much a foreigner to this land. I fear I do not carry what you would consider a verifiable credit card. Will payment by cash, in advance, for each day's stay be acceptable?"

Geez. Eric glanced helplessly about, rather relieved to see the rest of the night staff watching. At a slight nod from the night manager, Eric said in relief to the stranger, "Uh, yes, sir, I, uh, yes."

The stranger flashed him another of those charming, chill smiles, smiled at all the others, then obligingly filled out the proper card. Eric glanced at it, not at all surprised that he couldn't recognize the address or even the country. "Very good, Mr., ah, Ahligar. Will you need help with—"

"That will not be necessary. I will find my own way. I am," Mr. Ahligar added, "quite weary from my . . . journey, and only wish to be left in peace. That can, I imagine, be arranged?"

"Oh, yes sir! Not a problem."

"That is very . . . fortunate," the stranger said.

And this time there was not even the slightest hint of charm to his smile.

Alone in the hotel room he had just rented, Kerezar slipped the odd little "Please Do Not Disturb" sign onto the doorknob, locked the door, did a quick, wary scan of the room, finding nothing alarming—and then, since there was no one to see him in this weakness, collapsed full length on the bed.

All that iron. The trip up to that eighth-floor lobby had almost been too much to endure after all the ordeals he had already faced this night, and the ride up to this floor . . . an endless trial.

But I survived. I will survive. To your regret, Ilaron.

TWELVE

Morning Has Broken

Morning had broken.

It certainly has, Denise thought wryly, hardly feeling rested, *and we're not going to be able to fix it.*

How much sleep had she had? Two hours? Three? It certainly didn't feel like much more. She forced herself out of bed, yawning, telling herself, *look, a triumph, we have achieved verticality,* stubbing her toe on the forgotten pile of books as she staggered toward the door—

Whoa, wait. She'd forgotten about her . . . guest out there in the living room. Fumbling in dresser and closet, Denise warily dressed in her bedroom, running a hasty comb through her hair Just In Case, and only then dared steal into the bathroom.

Heh, said guest had already been in here. The room was spotless, but a still-damp towel and condensation on the mirror gave him away. He also seemed to have made free use of one of her moisturizers, the one that touted its sunblocking abilities.

It all wasn't some fantastic dream, then. He's real. And that means, alarming thought, so is the rest of it.

As Denise started toward the living room, she was sidetracked by the smell of brewing coffee. Ilaron was standing in her little kitchenette, watching a pan on the stove like a sorcerer watching a cauldron, spatula in hand, apron protecting his clothing, and sunglasses firmly on his face. The sight of him in all his exotic elegance in such a mundane setting was enough to make her pause. He looked disgustingly unrumpled for someone who had slept in his clothes; evidently Ilaron had some spell that repelled dirt and wrinkles.

I must, she thought with a flash of wry humor, *ask him for the recipe.*

Realizing that she was there, Ilaron turned to salute her solemnly with the spatula. "The coffee will be done in a moment. I trust you eat breakfast?"

Returning his attention to the stove, he added, "And no need to stare in such wide-eyed amazement. There is nothing surprising about my knowing how to cook."

Turning off the gas, Ilaron began portioning out something that smelled wonderful onto two plates. Handing her one, he continued, "I do have to eat, even as you humans, live alone, and do not wish to eat out for every meal."

"Of . . . course. I just never saw a cook in suit and sunglasses before."

That forced the barest twitch of a smile from him. He gestured approvingly with the spatula at her cuneiform markings over doors and windows. "I can't read the markings, but I can feel their power."

This sudden reminder of last night and all its weirdnesses sent a shiver up Denise's spine. As Ilaron dumped the spatula in the sink and settled himself at her little kitchen table, she sat down in the other chair with a thump and switched on the radio. Eating one-handed (some sort of nicely spicy omelet, as it turned out, more tasty than she would have thought possible considering her sparsely filled spice rack), she hunted for one of the all-news radio stations.

". . . in the West Village."

Her hand froze on the dial.

"Five bodies have been pulled from the wreckage so far, though the names have not yet been released pending notification of next of kin. The police have refused to speculate on the cause of the explosion at this time, although the likelihood of a bomb or possibly even of a bomb-making facility has not been ruled out."

"Wait," Denise muttered, sipping her coffee. "Sooner or later, someone is going to bring up that current buzzword: terrorism."

"And they will continue to toy with the bomb-making facility concept," Ilaron agreed, "even though the experts will never find even the slightest of chemical traces. Yes," he added wryly, "I've listened to these stations, too."

But the start of a second story made Denise freeze again, coffee cup in hand:

"In an unrelated item, the body of an adult male, identity not yet disclosed, was found within a block of the explosion. While eyewitness accounts claim that marks on the body bear similarities to those left by the African Ebola virus, the Board of Health is strenuously denying the presence of any strain of the Ebola virus in New York City."

A pause, as though the newscaster was listening to something off-mike, then: "We switch now to a live statement, already in progress, from Board of Health spokesperson Dr. Nathan Carson."

Carson, who had what Denise suspected was a deliberately dull, calming voice, was announcing, "I repeat: There is *no* evidence of any case of the Ebola virus anywhere within North America, and certainly none within New York City."

But a shrill voice, presumably belonging to a die-hard reporter, shouted, "What about the body? Didn't that show—"

"There are no cases of the Ebola virus within New York City," Carson repeated firmly. "Nor is there any indication that the virus might have mutated."

"But, Dr. Carson, can you speculate on what might have been the cause of—"

"Speculation would be premature. I have no further comment."

With that, the station switched back to its regular news anchor, who went on to discuss the crimes of the day. Denise settled back in her chair. Ebola . . . sudden disease . . . near where she and Ilaron had been, near the explosion he had said was a demon's emergence . . . the Children of Sumer . . .

Her late-night studies hadn't been in vain. "Lamashtu," she gasped in sudden comprehension. "That's who—what—it is. They've conjured Lamashtu. Trust a cult not to even get the culture right, but—Ilaron, it's she, it can't be any other."

He managed without moving a muscle to go from casual listener to alert hunter. "Go on."

"Well, Lamashtu's from ancient Mesopotamia, all right, that's probably how they—how they reached her or whatever it is they did, but she's not Sumerian. She's Assyrian, maybe, or Babylonian, and she's supposed to be a—a weird mix, woman's body, talons, wings, lion's head. Lamashtu's said to be the child of Anu, god of the heavens, but she chose to be a demon—very specifically the Demon of Disease!"

Ilaron never stirred, his chill calm reminding Denise with a shock that he had probably seen and maybe even dealt with demons. His lack of reaction grated on her nerves so badly that she stammered, "Wait, just—just wait here," and went to snatch up a book, returning, leafing frantically through the pages. "Ha, here, listen. This is what we're up against:

" 'She is fury, she is rage, she is dreadful sorcery,
　She slays the old, the young, the baby in the womb,
　Her name is fever, fire, death,
　Her name is Lamashtu—'

"Dammit, Ilaron, don't just sit there, say something!"

"An incarnation." His voice was not precisely calm. Rather, Denise thought, it held the very antithesis of emotion. "Enough of humanity believed that there must be an incarnation of disease, and so a Demon of Disease was born."

"I—I don't care about Demonology 101!"

"No," he said drily. "You'd have had no need. Till today."

"Oh, right, but now—"

"But now, I agree, we have a complication. A plague in New York City is . . . hardly desirable."

"Ilaron!"

He blinked. "Ah, I'm sorry. I was merely trying for a . . . I admit it, a feeble attempt at humor."

"It was very feeble! And she, the demon, the incarnation, Lamashtu, Ilaron, don't be so damnably calm! Lamashtu *knows who we are.*"

"Yes. She does. Do not stare at me in such horror. This isn't the start of . . . what is that mythic final battle? Arma . . ."

"Armageddon. But what—"

"Exactly. Nor," he added before she could interrupt, "is it our personal Armageddon. We are reasonably safe during the daylight hours. Just as the human tales all claim, nothing of supernatural evil can walk under this realm's sun."

" 'Reasonably'? You said that last night, too! What does 'reasonably' mean? Is that like being only *slightly* pregnant?" His start told her he'd never heard that term before. Denise didn't bother to explain. "We can't go to anyone—"

"Hardly."

"Then—what are we going to do?"

He shrugged. "Drive the demon out."

"You make that sound so simple!" She stopped short, not quite hopeful. "Is it?"

"Ah well," Ilaron admitted, "under different circumstances, it might have been. Unfortunately, in this case, it isn't. I'm afraid that I know nothing about Lamashtu, which means that I also know nothing about how she may be banished. I don't suppose you . . . ?"

She shook her head. "All I know are some of the incantations, such as the one I just read. People wore them carved on amulets meant to ward her off. You know the sort of thing I mean: like the holy charms people wear today."

"Ah. Not strong enough. We need a true spell of banishment."

Denise looked at him in fresh alarm. "And you— she—you—"

"No, Denise." His voice was wry. "I am not a foe, nor the ally of the foe. Her sudden materialization last night caught me off guard. That will not happen again."

Breakfast had lost all its appeal. Denise, biting her lip, got up to put her plate and coffee cup in the sink. "I'm going to work."

"No. There are too many unguarded entrances to the museum."

"Whoa. What happened to that 'reasonably safe'? You just told me that nothing evil can endure daylight."

"Let me remind you that there is more than supernatural evil. Denise, we have no proof that all the Children of Sumer are dead."

She glanced at him, a little startled at his concern. "If we're going to learn how to banish Lamashtu— and I *don't* believe I just said that—I'll need to do research. The reference books I'll need are in my office."

Ilaron hesitated, then finally nodded in grudging approval. "As long as you keep the office door locked and go nowhere without a guard, you should be safe. I plan to spend the day in research as well."

Denise waited, but he didn't specify details.

"And," Ilaron added, absently helping her clear away the dishes, "I mean to escort you to the museum and will escort you from the museum, especially if you must work late."

Denise, seeing his grim expression, agreed without question.

But Ilaron wasn't finished. "I've had some time to think this over while waiting for you to wake: The Darkness may or may not be truly aware of you by this point, but the Children of Sumer certainly are."

"Yes, but—"

"I do *not* want you returning here."

"Oh come *on,* this is a safe building!"

"Against humans. Warded though it is by those cuneiform charms, it still could not withstand strong magic."

Denise straightened. "Are you *expecting* strong magic?"

"I don't know—"

"But—"

"*But,*" he continued firmly, "the risk is real."

"Then what am I supposed to do? Live in my office?"

"You will stay with me."

It was more of an order, Denise thought, than a suggestion. "I can't just—"

"There is an unused guest room in my apartment." He added impatiently, "This isn't some foolish human 'come-on,' or whatever that ridiculous phrase may be. You are an attractive woman for a human, but you *are* human, and my will is hardly that feeble. If you will feel more comfortable, I will swear to your safety!"

"Oh, that won't be necessary, because I have no intention of going to—"

"And I assure you," Ilaron continued over her protest, "I am not thrilled with sharing my privacy even with someone whose company I can tolerate."

Now there's a nice backhanded compliment, Denise thought. "Yes, but—"

"But I will be able to guard us both more effectively there! There *are* limits, Denise: I can't be in two places at the same time! In an ideal situation, you would never have been involved in magic, you would have gone on with your scholarly life and all would have remained as it should be in a logical world. But it's too late for 'should have been,' the Children of Sumer saw to that! Come now, are we in agreement?"

Denise hesitated, trying to find the right words. *I don't like this, I don't like the whole idea, and I really don't like his arrogant tone.*

But then, odd thought, this was probably the first time he'd ever shown concern for another, or needed to show concern, and didn't quite know how to go about it.

"Attractive woman for a human." Huh.

"All right," she admitted reluctantly. "I confess it: After last night, I do *not* want to face Lamashtu or whatever else is out there alone, and would much rather have your, ah, magic nearby, thank you very much! But how long is this 'visit' going to last?"

Ilaron sighed, shrugging gracefully. "There is, alas, no telling."

Suddenly small things seemed terribly important; Denise realized that she was clinging desperately to the last shreds of normalcy, but couldn't seem to stop.

"My clothing—"

"Surely you have a suitcase? And sufficient clean clothing to hand?"

"But—the plants—"

"Will survive. Or can be replaced."

"My mail! Ilaron, I can't go, I won't have time to stop the mail!"

"Supernatural entities," Ilaron countered blandly, "are hardly likely to want your mail. Now, are you quite finished dithering?"

"I am not dith . . . yes, I am. Sorry. Let me just get my things."

Ilaron waited with an inhuman stillness that was more unnerving than human impatience for Denise to pack what she thought she would need. "For now," he volunteered, "I will store it in my gallery office, so you won't have awkward questions to answer."

She nearly dropped the suitcase, taken aback by this new touch of concern. *But then,* Denise reminded herself, *nothing else in this past day and a half has been predictable!*

Together with her odd, handsome bodyguard, she set off for the museum.

Kerezar sat alone in his room in the Marriott Marquis Hotel. Granted, he had chosen this particular hotel primarily because of its vastness and one guest's relative anonymity. But rather to his surprise, the room he'd been assigned was large and, he thought, pleasantly comfortable; he had expected far less from something built by humans.

A good neighborhood, this, too, if a virtual chaos of noise and confusion. Despite the early hour, the street outside—called, he believed, Broadway—already teemed with life. And if he extended his senses as much as the cursed iron in the building allowed, he could feel delicious hints of Darkness in the district: many predators here and many potential victims.

There were advantages to a city this size, a city where activity never quite stopped and everything was available, if one was but logical about it.

Outside, it was almost fully dawn, but the first thing that Kerezar had done on entering the room was firmly shut the curtains. Although some light still leaked in around the edges, the room was comfortably dark as he went over the so-cleverly named Yellow Pages, hunting. He had already requested that he not be disturbed, and he doubted that the young human to whom he'd spoken would dare to disobey him. Besides, something as simple as that "Do Not Disturb" sign on the doorknob should doubly ensure privacy.

Fascinating, these listings . . . so many of them and in so many fields. He wasn't sure what many of them meant, but Kerezar was almost impressed.

I had no idea that humans could be so clever, so inventive!

Most of the names involved meant nothing to him. What, for instance, was this "telecommunications" that seemed important enough to have so many entries? "Communications" was obvious enough, but—wait, now, "*tele*phone," "*tele*vision"—so now, here was the humans' answer to magic, the use of the force they called "electricity" to summon sounds and images through the air. Close enough to magic, after all!

One thing he noted in particular, and which intrigued him: corporations like so many vast spiderwebs . . . containing who knew how many lives, how much power . . . and all of it, amazingly, controlled without the use of magic.

Kerezar leafed through the Yellow Pages again, his mind working on a dozen different angles at once. He hadn't forgotten about Ilaron, nor about the urgency of returning to a throne left perilously unoccupied; on the contrary, he was considering that aspect even as he considered these new themes.

Intriguing themes, indeed. Eight million lives in this city alone, and all of them, no doubt, linked in some way to this intricate telecommunications web. All of those lives, as a result, influenced by what they saw, heard, were told. Kerezar frowned ever so slightly, pondering possibilities.

Whoever stood at the head of one of these telecommunications empires would be an emperor, indeed.

Interesting thought. Very. More interesting was what it might mean for one of his race . . . someone with sufficient cunning and will might well find himself ruling not one but two realms.

Did humans think of ambition in the same terms? Probably not, animalistic as they were. But Kerezar's realm was always in peril of a fatal imbalance; his was a slow-breeding, rarely fertile race, the High Nobility and their underclasses both. His search through the Yellow Pages with that wild diversity of subjects showed him a fundamental difference between his realm and this: There, little that was new was created, while this realm was constantly reinventing itself.

How nicely this crass but vital humanity would feed his realm! There could be a never-ending source of human cleverness, human resources, human sacrifices—and none here would ever suspect. But first the two realms would need to be linked, a subtle link, so that no human might voluntarily make the crossing.

Linked, though, by what? There was the real problem. It must be some force common to both realms, yet something powerful. . . .

Of course, that "electricity" they used so commonly here, that should definitely serve.

Interesting, indeed. Perhaps in the future . . . Of course the will was not the same as the deed; there was much to be done first—

Including destroying Ilaron.

Yes, and finding a way to deal with those twin perils

of this realm, sunlight and iron. *How,* Kerezar wondered, *does Ilaron endure?* He shuddered at the cold burning of iron all around him. *Ilaron must have an incredibly powerful spell of protection. I will be careful to twist every detail of it from him before any official punishments take place.*

But first he must find Ilaron. When he'd sent out those ugly young creatures to do his bidding, he had never dreamed that there could be so many art galleries in one city! Ilaron surely was in a better part of the city—but Kerezar had no idea what or where that might be.

Time, I think, to make a few inquiries.

The front desk, fortunately, had no windows too near to it; no perilous rays of that rising sun could touch him. The young man of the night before was, of course, no longer there, but Kerezar, smiling *so* urbanely, charmed the young woman behind the Guest Services area into pointing out exactly where the most prestigious galleries, auction houses, and museums—indeed, every business dealing in art—were located. He "tsked" with her over the amazing variety and briefly debated turning this helpful and fresh-faced young woman into a . . . tool.

No. She would surely be missed.

There would be others who would not.

Besides, the continually brightening day was beginning to pull at his concentration, weakening his will. Armed with maps and brochures, Kerezar, gritting his teeth against yet another elevator ride, headed back up to the sanctuary of his room to continue the hunt.

With the coming of dawn, Lamashtu settled down to a state of dormancy within Sedgwick's mind, barely aware of the outside world.

Go on, my human toy, she murmured drowsily. *Go*

*out and do what you will. Which is   . what . . .
I . . . desire.*

Sedgwick had a vague memory of having wandered
the streets all night, no goal in mind, dimly knowing that
something was not right but not at all sure what that
something might be. Not really worried that he
couldn't remember. If he concentrated with all his
might, he could *almost* remember . . . an explosion . . .
there had been an explosion . . . yes, and the rest of
the Children of Sumer were dead.

The Children of Sumer were dead.

No. That meant nothing to him. Nearly nothing.

But something was changing. Last night, he had
rambled aimlessly. This morning, Sedgwick headed
with definite purpose not for home or even for the
job he probably no longer had, but for the museum.
He had no idea why, save for this one thing. This one
person he remembered. This one foe was there.

Denise Sheridan.

Yes, that was her name. The woman who mocked
the past, the sacrifice who had escaped.

No longer.

Dimly, Lamashtu stirred from lovely dreams of
blood, sensing Sedgwick's sudden surge of hatred. *Yes,*
she sleepily prodded Sedgwick, *the museum.*

There was a place within it she wished to reach, a
place of interesting possibilities.

*The museum, my human. To the humans' place of
art and antiquity. We shall work wonders there.*

THIRTEEN

To Have and Have Not

To Ilaron's relief, he and Denise arrived at The American Museum of Art without the slightest of challenges, then reached her office equally unchallenged. With a polite if slightly tongue-in-cheek flourish, he delivered Denise to a blushing, all but giggling, Sarah, bowed with equally tongue-in-cheek elegance, and went on his way.

But he went with senses still very much alert. Nothing untoward in the still-tranquil museum, not yet open to the public, nothing untoward in the more lively surrounding streets as he headed to his gallery. The usual crowds of pedestrians and commuters in vehicles, all intent only on one thing: getting to work on time. Normal bustle, normal traffic noises and smells.

Not at all reassured by the ordinary world about him, Ilaron entered his gallery, but only long enough to greet his staff, see that everything was progressing well there, too, and casually to leave Denise's suitcase in his office.

"I will be gone for perhaps an hour or two," he told Ms. Daniels and the others. Then, without waiting for more than their nods, he headed out onto Madison Avenue and hailed a taxi to take him back down to the West Village.

I doubt that there will be anything much to be

learned after so many humans have trampled the site. But any clue will be valuable.

The driver had a *Daily News* on the seat beside him, and Ilaron, catching a glimpse of the newspaper's front page, which featured a photo of the demolished town house, asked, "May I borrow that for a moment?"

"Help yourself. Finished it anyhow."

It was not true, Ilaron mused, that no cabdrivers in New York spoke English. This one most certainly did, and with apparent relish:

"How about that building exploding like that? Crazy, right? Whaddaya think? Terrorists? Or maybe a bomb factory. You know? That sorta thing's happened before, right? Right. In the Village, too, few years back. Think it's that? Buncha idiot terrorists blowing themselves up?"

"In a way," Ilaron said drily, and began to read.

Mercifully, the driver became too involved in fighting the morning's traffic after that to continue the conversation.

As Ilaron had expected, the lead article about the explosion was remarkably vague, mentioning only that the blast didn't seem to bear the earmarks of a "normal" bomb. That forced a bemused "huh" from him; strange society, this, when a bomb could be described as normal. His attention was caught by a second, related article concerning the possible non–Ebola virus nonvictim found nearby, which was equally vague regarding solid data, while a third—

Ilaron stiffened, staring at the third article. One teenage male and one adult male found dead in the West Village within blocks of each other, both the victims of stab wounds that, according to the scanty facts and a reporter's speculations, looked as though the victims had been cut down by a swordsman.

A swordsman, he thought uneasily. *Too close to the*

site of the demon's appearance, yes, and to that mysterious death by disease, to be coincidence.

A little shiver of alarm ran through him. The killer *might* have been a human lunatic, but in his experiences in this realm so far, few human lunatics were skilled in swordsmanship. Who else? Those from his realm, yes. Yet if his kind had entered this realm in any force, he would have sensed it.

Then again, what if only one or two had slipped through, pulled along by Lamashtu's materialization? Perhaps even after having made a pact with the demon? Not impossible. In fact, this uncomfortable possibility had been at the back of his mind since he'd awakened.

Unfortunately, there are just too many auras in this crowded city. I can't locate any specific one.

Of course, that worked the other way around as well: A magical foe would have just as much trouble trying to pick out his aura.

Assuming, of course, that the slayer really had been a swordsman. And from his realm.

Maybe it really is *nothing more than some lunatic human swashbuckler out there. There's been no proof one way or the other. And maybe I really* am *growing paranoid. Still . . .*

"Hey, mister," the driver cut in. "This is as far as I can get. See? Cops have the whole area sealed off."

"Never mind. You've gotten us close enough."

He paid the driver and got out, acting the part of a casual passerby. As Ilaron had expected, the police investigation was still very much in full swing, with cranes and other machines totally filling the street and officious-looking folks scurrying about with mysterious instruments. Half the block was sealed off from pedestrians with the familiar yellow "Police Line. Do Not Cross" tape, which obviously meant that he couldn't get too close. That wasn't truly a problem; Ilaron al-

ready knew that there was nothing to be found there,
at least not on the magical level.

*Now to find the spot where the non-Ebola nonvictim
collapsed . . . ah.*

He easily located the area—but it was also still
under investigation and sealed off by lines of yellow
tape. It would have been nice, Ilaron reflected, to have
gotten a bit closer here, too.

*But since I already know that Lamashtu was the
killer—no doubt about that—there isn't much new information to be gained here, either.*

He found a third site, one of the murder scenes,
also taped off, *also* under investigation, and stifled a
sigh. A busy day for New York officials, a frustrating
one for him.

But Ilaron walked all over the general area anyhow,
wearing the look of someone purposeful; humans, he'd
long ago learned, tended to ignore those who acted
as though they had a right to be where they were.

As he pretended to be heading toward a specific
goal, Ilaron magically scanned as best he could, despite the handicap posed by daylight, for any trace of
an aura that just didn't fit. . . .

Wait. What . . . ?

Ilaron stopped, staring at a ramshackle wooden shed
half-hidden behind a building, heart suddenly racing.
Warily, making sure that no one spotted this "eccen-
tric" behavior, he entered the shed, holding his breath
against the stench, delicately touching the walls, the
floor, then backed out, straightening with a hiss.

Kerezar!

The identity had just hit him with the force of a
blow. There had been only the barest trace of an aura,
already dissipating in the sunlight, but—Kerezar, yes,
Kerezar had definitely been here, was here now, somewhere in this city!

And, more, Kerezar was . . .

For an irrational moment, Ilaron felt a surge of pure fury, just then knowing with every magical sense that it had been Kerezar who'd won the power struggle Ilaron had left behind him, Kerezar who sat the throne that should be his—

Oh, you utter idiot! What difference can it possibly make who sits the throne of a realm you abandoned? One to which you never wish to return?

Let Kerezar have the throne! Let him rule and never know a moment's joy of it!

Forcing his mind back to rational calm, Ilaron considered what he knew of Kerezar's nature: cold even for one of their race, cruelly analytical, totally without the slightest hint of any tempering warmth.

It isn't like him to do anything as rash as follow me here alone. And yet, alone, he definitely is.

That could only mean one thing: Kerezar had made a mistake, very probably by having failed to bargain quite accurately enough with Lamashtu. It wasn't unthinkable; demons were notoriously unpredictable and sly, and, Ilaron thought, even his kind could err.

But Kerezar never was the sort to let anger at himself or others handicap him. He wouldn't have jumped blindly between realms, either.

Still . . . assuming that Kerezar truly hadn't located this realm until after Reschet's return home, which seemed the only logical possibility, he wouldn't have had sufficient time to make too careful a study of humanity.

Given, then: a Kerezar with a working knowledge of the human language, probably written as well as spoken. He would know what clothes to wear, even have a grasp of the surface layer of human customs. He could, no, more probably would, be passing as a foreigner to explain any incongruities, perhaps as a businessman of some innocuous sort. By now, he would have found himself a sanctuary from which he could hunt—all the while aware that every moment away from his throne meant an additional risk of usurpation.

He must find me swiftly. Particularly since he will have no chance to build up any immunity to iron or tolerance for sunlight. There's my edge . . . if only I can find a way to use it.

But where *was* Kerezar's sanctuary? Knowing him, somewhere comfortable, even elegant. That had to be why a man had been slain, if not the teenager, to help fund such a retreat. Ilaron thought with dark humor that there was surely at least one more body bearing fatal sword wounds lying somewhere in Manhattan; Kerezar would have quickly figured out how much money he would need, this land using such a basic decimal system of currency, and would have had no qualms about gathering it.

And the demon? Where was she? Were she and Kerezar working together? It didn't seem likely, not after she had tricked him, but right now nothing could be ruled out.

Eight million people in this city, perhaps twelve or more millions in the Greater New York Metropolitan Region, or whatever they name it. How am I to find him in all that? Yes, and find him before he figures out a way to find me?

There was nothing more to be learned here. Ilaron found himself a taxi on Seventh Avenue, got the driver—who was one of the mostly non-English-speaking variety—turned properly around onto northbound Sixth Avenue (he'd been in this city long enough to know no New Yorker ever called it by its official name, Avenue of the Americas), and hurried back up and across town to his gallery.

"Mr. Highborn!" As he entered the gallery, Ms. Daniels all but pounced on him, looking almost indignant. "We've already had two customers this morning asking about the Shang Dynasty vase, and we—"

"Ms. Daniels, I know you are competent to handle the situation as you see fit."

With a nod to the startled woman and the two younger members of his staff, who were staring at him almost in wonder at his sharpness, Ilaron rushed past them, on into his office, slamming the door behind him in his haste. Switching on the computer with a glance, he set about a magically enhanced search for anyone who had checked into a Manhattan hotel the night before, knowing how nearly hopeless this would be.

Sure enough, the resulting list was far too long. He narrowed it to lone travelers.

Still too long. He would, Ilaron thought drily, love to restrict the search to "men with silver hair, eerie eyes, exotic accents, and the quirk of paying by cash," but there *were* limits. It would be easy enough for one of their devious, magical race to establish a false identity.

After all, I did it, with a minimal use of magical persuasion, too: credit cards, Social Security number and all.

Devious, yes. Could Kerezar already have human agents aiding him? There hadn't been much time for enlistment, but Ilaron was well aware of the perils of underestimating his foe.

Ah, and then there's Reschet. Did that tricky little creature give Kerezar any vital clues? Such as, perhaps, art?

Too many unanswered questions. The computer was beginning to narrow down the search, but he saw that there were still over a hundred possibilities.

Ilaron called out, "Ms. Daniels."

The door opened just enough for the woman to glance warily into the office. "Yes, Mr. Highborn?"

"Ms. Daniels, pray forgive my brusqueness just before. I have a rather difficult task for the staff. You see, I am trying to track down a rather enigmatic . . . colleague who happens to be visiting this city, but who was foolish enough not to leave me any telephone number or address. I know he must be staying at a reasonably good hotel, but . . ."

"But you'd like us to start making phone inquiries? Of course."

She left, closing the door behind her.

Competent, indeed. And blessedly free from excess curiosity.

Ilaron sat for a moment, fingers steepled. The humans would probably assume they were trying to track down some foreign dealer in antiquities, possibly even one from his homeland. Good enough. But he had few hopes that any reputable hotel would give out any really useful information.

Ilaron straightened with a startled hiss. Something wrong, very wrong . . . Darkness . . . something at the edge of his magical senses . . . something . . . not here . . . nearby . . .

Yes! He leaped to his feet, flinging open the office door. "Keep trying," Ilaron called over his shoulder to the once-more startled staff as he sped out of the gallery. "I, however, must hurry back to the museum."

"Ah . . . are you in there?"

That was Sarah's voice. Denise peered around the mound of books and journals covering her desk, and heard the young woman fight down a giggle. "What?"

"Sorry. You look like you've been buried alive in books! Here's another one."

"Good. Put it . . . ah . . ." No clear floor space, either. "On that pile. Right. Thanks."

Wearily, Denise dived back into her work, poring over volumes in English or French, German or Baby-

Ionian, hunting down all the mentions of Lamashtu she could find. And there were a great many.

Not surprising, when you consider the region. Mesopotamia, what with its hot climate and the stagnant marshes along the Tigris and Euphrates Rivers, seemed designed to be a breeding ground for disease.

And high infant mortality, poor kids. And poor parents! No wonder they thought a demon was involved.

Was one?

No. She wasn't even going to consider that Lamashtu could have played an active role in human history. She wasn't ready for that much of the fantastic to intrude upon the real world.

Such as Ilaron?

Ilaron, whatever else he might be, was hardly a demon out for human lives. *Back to work, Dr. Sheridan.*

Or maybe not. The sudden shrilling of the telephone made her jump. One ring, two—ah, Sarah had gotten there in time. Hopefully it would be nothing much.

Hah. "Uh, Dr. Sheridan, I know you're busy, but—"

"But it's Alan Atherton, right? No, Sarah, I'm not getting psychic." As Denise picked up the receiver, she continued, "Just the way things have been going so far. And—" sweetly, "hello, Mr. Atherton. What can I do for you today?"

Her chirping caught him off guard. There was a brief hesitation on the other end, then, "I've been thinking, Dr. Sheridan."

Oh, congratulations. As blandly as she could manage: "Yes?"

"About your department. The galleries, rather. I'm afraid that they—"

"Just aren't exciting enough? Oh, I agree," Denise gushed, "and so, guess what? We've come up with a really thrilling concept—'The Assyrians: Civilized Killers.' Play to the public's love of horror and at the same time teach them something about the past-as-present. Isn't that something? We wouldn't even need much of a budget, you know, just some flashy graphics. Quick, colorful, educational, and exciting—isn't that wonderful?''

"I, ah, that is—"

"Oh, you *do* like it! How splendid! I can get a proposal off to you in . . . mmm . . . in about a week, I'd say, if that's all right with you? It is? Perfect. *Such* a pleasure talking to you, Mr. Atherton, and I'm so glad you like my idea. Now, I wouldn't think of taking up any more of your precious time, so, good-bye for now!"

She hung up, then sat with head in hands for a time, catching her breath. *God, what a . . . no, never mind what he is. That's one of the few times I've been able to cut him off in mid-intimidation. Thank you, Ilaron, thank you! I never would have thought up that Assyrian idea so quickly on my own.*

"Sarah," she called out, "unless it's someone like our Fearless Leader—and you won't repeat that outside this office now, will you? Unless it's someone that important—or someone like Ilaron Highborn—please hold all my calls."

A cheerful chirp, "Can do!"

"Thank you."

Denise dived back into her research. *No more museum business, no more complications, please, please, let me just get this over and done!* So far she'd come across Lamashtu in all her dreadful aspects, stalking cattle, humans, killing all she touched:

"Hers is the ravening lion's face," Denise read, "her hands are gory with flesh and blood," then stopped with a shudder.

Plenty of Lamashtu data. But so far the only evidence that she'd been able to find regarding how one actually got rid of the demon was a flat statement that first she must raise *another* demon, Pazuzu.

Right. I've seen the incantations often enough: simple charms, like the ones I mentioned to Ilaron. Take seven strands of dyed wool, hair from the right side of a male donkey, hair from a white pig, and so on.

Yes, and there were all those little bronze amulets, with Pazuzu keeping a wary eye on Lamashtu . . . wishful thinking, those, to ward off disease and protect babies.

Very human, too, the sort of thing everyone must have carried around. But there's nothing in any of them in the way of true conjurations or banishments

And how, she asked herself drily, had she so suddenly become an expert on conjurations and banishments?

Life is a Learning Experience. And I would like the chance to go right on learning, thank you very much!

Ah well. Onward. Pazuzu, Denise knew, was every bit as inhuman and perilous as Lamashtu. Ugly fellow, too: doglike head, taloned hands, a double set of wings—but unlike Lamashtu, he had a good side, or at least a not-so-nasty one. Even though Denise remembered a horror book and movie that had portrayed him as a child-possessing scion of utter evil, Pazuzu was as much deity as demon. He was, in fact, son of Hanbi, the equally demonic god or godlike demon King of the Winds. And sometimes (apparently if properly moved by whim or human prayer) Pazuzu used his father's winds to drive away disease.

Hopefully we're not just talking about metaphors.

At least all the myths agreed on one thing: Pazuzu hated Lamashtu. And since he hated her with such fervor, Pazuzu was always eager to drive her away. Well and good, even if those myths didn't spell out whether or not Pazuzu safely vanished after that.

But then, that wasn't really a problem—because not

one of the references spelled out how to raise Pazuzu in the first place!

Too much data, Denise thought, looking with a jaundiced eye at the stacks of books and magazines, *far too much to go over in one day.*

"Sarah," she called, "I'm afraid I have a rather onerous job for you." As the young woman warily poked her head into the office, Denise told her, "See all this? I need a copy of every marked article."

Sarah, to her credit, didn't flinch, although her smile was a little forced. "I'll go get the cart."

At least, Denise thought, now she'd be able to study the material at home . . . or rather, she remembered with a little shock, at Ilaron's home. Her mind conjured up visions of some dark, sinister but palatial setting, like something out of an epic fantasy novel. . . .

Oh, don't be stupid!

But . . . what *was* she going to find?

Ilaron froze on the main stairway, a hunter suddenly sighting prey. There! That furtive figure hurrying across the Great Hall was definitely the man who had attacked Denise last night. More than that, worse than that:

There is the Darkness, the demon, there within a human host! He sensed it as strongly as a sudden chill. *It—she—Lamashtu is lying dormant, helpless by daylight—but the human is not helpless!*

Ilaron started in pursuit, weaving his way through the early throngs of visitors—only to nearly collide full-on with a tall, tweedy figure: Alan Atherton.

"Here now, steady—why, Ilaron Highborn!" The museum's director feigned a warm smile, a flash of teeth that, Ilaron thought, could just as easily have been a snarl. "Where are you going in such a hurry?"

"There's a man who just entered," Ilaron snapped.

"No, I don't know his name. But you must have him thrown out of the museum!"

Wrong word, that *must*. Atherton clearly didn't care for the autocratic command, nor the autocratic tone of voice. "But this is ridiculous!" he all but blustered. "On what charge? We can hardly go about throwing out some harmless—"

"He is far from harmless."

"I know you aren't a native English speaker, but haven't you ever heard the expression 'don't make waves'?"

"Yes, of course, but—"

"My dear Mr. Highborn, the man hasn't done anything illegal!"

"Not here, but—"

"Well, then! If he's broken no laws—"

"Surely attempted assault is proof enough." It came out as a snarl, and Atherton started. "Yes, Mr. Atherton, he attempted an assault on Denise Sheridan last night."

"What, *here*?"

Is it less of a crime for having happened off museum property? "No."

"I see. And has Dr. Sheridan filed charges?"

"No, but—"

"No? Well, then." Atherton threw up his hands. "There is nothing I can do. Surely you can see that. If he ever does commit a verifiable crime, or if Dr. Sheridan does, indeed, file charges, then do feel free to come to me. In the meantime— Ah, good day to you, Mr. Highborn!"

That was called after him. Ilaron, fuming over the stupidity of humans, had already brushed past Atherton, doing some careful stalking. Yes, there was the human prey, or rather Lamashtu within her human host, already on the far side of the Great Hall and headed down one of the side corridors flanking the main stairs.

And going away *from Denise's office. Odd.*

Did the demon sense that Ilaron was watching? Possibly. Or else what was left of the human host was just too edgy to stay put and too fragmented to be logical.

One or the other. To Ilaron's satisfaction, the man turned and slunk out of the building. To his frustration, that sly exit was from the far side of that well-named Great Hall, too far away for Ilaron to reach him in time without breaking into a very suspicious run.

And then I'd *be the one banished from the museum. Or asked some very awkward questions. Ah well, at least Sedgwick, or rather Lamashtu-in-Sedgwick, is gone for now. But will they be back?*

Probably.

And that idiot of a director will do nothing!

In that case, Ilaron decided grimly, *I will,* and stalked off to Denise's office.

FOURTEEN

On the Town

Kerezar's shaven-headed human army was not having a good day. Too damn many galleries to check, and most of the snooty bastards running the places wouldn't even let any of them inside. By now, after almost a whole day spent wandering around Manhattan, the teens were footsore and frustrated, beginning to wonder if this had been such a good idea.

"Look," one of them said suddenly, "what if we just, you know—quit?"

The others stared at him. "You crazy? You fuckin' *crazy*? You don't back out of a deal with the Prince of Darkness!"

"Well, maybe he isn't . . ."

But that suggestion trailed into silence. They all knew. They had all seen the force of Evil in that cold face and those endlessly black eyes, they had all felt the bite of his sword, seen him taste their blood, known that Evil had surged over them, making them its own.

And there was the dimmest, least-sure memory that there had once been another of them, slain before their eyes, his blood also tasted by. . . .

"Hey!" someone yelped. "Where're Bulldog and Fangs?"

For a second, pure horror swept over them; they'd all seen *that* movie, with the party disappearing one by one.

But then wiry Razor snickered. "You idiots! Nothing's picking us off, not us. The two fags wussed out, that's all. Saw them sneak off into a church."

But the idea of Bulldog and Fangs suddenly finding religion wasn't as funny as it should have been. For if Satan was real, they all realized, then so was the Holy Opposition. And if it came down to choosing sides . . .

"Hell." It was a defiant bark. "Coupla faggots. They never had any guts anyhow."

"Yeah. We're tough, right?"

"Too tough for wussing out like a coupla li'l fagboys."

Right. They would stick this out: The rewards would be worth it. As for failure—they'd find a way out of trouble, wouldn't they?

Hell, yes! They always did.

Meanwhile, their "Prince of Darkness" was having his own troubles.

Kerezar, sitting on his bed in the hotel room, since the bed was farthest from the window and the cursed sunlight out there, was going over his maps and brochures again and yet again, and beginning to feel an unfamiliar sensation of savage frustration. He had been away from his realm for . . . how long? How differently did time run between the two realms? Did it, for that matter? No way of knowing, not here and now.

But every moment spent away meant more of a risk, more of a chance offered to some other contender trying to claim the throne. *His* throne.

What will be waiting for me when I return?

No. Useless to consider that. He must think only of Ilaron. Returning with the traitor in tow would give his reign status far beyond anything any would-be usurper could claim.

Back to the brochures. Kerezar frowned at them,

thinking. He had narrowed his search a bit by now, down to the midtown area below Ninetieth Street and above Forty-second Street and east of Fifth Avenue since, after various consultations with that so-helpful concierge and an organization called the Chamber of Commerce, that seemed to be the most prestigious area, and therefore the most likely for Ilaron to be doing . . . whatever it was he was doing.

But that didn't mean that his guess was right. And even if it was, there were still an annoyingly large number of art galleries in that area. And while some of their names sounded promising . . .

At least he thought that they did, though who knew how humans named things . . . ?

Kerezar stopped, alarmed at how muzzy his mind was growing once again, and rubbed a hand over his eyes.

That didn't help. This realm with its obscene sunlight was making his head ache. Even with the curtains firmly drawn, some light was still seeping in around the edges; it was becoming increasingly difficult to think clearly. He could all too easily just let himself slide into . . .

No!

With that mental shout, Kerezar forced his attention back to the brochures. He would *not* give in, he *would* focus his vision, his will.

So, now. In addition to galleries, he saw that there were also museums of art and culture. Far too many museums—these humans must be obsessive about their past!

Never mind what the humans felt. The grandest museum of the lot, certainly the largest, would seem to be The American Museum of Art . . . yes, there on Fifth Avenue, the westward boundary of the area he'd selected, and well within the other parameters.

The American Museum of Art . . .

Surely Ilaron would have some connection there . . .
would have . . .

Kerezar bit back a most uncharacteristic shout of
pure rage. If only he could think! Too much iron—
almost every artifact in the cursed realm seemed to
be made of it; iron screamed from the walls, the ceiling, even from the frame of the bed he sat upon.

Kerezar grit his teeth in renewed frustration, furious
at himself—and furious at the illogic of being furious.
He sat reciting every calming discipline he knew, just
to fight off a growing sense of total, irrational panic.

They weren't working all that well.

*Ridiculous, ridiculous! If Ilaron can function here,
so can I!*

Could he?

At last, head pounding painfully, Kerezar surrendered, facing reality with cold honesty. Absurd to com-
pare himself to Ilaron, who had, after all, had more
time to adjust to this realm.

All he could do, Kerezar acknowledged, was try to
sleep, and wait for the restorative powers of the night.

Denise looked up with a start at the sound of a soft
"Ahem," then glanced wildly at her watch. "It *can't*
be five o'clock already!"

"Yes, it can," Ilaron said mildly. "And is."

And he, good as his word, was here in her office
waiting for her. "I will never get used to that," Denise
commented. "Those sudden appearances of yours,
that is."

He almost chuckled. "No great magics. I merely can
move softly and . . . unobtrusively when I wish. How
did your research go?"

"Ah. Well." She gestured at the wild disarray of
books and journals covering her desk and, by now,
most of the floor. "That should give you some idea.
And of course even with Sarah fielding most of my

calls, the real world kept getting in the way." His nod told her that he quite understood that problem. "I still haven't found the right reference," Denise continued, "although Sarah, bless her, has photocopied reams of material that I can take with me to study tonight."

"Excellent. Shall we?"

Feeling like someone diving blindly into unknown waters, Denise snatched up her coat and the now-bulging attaché case full of photocopies, staggering a little. Ilaron, seeing her difficulty, took the attaché case from her, though she suspected it was done more from practicality than chivalry, and they left together, Denise trying desperately to pretend she was just going off to some perfectly ordinary, innocuous, after-hours business meeting.

Right. Business meeting. Denise caught Sarah's wondering stare and felt herself redden.

Ordinary.

And I'm King Sargon of Akkad.

As she and Ilaron left the museum, he said suddenly, "Ha, wait, your suitcase. We'll make a brief stop at my gallery to retrieve it."

But the moment he entered the gallery, Ilaron was cornered by a competent-looking, well-dressed woman—Ms. Daniels, of course; Denise had met her once and occasionally spoke with her over the phone.

"Your pardon, Mr. Highborn, Dr. Sheridan." Her tone was this side short of exasperation. "I can see you're in a hurry, but . . ." She flourished a handful of documents almost under Ilaron's nose. "If you don't sign these, they are *not* going out overnight."

"Ah." A quick glance at the papers. "Indeed. Denise, if you will excuse me for a few moments?"

Amused to see the great and mighty Dark Elf (or whatever he was) brought low by the demands of bureaucracy, Denise obligingly sat waiting, trying not to swing her legs like a child, just as glad for the moment not to have to think about where she was going after this, and made small talk with the other two staff members.

Barely more than kids, both of them.

Right out of college, no doubt, like her Sarah, but with the sharply ambitious eyes she'd seen in other youngsters in the art world. They'd be out of place in a museum but, she guessed, made very useful employees in the more mercantile world of the art gallery.

A gallery such as this one? Testing, Denise asked the two kids in the mildest, most casual of tones, "What's it like working here?"

Well now, that got beneath those studied veneers!

"Oh, it's marvelous!" Sharon all but squealed, suddenly no more than the kid she was.

"A great place to work," Kevin agreed, just as warmly. "You never know what time period's going to be on display next, so it really keeps you on your toes. And," he added in awe, "Mr. Highborn knows so much about all types of art. I never saw him once make a mistake, not once."

"He's a wonderful employer," Sharon summed up, so warmly that Denise had to bite back a smile.

Handsome, too, eh, kid? You and Sarah ought to get together!

Of course, neither of the youngsters was going to say anything bad about Ilaron, not to her. But at the same time this unfeigned enthusiasm was, well, heartening.

Here came Ilaron now, with her suitcase. The two kids had already learned how to school their expressions to blandness; the more experienced Ms. Daniels merely smiled and wished her employer and Denise both a good night.

Of course. I'm just going to spend the night with her boss. No big deal. She shot a sly sideways glance at Ilaron. *Too bad this is something other than it looks.*

Not that I would . . . ah . . . I mean, I might, but . . .
I really do prefer my men human!

A line from a science-fiction film raced through her mind, and she nearly choked suppressing laughter over *"You know that interspecies romances never work out!"*

Not a word from Ilaron as they walked on. Nice of him to carry both the suitcase and the attaché case, though she suspected once again that he was doing it more from pragmatism than good old human-style chivalry.

But then Denise realized that their course had become decidedly erratic, sometimes crossing streets in the middle of the block, sometimes at the corner, sometimes even going back and forth, almost always keeping to the sunlight.

Finally, she couldn't stand the mystery any longer. "What *are* you doing?"

He spared her the quickest of wry grins. "Being paranoid. Two together leave a much clearer psychic trace than would only one. The more erratic our path, the more difficult that trace becomes to follow."

"A moving target being harder to hit, eh?"

He raised a bemused eyebrow. "In a manner of speaking. And by keeping to the sunlight, which is so alien to . . . that realm and anything demonic, we further confuse the trail."

"Oh." *God. I'd think he really* was *paranoid if I didn't know—if I hadn't seen—felt—that explosion, that sense of evil so powerful that I—*

"There," Ilaron said all at once, much to her relief. "That is the building in which I live."

Denise allowed herself the moment's luxury of gawking like a tourist, looking up and up at it. *Impressive. And I bet the rent's just as high.*

Like Ms. Daniels back at the gallery, the doorman showed not the slightest trace of emotion other than a polite, vague smile as he held the door open for them, touching his cap to them.

He sees nothing, Denise thought drily, *but I bet he gossips plenty. Or maybe not. I wouldn't want to be caught spreading tales about our Mr. Highborn!*

The building must have been post-War, judging from what she'd seen of its sleek brick exterior, but the lobby definitely harked back to an earlier age, one of those slightly overblown ones that spoke of money and not-quite good taste. Ilaron clearly was so used to the extravagances that he didn't even see them anymore, but strode determinedly along, leaving her in his wake.

"Denise? My elevator is this way."

His elevator?

By God, it really was his and his alone, a private elevator opened by a special key. Denise tried not to show how impressed she was as it carried them smoothly up, to the penthouse floor, no less.

Ah. And now she had to try not to show her uneasiness as well as Ilaron stopped in the antechamber to check various security measures. The standard burglar alarm systems Denise understood, the more . . . well . . . James Bondian systems she more or less could figure out, too.

But when he stood frozen for a moment, murmuring something that made the air shimmer and her skin prickle—that was blatantly some magical safeguard.

And blatantly disconcerting.

The whole procedure took only a few seconds, but it was hardly reassuring to see still more proof of how he lived, forever on his guard.

However, Denise thought, trying to calm her racing heart with something closer to normalcy, *however, I suspect he's down-to-earth unmagically uneasy as well. Not used to having visitors, are we, Ilaron?*

"Please, enter."

Of your own free will, her mind blathered. *Wonder if he does drink . . . wine?*

Never mind the movie quotes. Here we go. Out of my realm into . . . what?

FIFTEEN

Be It Ever So Humble

Nothing dramatic happened as she passed through the doorway. Denise let out her breath in a slow sigh, daring to look around. Ilaron's apartment . . .

. . . wasn't what she had expected. Nothing of Darkness here, nothing alarming or overblown at all.

The living room was large, dimly lit but filled with tranquil beauty—as well as a good many bookcases.

Of course. He'd have to keep adding to his knowledge of this realm somehow. Probably he's a prolific reader!

The sofa and chairs were upholstered in some rich beige weave that she suspected was sold by the "don't ask the price" yard. Despite that costly fact, Denise thought drily, they still looked comfortable. The carpet was definitely a genuine Kurdish weave in lovely muted reds and blues, and scattered about the room and on the walls were quite a few well-placed sculptures and paintings of several eras.

The room also, reassuringly, wasn't flawless. Denise hadn't expected the mess of a stereotypical bachelor apartment, but there was something almost heartening about the open *Art Times* lying abandoned across the arm of one chair, and the books stacked haphazardly in a corner as though their owner had forgotten about reshelving them.

Oh, and look! A coffee cup on that end table, hurray! He may not be human, but he's not perfect, either.

Daring to look around more openly, Denise decided that the overall effect was . . . decidedly eclectic. Just like his gallery. And just like the gallery, it all somehow managed to blend into a satisfying whole.

Hey now, that's a genuine Monet on that wall, I'd swear to it. Don't recognize the abstract next to it, but that figurine on the table is definitely a Roman bronze, maybe First Century A.D? And there's a . . . Brancusi? All those sleek, abstract arcs and curves, has to be Brancusi.

And that . . . Denise took a closer look at the elegant, silvery sword, at the clasp that would make it easy to snatch from its wall mounting—

"It's not ornamental, is it?" she asked warily.

"No."

Something about that response told her she'd better say something else, quickly. "You have a lovely apartment."

Was Ilaron pleased or annoyed at her appreciation? There was no way of telling from his calm mask of a face.

At a gesture from him (*Everyday magic,* Denise wondered, *or just showing off for company?*), a sound system switched itself on: Bach, she realized, the civilized notes of the Double Concerto. She glanced at him in appreciation and caught the faintest hint of pleasure cross that cold face. There were, it seemed, a good many unexpected layers to Ilaron.

But Denise was tired, physically and emotionally both. And suddenly she was so overwhelmed by the day's events, the events of the night before, and her relief that the apartment should look so normal, so *human,* that she couldn't bear it.

Sinking to a sofa, Denise, to her utter embarrassment, burst into tears.

Ilaron's reaction was alarming. "Stop that!" he commanded, eyes fierce. "Stop it!"

Without another word, he rushed into the next room, slamming the door behind him. Denise was shocked enough nearly to choke, and frantically struggled to get herself back under control, wiping her nose and eyes with a tissue hastily scrounged from her purse.

What in hell . . .

But she didn't quite dare go and knock on that intimidatingly slammed door. After a time, though, a wary Ilaron opened it, peering cautiously out at her, then returned to her side, face rigid. "Forgive me," he said shortly.

"What was all that about?"

"A small thing."

"That was no small thing! Ilaron, please! If I'm going to stay here even a short while, I don't want to have to worry about every word I say or move I make."

He sighed. "Fair enough."

"Well?"

"Very well, if you must know: In my realm, only slaves weep. Your tears sparked what you would, I imagine, call the predator response in me."

"Oh."

"Don't fear. I will not let it happen again."

Denise stared at him, no longer at all in the mood for tears. God, he *wasn't* human, was he?

But, amazingly, right now that thought somehow wasn't frightening. She was too aware of something there behind the rigid mask, the slightest hint of . . . was it despair?

"What a terribly difficult life you must lead," she burst out before she could stop herself. No going back now, so Denise continued boldly, "I guessed at it before, but . . . seeing this . . . seeing you . . . watching you fight your upbringing, your very nature . . ."

Ilaron shrugged, clearly not accepting her pity. Possibly, though it was impossible to read emotion in that inhumanly still face, he was even embarrassed by her concern.

"I made the choice to live in this realm." His voice held no inflection at all. "For all the admittedly never-ending difficulties, I do not regret it. Come, I will show you to the guest room."

Right. Guest room. Safe topic. God, when will *I learn to keep my mouth shut?*

The guest room was as comfortable and handsome as everything else here, with a large, canopied bed and sleek rosewood dresser, table and chair, though everything had the carefully precise look of a room rarely used.

No women friends, then? Denise couldn't help but wonder. *No, that's right, no visitors at all. Aren't you lonely, Ilaron? You never really did answer me when I last asked that. Do you even understand loneliness?*

Ilaron, not noticing or perhaps not wanting to notice her sudden uneasiness, swiftly pointed out the amenities, a walk-in closet, a separate bathroom, then left her to settle in.

Denise, being, after all, only human, promptly prowled through the closet and the dresser drawers. No sign of prior inhabitancy, though the fact that the closet held hangers—plenty of them, no cheap plastic types but nice, sturdy wooden ones with a pleasant whiff of cedar to them—and the bathroom clean towels and fresh soap (mm, nicely perfumed, too), when Ilaron couldn't possibly have known till this morning that she would be here, made her wonder.

Ah well, maybe his cleaning woman did a very thorough job. Or maybe he kept the room ready Just In Case. Or maybe, she thought wryly, it was simply magic.

When Denise reappeared, feeling a little less uneasy for no reason she could have named—all those hangers, maybe, or the scented soap, items showing a concern for her comfort—she found the living room empty.

"In here," called Ilaron's voice. "In the kitchen."

She followed his voice into the beautifully appointed room, feeling a quick pang of envy over all that lovely counter space and shelving, and found Ilaron at the stove, already preparing an early dinner.

"The sun won't set for another hour or so," he said over his shoulder, "and I thought we would both enjoy a brief respite."

"Excellent idea."

But then Denise spotted a Zabar's shopping bag sitting in a corner of the gleaming kitchen. She pictured Ilaron, in all his elegant, alien aloofness, at Zabar's, that quintessentially New York superstore of food, and dissolved into helpless laughter.

This earned her a puzzled frown. "What do you find so amusing?"

Unable to explain, Denise hastily asked, "What can I do to help?"

He was still puzzled, but pointed to a plate of scallions. Denise set about chopping with a good will until it hit her that the act of preparing a dinner together was one of those awkwardly intimate situations. She glanced subtly at her host. Did Ilaron feel that, too? No telling.

"Attractive, for a human woman." Heh.

Fortunately, the meal was soon ready, some concoction of hot smoked salmon and warmed salad that smelled good enough to make her mouth water.

"Since the day is still so warm," Ilaron said, filling a pitcher with ice water, "I suggest that we dine out on the terrace. No alcohol," he added casually. "We have work facing us, and don't want our alertness blunted."

"Uh, no. Of course not."

They carried their plates and glasses outside, and Denise glanced about appreciatively. They were on the south side of the apartment, and to west and south was a vista of wildly varied cityscape, intricately wrought Gothic rooftops vying with the flat, glass-and-steel sort of the fifties and sixties, plus a few ultramodern, quirky variations with curves like the tops of old-fashioned furniture. To the east, the city flattened out, offering a view that stretched out over Long Island.

He must get some spectacular sunrises. Does he, can he, enjoy sunrises?

The terrace, which rimmed the entire apartment, was attractively landscaped with low, flowering plants. *Azaleas?* Denise thought doubtfully, used to whatever would grow indoors in pots. *And impatiens?*

Then she realized with a sudden renewed stab of alarm why there was nothing tall, nothing bushy. *There are no places for anyone to hide.*

She didn't want to think about that, or indeed of much of anything else. All she wanted, Denise decided, was just a peaceful interlude of nothing but sociable dining. Good for the nerves.

And for Ilaron's nerves as well? The cold, beautiful face was, to her surprise, almost relaxed, almost smiling. "I do like this view," he said suddenly.

Ah, innocuous small talk. Good. Denise glanced about at the sweeping panorama again. "I do, too."

"I admit I was thinking more of defensive capabilities when I took this apartment. But," he added hastily, seeing her flinch, "the view is decidedly a bonus. A fascinating city, this."

"Tell me," Denise said, determinedly forcing the theme back onto the small-talk track, "do you really enjoy running an art gallery?"

"Oh, I do." Again she saw a trace of that quick, awkward, almost innocent smile. "Denise, you grew up in this world; no matter how you try, you just cannot possibly appreciate the never-ending *newness* that is human creativity. Or, for that matter, the continued link of each artist's joy in that creativity down through the human ages."

She studied him. "You can feel that, can't you? Literally? That's how you know truth from forgery."

He nodded. "Every time I touch a statue or painting, I feel its . . . ah, I don't know if I can put this into your language's words. I feel its *trueness*, I feel the artist's joy, and the joy of being surrounded by—

"Ah, enough."

The cold mask had dropped back over his face, as though he were angry at himself for revealing so much. After an awkward moment of silence, Ilaron continued, almost convincingly lightly, "As for the everyday matters of the gallery, all those 'ordinary' little details, remember that what seems ordinary to you is still nicely exotic to me."

"Even the taxes?" she teased. "And the rent?"

"I am," he told her in mock solemnity, "a legal taxpayer. If not exactly a legal citizen. And as for the rent, both at the gallery and here . . ."

A meaningful silence. Ilaron, Denise realized, had little to do with human concepts of morality. He would hardly be averse to using magical persuasion to smooth his path a bit. Including keeping the rents on gallery and apartment unusually low. She felt laughter bubbling up to the point where she couldn't hold it in.

"What?" he asked, a hint of amusement in his voice.

"I was just thinking that you—you really have adapted nicely, you really have!"

"I will," Ilaron said drily, "take that as a compliment. And you?" he countered. "Do you enjoy running a museum department?"

"I do. Of course I can't feel the same, well, psychic joy you do in handling artifacts, but I *do* get a thrill in knowing I'm reading a cuneiform text no one's seen for maybe four thousand years, or in seeing a scrap of fabric or a necklace and finding some clue that connects it to some perfectly ordinary human being who lived in ancient Nippur or Lagash. There's so much we still don't know about our own kind, how they lived, how they thought, what they hoped or dreamed—"

She hesitated, now a little embarrassed herself at having revealed so much. "Well. What else do you want me to say?"

Ilaron's wave of a hand was downright regal. "Whatever you wish." A pause. "Very well: What led you to archaeology in the first place?"

"I . . . don't even remember! I discovered the ancient Mesopotamians at a pretty young age, yes, at the museum, and got hooked. Decided then and there that I wasn't going to be a corporate type, but I never dreamed I'd be lucky enough to wind up where I am. And it's always a thrill to learn that the chain's unbroken."

"Eh?"

"That the next generation's been hooked the way *I* was hooked." Denise smiled. "There's nothing like getting a letter from some schoolkid saying, 'I thought history was boring till I saw the Sumerian stuff, it's so *kewl*,'"—she spelled that out for him and caught a faint smile in return—"or 'I want to be an archaeologist when I graduate.' It's all worthwhile at times like that."

Ilaron raised an amused eyebrow. "Even the museum politics?"

"Even the museum politics. Even if I can't magick Alan Atherton into a lapdog!"

That actually forced a laugh from him. "Neither, I assure you, can I!"

They fell into companionable silence, enjoying the

vista about them, pointing out the quick, unexpected swoop of a hawk across the skyline or a jet contrail high overhead suddenly turned to a line of bright silver as the sun caught it.

But the sun all too soon slid behind the western buildings, and the daylight faded. Far below them, the canyons of the city streets grew blue with shadows as the twilight deepened, then blazed with new gold as lights came on all over the city.

And Ilaron, dropping the mask of affability, got to his feet. "We must go inside now," he said shortly. "You, to do your research."

"And you?"

"I have research to do as well."

He didn't specify the type.

And she, seeing how his face had once again gone cold and unreadable, alien, did not ask.

SIXTEEN

Moonlight Sonata

They were plotting against him, Setheatel and Ertia, two more ambitious nobles were plotting against him there in the cool, velvet darkness, whispering that they cared not how he'd slain Ahligar, whispering that he had left his throne untended, whispering that now they could dare to act, while he, he could not touch them—

Kerezar stirred, groaned faintly, then suddenly came fully awake, sitting bolt upright on his bed, instantly knowing that he was in the human realm, in the hotel known as the Marriott Marquis, and feeling the night outside the room even through the closed curtains.

Yes, ah yes. At last.

The dream . . . had been only that, nothing of value or import. Yes, there almost certainly still were those who plotted against him, he would be amazed if there were not. But he would deal with them firmly enough in time.

He rose, found what served these humans as bathing facilities, and did the best he could without touching all the cursed iron knobs and handles, muffling them in towels so that he could safely turn them on or off.

Better. At least I can think again.

Kerezar paused, dripping, smiling ever so faintly.

Yes . . . indeed I can . . . Now that the night has fallen, there is work to be done. On more than one level, I think . . .

As he worked out the details of what was to be

done, and how, his smile thinned till it was sharp as the edge of a blade.

It is not, I am sure, to be work that my noisome young helpers will enjoy. But what they wish or do not wish is irrelevant. They shall still prove useful.

More so than ever one of them has imagined in all his short, ugly life.

But where were they to meet? The West Village was too inconvenient. The area directly about the hotel would not do, either, convenient though it might have been: Kerezar had quickly realized that due west and east on all the side streets were various houses of human entertainment, theaters, he believed they were called, and with the theaters, a good many places designed specifically for dining: restaurants. Too many people would, therefore, be about, presumably at any hour since he'd seen that this city never ceased activity.

But farther west, nearer to what the humans called the Hudson River, seemed to be, according to the maps, a district consisting mostly of warehouses, an area that would be almost totally empty and barren at night.

Excellent.

Freshly groomed, disguised once more as human, Kerezar hid his sword in a fold of his coat. Then, grim-faced and determined, he made another ride down in that cursed iron box of an elevator, refusing to wince at the nearness of the deadly metal. Exiting on the ground level, he slipped his way through what seemed like impossible crowds of humans, trying not to flinch at their cheerful noise and animal smells, out to the driveway that cut through the hotel. There, struggling not to cough amid the various chemical and mechanical reeks, he watched the humans for a careful bit till he was certain of the right action.

Yes. That was how one gained transport. Kerezar

stood on the proper line like a law-abiding human, and waited for a taxi.

"The West Village," he told the driver, and gave curt directions, then settled back on the seat.

The West Village, yes, where he would meet his human . . . allies. Who would, he assumed without hesitation, be there.

As indeed they were. Kerezar, having warily left the taxi several blocks back and walked the rest by a circuitous route that would throw off any potential watcher, stopped short, smiling inwardly at the sight of the teens waiting for him just where they should be. He had come up behind them, giving him the chance to study them unhindered. Were they somewhat fewer in number? Perhaps. The more cowardly would presumably have fled when they could. No matter; they could not work harm against him.

He cleared his throat. His teenage aides whirled, stifling yelps, then stood shifting nervously from foot to foot, trying not to meet his gaze, clearly shamefaced. And, he sensed, behind those vicious young facades, they were genuinely terrified.

Tsk, you've failed me, haven't you? "Well?" Kerezar asked mildly, already knowing what answer to expect.

Sure enough: "We hunted, we really did!"

Ah, look at them, so clearly in fear for the safety of their . . . what was the phrase humans used so lightly? Their immortal souls. As though he had any use for souls, human or otherwise.

Still, Kerezar thought, *I do have a role to play if I am to keep these tools my own.*

So he merely . . . stared, gaze cold and unreadable, letting them squirm and give off such a charmingly tantalizing aura and scent of fear. Yes, oh yes, it was almost unbearable not to attack, not to slay one just for the delight of feeling the sweetness of a victim's death.

But Kerezar reminded himself sternly that he had never yet given in to the flaw of self-indulgence. And he was hardly about to weaken now.

"It is not a problem," he soothed in false, wonderfully feigned concern, and felt the miasma of their fear lift just the tiniest bit. Poor little things, how they wanted to believe that he cared about them!

Fools.

"I knew that I had set you an almost impossible task," Kerezar continued, still in that almost comforting voice. "It was a test, no more."

He let them wait a few moments more, just to keep the weak creatures from becoming too complacent, then added, almost offhandedly, "And you have passed. From now on," Kerezar continued over their half-stifled gasps of relief, "you are to meet me farther uptown whenever I require. There is still much for you to do. As to where . . ." He gave the humans the address of the specific site he had chosen. "You will meet me there whenever I so command. Is that understood?"

Nods and mutters of agreement. But judging from their uneasy sideways glances at each other, it was either a region they didn't know very well or one they feared.

Or could it be that they thought the site might have a magical significance? No matter.

No matter. They have no choice. Even were this site not so inconvenient for me, it is no longer safe. There have been far too many human investigations in this area recently. And even humans may make inopportune discoveries.

"Tomorrow," he told his human followers, "you will do my bidding again—but warily. Do you understand me? I do not wish your families, your acquaintances to wonder unduly at your absences."

Shrugs, indifferent grimaces: Obviously, he thought, their families cared little what they did, or they would not already have such freedom.

"Of course," Kerezar added, just in case, "you will not let anyone even begin to suspect that you are leading a second existence as my . . . aides."

Unspoken but quite obvious on his face was: They'd best not be so foolish.

Satisfied at the renewed rush of fear he sensed from them all, Kerezar continued coldly, "I wish you to travel to the new site I have mentioned. Wait for me there, no matter how long the delay, and you shall receive my orders. Now, go."

But then he pointed, selecting one boy at random. "You, no. Come with me. The rest of you—go away."

Leading his chosen one on, Kerezar hunted until he found a dark, quiet alley faced on both sides by windowless walls.

"Perfect."

"What . . ."

"Ah no, boy. It's not for you to question me. Tell me, have you ever heard of an augury? No? You shall learn."

Enough speaking. A pity he had none of the proper sacrificial tools, but a glance about the alley showed broken glass, rough, abrasive bits of rock . . . True nobility, Kerezar noted, made due with what was at hand without complaint.

And the augury would be just as useful no matter with what tools it was performed.

A quick, viciously elegant blow crushed the victim's vocal cords: There must be no distracting screams or needless noise of any sort. An equally vicious thrust of magic hurled the victim flat, pinned helplessly against the ground, limbs outstretched. Improvised

spikes of metal and wood through hands and feet ensured the victim's proper placement. Desperate, terrified eyes stared up at him, wide with shock, but their
pleading was meaningless.

Working with swift efficiency, Kerezar stripped
away the victim's clothes. And then, slowly, gracefully,
with sword, abrasive rock, and shards of glass, he
began to sacrifice the chosen victim to the Darkness.
Pain and terror swirled about him as he worked, and
Kerezar drank in the dark glory, offering it back to
the Darkness. And Power swirled about him, rising in
strength, drawn from agony, growing as agony grew,
growing Power, growing . . . yes, yes . . . he forced
the Power into the form he must have, into the augury, into one fierce blast of scrying and—

Ilaron!

He nearly shouted out that name. Without a doubt,
he had just sensed Ilaron, here in this city, no doubts
now, Ilaron was here and—

What was this "Highborn Gallery"? He must have
seen it in the brochures before too much iron had
overwhelmed his mind, seen it and stored it uncon-
sciously away in his memory.

"Highborn Gallery." That could be a very loose
translation of "High Nobility." Could Ilaron be so arrogant? Possibly. Perhaps he—

Without warning, the victim died. The swirl of
Power snapped out of being, and Kerezar straightened
with a hiss, dazed for a moment by the suddenness of
the return to the mundane human world.

Humans, he thought coldly as his head cleared, *are
far too fragile.*

But . . . "The Highborn Gallery," Kerezar murmured. This one touch of information he had just
gained might well prove valuable.

Kerezar left the remnants of the sacrifice behind
him. Let the humans make of it what they would.

There was enough crime in this city, surely, for them to think it no more than the result of one gang taking their petty vengeance on another.

It no longer held any interest for him.

Ilaron sat alone at his desk, before him a silver knife, a mirror, a bowl of distilled water. There in the night, he was engrossed in his own forms of scrying, murmuring spell after spell, staring into the mirror, the smooth, shiny blade of the knife, seeing . . . seeing . . .

Ah, nothing. Nothing more than useless swirlings of fog. He put down the knife, brushing stray strands of damp hair back from his face. Scrying was awkward in this realm, sadly limited, and—

. . . *and at the back of his mind the Darkness whispered, unwanted, that all he needed for a true reading was blood, pain, terror—*

Wearily, he shut the whisper away, sealing it behind a wall of will. These nonbloody, nonsacrificial forms of scrying were difficult to work only because of the need for caution. Particularly now. He most certainly did not want to risk leaving his mind open even for an instant, not with Kerezar in the same realm.

Of course, Ilaron admitted, even in safer days, when he had dared the risk of opening his mind, there'd still been a problem: In that heightened sense of awareness, he had been far *too* aware of all the human waves of emotion in this crowded city to be able to totally concentrate, too aware, as well, of their dark side, their tempting darkness . . .

No. And no again.

With a sigh, Ilaron pulled the bowl of water to him. He would try once more—no, curse the Darkness, he would not merely try. He would *succeed.*

And he . . . saw . . . yes . . . He sensed . . .

"Kerezar!"

* * *

Denise sat cross-legged on the guest room's bed, still fully clad save for her shoes, sheaves of paper spread out all around her—and nearly fell over with the force of a sudden, immense yawn.

Ah, ridiculous. She set to work again, only to realize all at once she was sagging, bent nearly double over the photocopies, peering at them, too bleary-eyed to make sense of the cuneiform texts.

Denise straightened slowly, hands on her lower back, trying to stretch the weariness out of her body, trying to force some energy back into her brain, thinking, *I am* not *ready to call it a night.*

No use. For all her determination, she was yawning all over again, and her eyes were burning.

Dammit, if Ilaron can keep working out there, then I'm not ready to give up in here, not yet!

All right. One more try. "Anu created her," Denise translated in a murmur, "Ea raised her . . . reared her? Educated—no, Ea never did that . . . what, then? Ea . . . damn."

Now that she'd gotten this far into it, the thing looked like just one more standard incantation . . . yes. That was exactly what this one was: nothing of any use at all.

With a sigh that wanted very much to turn into another yawn, Denise put the useless page aside and stared determinedly at the next photocopy, which was even less clear, trying to make sense out of the blurry symbols by sheer force of will. They were blurring even more as she looked at them, and she was starting to slide sideways. . . .

Denise came starkly awake, staring wildly. What the *hell*? A shout! That had been a strangled shout from the living room!

Ilaron!

She nearly fell off the bed in her hurry, hunted for and couldn't find her shoes, found one, only one, tossed it aside in frustration and rushed out, barefoot—only to stop dead at a hiss of startled pain. The living room seemed pitch-black after the brightness of the guest room—ah, right! The sudden blaze of light must have really hurt. Hastily she shut the door to the guest room.

"Sorry, I wasn't thinking. Are you all right?"

Ilaron, of course, could see perfectly well in the darkness. As he lowered the hand he'd flung over his eyes, they glinted eerily at her, greenish, like those of a cat. "Yes," he said after a moment. "You may turn up that light. By your left hand. *Gradually.*"

As she turned it up, very slowly and gingerly, just enough to let her see clearly and feeling guilty about even that much light, Ilaron added, "I didn't mean to alarm you; I was . . . startled, that's all."

"By, uh, what?"

He snorted. "You needn't look so alarmed. There's nothing lurking in the apartment. I merely learned that I was right: Kerezar is definitely in this realm."

"Kerezar."

Ilaron hesitated, as though trying to find a way not to frighten her. "He is one of my kind," he finally said. "A singularly cold, deadly one of my kind."

"There's more to it, isn't there?"

"Yes. Kerezar is . . . the ruler of that realm, and 'ruler' is not exactly the hereditary title it might be here."

Something in his voice set off a warning. "Ilaron . . . ? Were you . . . ?"

"Yes," he admitted reluctantly. "Or rather, I could have held that rank. But I . . . had no wish for it, or for the endless ruthlessness that came with it. Quite simply, Denise: The ruler of that realm gets his throne by killing those who oppose him, then holds by being more devious and brutal than any other schemer."

"How charming. And he's *here*?"

"Alone," he assured her and, she guessed from the fleeting hint of emotion she caught on his face, assured himself as well. "There is no Otherly army with him. I suspect that while in the process of hunting me, he made some not-quite-successful pact with Lamashtu, and she tricked even him."

"And stranded him here without anyone else to help him. Score one for the demon."

"Don't underestimate Kerezar. He may be alone, but he's not exactly helpless. In fact," Ilaron added almost casually, "Kerezar has just sacrificed a human to gain a temporary rush of Power. That sudden surge of Power was what startled me."

Oh God!

Now that her eyes had adjusted to the dimness, Denise could see a hint of something . . . odd glittering in Ilaron's eyes, something decidedly unpleasant and . . . alien. Evil?

And here I am, alone in an isolated penthouse with—with—what?

No. She wasn't going to be afraid of him at this stage of things. Forcing out the words, Denise asked, "D-does this mean that Kerezar has found us?"

"No."

But then, Ilaron rubbed a hand over his face in a very human gesture of weariness. "No," he repeated, and now his eyes, to her great relief, were sane again. "The double-edged hunt must, and will, continue.

"Oh, and by the way, I have a name for our crazed cultist, the one who would have sacrificed you: Sedgwick. I caught that data in passing. But I would not worry about either peril just yet. For now, you need not fear."

Ilaron's voice was all at once smooth and soothing. "You are safe here. You may sleep."

And, overwhelmed by the suddenness of his spell

and utterly exhausted, she staggered back to the guest room and did just that.

Kerezar, still feeling the pleasant surge of Power warming him, found transportation uptown, to the warehouse where his human tools had gathered to wait for him.

How fortunate for them that they did so.

Their eyes were weary; they were not, for all their wishes, truly creatures of the night. But they need stay awake and alert only a little bit longer. Efficiently, Kerezar included them all in a web of glamour. They would not ask about their missing fellow; they would not even remember him.

"Tomorrow," Kerezar purred, "I have a specific site for you to search, a specific midtown gallery: the High-born Gallery, which lies at the intersection of Madison Avenue and Seventy-eighth Street. Do you know where that is? Are you sure of it? Good. You are to be wary and arouse no suspicions. Is that understood? No suspicions! Ah, you do understand. Splendid. Tomorrow, my assistants," Kerezar added, "you should have far better luck in your hunt."

Unspoken was: They must.

All that night, Lamashtu prowled the city in Sedgwick's body, not yet attacking, merely enjoying the novel experience of . . . anticipation

So much promise here, all these nice, fresh lives about her, more than she had ever seen in one site! Lovely, sweet and rare and intoxicating. So many lives, and all she would need to do when she was sated with this new and thrilling act of waiting was reach out a hand . . .

But, to her disgust, Sedgwick's body, being mortal, was wearying, and far too quickly. She must, Lamashtu realized, let her host eat and rest—

In short, she must waste the rest of the night! Rage stirred within her, aching to be loosed. Let the human shrivel, let him die!

But, no. No. Not quite yet. That would mean the inconvenience of finding a new host. And as for freely manifesting herself—no, again, not just yet. Lamashtu knew that she wasn't sure enough of this new realm for such a drastic step.

So she soothed the rage, contented herself with touching a few homeless street people in passing, and smiled to herself to see them stagger and fall lifeless. A small satisfaction, but satisfying none the less. And anticipation really was a delicious change, particularly with the promise of so much rage to be unleashed, so much death to be released, at the other side of it.

Tomorrow, Lamashtu mused, pleased that there would *be* a finite, measurable tomorrow after so many ages of timeless boredom. Tomorrow, she would see about getting Sedgwick to obey her more efficiently. Tomorrow, too, she would see about eliminating the troublesome human he worried at, the scholar-woman who knew too much about her—who might even know the secret of her banishment.

Tomorrow, Denise Sheridan would die.

SEVENTEEN

. . . Where the Shadows Lie

The faintest sound of motion outside the guest room woke her. Denise lay in bed for a moment, blinking, gradually remembering where she was, then trying to figure out what she was hearing . . . the softest whisper of *something* cutting the air . . .

She gave up. Hastily washing and dressing, finally finding that recalcitrant lost shoe, Denise opened the door a wary crack, not wanting to blind her host again.

No problem this time. The living room curtains had been drawn aside just enough to let some daylight in, sufficient to let her see Ilaron, lithe in black exercise clothes, sword in hand and unbound hair tossing about his head in dark waves. He was going through an intricate, elegant dance of an exercise, moving with such swift, deadly precision that Denise stood frozen in sheer wonder. Was he aware of her? He gave no sign, his alien eyes unreadable, his face coldly tranquil, clearly concentrating only on completing the exercise.

Beautiful, Denise thought, and wasn't quite sure if she meant the dance or the dancer.

At last the intricate routine ended with a final lunge that would have neatly spitted any opponent. Ilaron straightened, turned to salute Denise briefly with the sword, his face still a mask, then vanished into another room. Denise heard the muted sound of running water and his voice, rising above it, "Perhaps you would care to start the coffee?"

Oh, yes.

She wasted a few moments in wandering about the kitchen, giving in to a very human urge to open drawers and cupboards.

Nothing alien. Ilaron liked his ingredients fresh and his cooking implements of the finest quality, but she'd already guessed that.

Ah. Coffee. Beans, of course; no instant nonsense for Ilaron! And here was the grinder and a *very* expensive brand of brewer. Biting her lip, she carefully measured out what she hoped was exactly the right amount of beans (you didn't waste a bean of this exotic Indonesian blend), then set to work.

Denise was listening to the cheerful sound of coffee brewing by the time Ilaron joined her. No sign of the tranquil, exotic swordsman now: He was the successful businessman, suit beautifully cut, hair neatly tied back, sunglasses hiding his eyes.

All in all, Denise thought, he looked both fashionable and disgustingly awake and alert. Giving in to a yawn, she asked, "Your people don't need much sleep, do they?"

"Not as much as yours. The sleep spell didn't help?"

"One of the few times quality didn't overcome quantity." *Oh Lord, I didn't mean a double entendre.*

Fortunately, he chose not to see it. "A pity," was all he said. "But come, the coffee is ready."

"Mm. I should have just set up an IV drip of caffeine." At his blank expression, she thought, with a foolish little spark of triumph, *Ha, he doesn't understand* everything *about us.* "Never mind."

As Ilaron quickly and efficiently prepared two omelets, breaking eggs, chopping herbs, cooking, all (to her disgust) without spilling a drop or wasting a leaf, Denise said, half-joking, "I have a question for you."

"Eh?" He was engrossed in neatly transferring the food to plates.

"Why are elves always swordsmen?"

"I am not an elf. And," he added, sitting across from her at the kitchen table, "as for swords . . . ah well, let me see. Sometimes it isn't convenient or safe to use magic; a sword is as useful as a wand or rod for storing spells; projectile weapons tend to be awkward and can run out of ammunition at awkward moments—"

"And you are an elegant people, and swords just look Really Cool."

That earned her a startled laugh. "And swords," he agreed, "look Really Cool. Denise, your pardon for spoiling breakfast, but I think it best that we listen to the news."

"I know." Denise took one last uncomplicated bite of her omelet, savoring the spicy-sweetness of the herbs. "I was only trying to postpone the inevitable."

". . . Ebola virus," said a solemn voice from the radio as Ilaron switched it on. "We'll be right back."

Denise groaned. She and Ilaron waited grimly through what seemed an endless barrage of commercials for cars and insurance until at last:

"To repeat our top story: The deaths of three homeless men and a woman last night in midtown Manhattan, within a block of each other, are under investigation, although health officials are strenuously denying the presence of any epidemic in the city."

Sure enough, the same Board of Health spokesperson, *Good old Dr. Carson,* Denise thought, *who's probably wishing he had some other job right now,* was saying in the same dull but this time not quite convincingly calm voice, "Let me state right up front that while these four deaths *are* currently under investigation, the victims categorically did *not* die of the Ebola virus. I repeat, there is *no* evidence of the Ebola virus either in New York City or the surrounding area, nor is there yet any indication at this time that the four deaths were at all related."

A reporter promptly picked up on that. "You say that the deaths weren't caused by the Ebola virus. Yet doctors on the scene reported massive hemorrhaging through the pores of the skin. Isn't this one of the symptoms of death caused by the Ebola virus?"

"Ghoul," Denise muttered.

"Yes," Carson was admitting, "but—" He had to raise his voice over the sudden uproar. "*But* none of the other signs match the symptoms of that virus."

"Dr. Carson!" another voice shouted. "Isn't it true that all four victims were found at the same location?"

"Within a block, yes, but—"

"Maybe it isn't the Ebola virus," someone else yelled, "but can you rule out any other disease? You say that there isn't any epidemic, but why were they all found in the same—"

"No comment."

Another uproar.

"No comment."

Denise glanced at Ilaron. None of the reporters were actually using the words "government cover-up," but the inference was clear enough.

Ilaron switched off the radio in disgust.

"Humans," he said, "and your pardon for the generality, seem to love terrifying themselves over imaginary dangers when there are very real dangers about."

"Lamashtu . . . ?"

"Oh yes, your Mesopotamian demon has had a good night playing with the helpless. I suspect that her touch alone would be sufficient cause for the mysterious and suddenly fatal disease."

Denise bit her lip. "Yes. All the stories of her say she kills by touch alone." She paused. "And what about your acquaintance?"

"Kerezar?" Ilaron shrugged ever so slightly. "Who

can say? By now he will have already lost the temporary Power lent by the sacrifice he performed."

"Ah . . . does that mean there are going to be
more sacrifices?"

"Probably."

Denise frowned at that offhanded coolness. "At
least I can do something about Lamashtu."

"Back at the museum, I assume?"

"Right. There is, unfortunately, nothing really useful in any of those photocopies you so kindly lugged
up here. But I've just begun the search through the
department's records."

He paused, as though about to argue, then gave the
smallest of resigned shrugs. "So be it. Come, my
lady." It was said with gentle sarcasm. "Your escort
waits."

Later, though, in her office in the museum, after
indeed having been escorted there by Ilaron (and having been met by a studiously bland-faced Sarah), Denise wasn't feeling quite so optimistic. First of all,
every time she got going, there seemed to be an
interruption.

Perfect. There went the phone again. Even with
Sarah fielding calls, Denise could hardly have refused
one from her counterpart in the British Museum (even
though said counterpart had nothing much to say and
was apparently just keeping in touch), or one from
Edgar Williams of Musical Instruments wanting to
know if, by any chance, she still had that copy of
Music of the Ancient Near East (she did), and could
he send over his aide to borrow it? (The aide, being
a healthy young man, had been more interested in
Sarah than books, and had at last needed to be chased
out by Denise.)

"Uh, Dr. Sheridan?"

Denise stifled a sigh. "Let me guess, Sarah: Fearless

Leader yet again. Yes? And . . . why, *hello,* Mr. Atherton. What can I do for you—yes, of course I was serious about the Assyrian exhibit. Why do you—of course I'll have the proposal ready for you in a week, just as I—what? Four days?" Fighting down the urge to snap, *Give me a break!* Denise said smoothly, "Of course. If I can't get it done in four days, why, I doubt I'll ever get it done. Yes, yes, of course I was joking!" *No, no, I was not.* "Till then. Bye, now."

Who knew? She might not have to worry about that stupid proposal at all, not with Lamashtu lurking and no one letting Denise do any serious research.

Not that she could! All these books, all these articles, and there was nothing specifically helpful, nothing!

Whoa. Wait. She was forgetting that there were still other sources; not all the department's texts were in printed, published books.

"Sarah—no, never mind. I'll look for it myself."

Someday, she thought, hunting through the department's overstuffed card catalog, *someday we'll computerize.*

Right now, no museum seemed to have ever reached the twentieth century, at least as far as office storage technology went. Yes, there were computers, but no department had the time or extra staff to transfer all the information on all the catalog cards into a computer database. Envying Ilaron his gallery's efficient computer system (and a budget that could fund a temp typist), Denise warily wiggled a stuck drawer. Something was caught in the back of the drawer, all the way in the back, of course, too far in for her to reach whatever it was—hopefully just a card and not something worse—with a hand . . .

Ha, wait . . . if she slipped this pen in there . . . yes. Gently, Denise worked the jam free, pulling out several yellowing record cards that probably hadn't been examined since they'd been written nearly a century ago. But they were in the right section . . .

Mm, and this one looked promising. It indicated a collection of handwritten papers from a Dr. Brandford Richards . . . couldn't place the name . . . a lot of less than fully accredited archaeologists and scholars back then . . . might not even have *been* an archaeologist. But then, Dr. Schliemann of the Discovery of Troy fame, hadn't been one, either. And the collection described on the cards did sound potentially useful—if at the same time weirdly occult.

Unfortunately, it wasn't going to be so easy to check. The collection, old and dubious as it was, wasn't stored either here in the office or in the museum's library.

The Tunnel, blast it.

Of course the papers were in the Tunnel, Murphy and his laws being what they were. Not exactly where she would have chosen to go hunting even on the best of days.

In the last century, a water tunnel had led under Central Park to the Forty-second Street Reservoir, where the main branch of the New York Public Library stood today. As far as she knew, most of the tunnel had been subsequently filled in, but the nearly four-block stretch directly under the museum still existed, and was used as a convenient storage space for less frequently accessed artifacts and records.

Convenient, hah. The last time I went down there, I came back with dust all over my clothes and a spider clinging to my sleeve.

"The things I do for science," she told Sarah.

"I'll go with you."

"No. Someone has to stay here, just in case. To answer phones if nothing else. Also, I'd like you to start thinking about what we could do about an exhibit using our Assyrian material and a miniscule budget."

Hey, I could *survive all this, I* might *still want my job!*
Denise shrugged. "I'll requisition someone from
Security."

It was museum policy that no one could go down
into the Tunnel alone, dating from the time someone
had done exactly that and had knocked himself cold
on a low-hanging pipe. Denise dialed the Security Department, and explained, "This is Dr. Sheridan. That's
right, from the Mesopotamian Art and Archaeology
Department. I need to check some of our records
down in the Tunnel, but as I think you know, Warren,
our departmental technician—that's right, he's still out
on medical leave, and—Jack Carlton? Fine. Tell him
I'll meet him at the entrance in about five minutes."

She hung up, grinning at Sarah. "How about that? If
only everyone in the museum was that cooperative!"
Including a certain Mr. Atherton. "Hold the fort,
Sarah. I'll be back as soon as I can."

Ilaron, his mind far from the everyday world,
stalked into his gallery, greeted his staff almost
brusquely, quickly checked that all was properly prepared for the daily opening, and disappeared into his
office. Seated at his desk, he began a quick scan of
those matters that absolutely required his immediate
attention, while all the while a growing awareness
nagged at the edge of his senses, though he could not
have said that there was anything specifically wrong,
telling him that he must return to the museum.

Denise, he thought. There was nothing as definitive
as a psychic link between them, and yet . . . and
yet . . .

A knock made him look up sharply from the papers.
"Ms. Daniels?"

"Sir." She poked her head inside. "Sir, I know
you're busy, but we really do need to talk."

He stifled an impatient sigh and signaled for her to enter and sit down.

"Mr. Highborn. I've been with you for some time now, so I think I can speak frankly."

"Of course."

"However, if I'm overstepping the bounds, please feel free to tell me."

"Ms. Daniels, please. The point of this?"

"Well. I think I've been here long enough that I'm justified in asking this." She leaned forward earnestly. "Are either you or the gallery in any trouble?"

He stared at her, taken aback. "Why should you think—ah. Because of the way I've been so mysteriously running in and out lately."

"And, quite frankly, by the way you don't seem to have your mind totally on what's happening here. Is it . . . something to do with your missing colleague?"

Ah. "In a way," Ilaron said evasively. "And no, Ms. Daniels, let me reassure you that the gallery is not, to the best of my knowledge, in any difficulty."

Unless Kerezar learns about—no. I can't see him entering anyplace so thoroughly surrounded by iron and security systems. Even Kerezar couldn't avoid setting off infrared alarms.

"Nor," Ilaron added with the slightest edge of dry humor, "has this matter anything to do with government agencies—including the Internal Revenue Service—terrorist groups, or crime syndicates of any sort. There, now. Does that set your mind at ease?"

"Not totally." Her tone was just as dry. "But I suspect that that's all the information you are going to give me. Thank you for your time."

She got to her feet, only to pause at the door. "Oh, and by the way," Ms. Daniels said over her shoulder, "I just thought you might like to know that we, Sharon, Kevin and I, we were worried about you."

As he sat there, speechless, she turned and smiled,

evidently pleased to have for once caught her employer totally by surprise, then left, closing the door firmly behind her.

So. And . . . so. What just happened here?

No answer to that. And now, Ilaron thought wryly, he had to set the staff's worries alive once more. Leaving his office, he told the three of them, "I must pay another visit to The American Museum of Art. I'll be back as soon as is possible."

Letting them make of that whatever they might, he hurried out.

And with him, just in case, Ilaron took his sword, disguised by simple illusion to look like nothing more dangerous than an elegant silvery walking stick.

Ilaron paused in the museum's main doorway, hunting. The *feeling* of something wrong, something involving Denise, was stronger now, beginning to focus itself . . . something, someone . . .

A nondescript figure was creeping about the main hall, and Ilaron straightened. Yes! There was the source of his uneasiness: Sedgwick!

This time, though, Sedgwick (or more likely Lamashtu) seemed aware of pursuit. By the time Ilaron had thrown money down at a register and gotten the button in the color of the day—garish red this time—which was proof of admission paid, his quarry had already vanished into the maze of corridors.

No use wasting time looking for Atherton, that useless socialite.

Instead, Ilaron headed straight for Denise's office—only to learn from a startled Sarah, "I'm sorry, but Dr. Sheridan isn't here."

"Isn't here! What do you mean? She can't have left the building!"

Sarah's fair skin reddened in her confusion. "Oh, no, I'm sorry, I—I didn't mean that. It's only that she's out of the office but still in the museum, gone to look up some old records down in the Tunnel."

"The . . . Tunnel."

"Y-yes. I can show you the way, but—"

"Do."

There was a great deal of persuasion behind that one word. Sarah, dazed and unable to protest, led him wordlessly through the museum corridors to a locked door of iron mesh, tucked away behind one of the administrative offices. Peering through the mesh, Ilaron could see a narrow metal stairway, almost steep enough to be called a ladder, leading down into a maze of low-hanging iron pipes.

"She's down there? *Alone?*"

"Oh no, Mr. Highborn, don't worry, one of the guards is with her. No one goes down there alone, that's the rules. I—I'm sorry, but I do have to get back to the office, you understand, no one's back there and . . ."

Ilaron absently waved her away.

"Uh, Mr. Highborn, sir," Sarah added over her shoulder, "I have to warn you, no unauthorized personnel are allowed down there."

He didn't even bother replying to that.

Nor, Ilaron thought, *am I about to explain myself. To anyone.* "Go, Sarah, back to your office. And," he added with a burst of will, "remember nothing of this conversation."

She went.

Jack Carlton, Denise thought, was as totally ordinary-looking a man as they came, balding and on his way to building a paunch, but he was a good, solid guard: dependable. She and he, joking lightheartedly about having to walk the gauntlet, made their way safely down the narrow steel staircase, ducking under the row of low-hanging pipes ("The ones that nearly did in that unfortunate fellow, you know, Dr. Sheridan, Professor What's-his-name?"), and came out into the Tunnel itself.

What they found was impressive enough to make Denise pause: utter darkness.

"Ah, Jack, can we have some light, please?"

"Right. The light switch is around here somewhere . . . yeah. Got it."

He quickly switched on the lights: a central row of naked bulbs hanging at widely spaced intervals from the ceiling.

And the Tunnel, Denise thought, *is revealed in all its splendor.*

It was the high-ceilinged upper half of what had been a brick circle, now bisected by the floor. Victorian bitumen hung down from between the bricks at the circle's apex in dingy black stalactites, and thick dust covered everything but the central aisle.

Directly behind Denise was the south end of the Tunnel, a blank wall set with a locked door, mysterious since no one had been behind it since the 1870s and no one knew what might lie on the other side.

No, you idiot. Don't think of that now. It's locked, anyhow. Firmly. So is the one at the far end.

She had to take that on trust, since the far end of the Tunnel, which lay somewhere under Eighty-fourth or Eighty-fifth Street, she wasn't sure exactly where, was lost in the dim light.

And in between, dusty cases and bookshelves lined the curving walls, some, from the looks of them, probably untouched since the museum had claimed the Tunnel back in 1878 or so. The occasional dark mound marked a tarpaulin-covered statue. Denise winced in spite of herself at the sight of one leprous white marble arm reaching out from under its covering as though begging for help. That was *not* what she wanted to see in her current frame of mind!

"Come on, Jack. I can't afford to waste too much time down here."

That sounded almost convincing, didn't it?

Denise walked as unhurriedly as she could to the section of Tunnel claimed by her department and started her hunt through ancient wooden file drawers, sneezing on dust and hoping that the sudden tickle that had just crossed her foot hadn't been another spider. She said jokingly over her shoulder to the guard, "This is almost too trite a spot for something spooky to happen, isn't it?"

No answer.

"Jack . . . ?"

Still nothing.

Oh no, Denise thought, *no. Not really.*

Yes, really. The Tunnel was suddenly darker than it had been. She whirled to see the bulbs, one by one, going out with small implosions.

And there before her, standing over the guard's limp body with knife in hand, was none other than Charles Sedgwick, last of the Children of Sumer.

EIGHTEEN

I Tremble When the Wind Blows Chill

For one desperate moment, Denise tried to convince herself that the imploding of the lightbulbs was due only to some weird sort of electrical short, that this *was* only Sedgwick, a madman certainly, standing over the guard's crumpled body with a bloody knife like something out of a low-budget thriller, but still only a man.

But what was looking back at her from Sedgwick's eyes had nothing to do with humanity. Denise realized that up to this minute, she hadn't truly believed in Lamashtu, not in her inner self.

So much for disbelief.

"All right," she said, keeping her voice as calm as possible. "All right. You are great Lamashtu, aren't you? Of course you are. I'm facing Lamashtu, daughter of Anu, whom all praise."

Sedgwick, which meant Lamashtu, stood motionless, watching her, disconcertingly without blinking.

She's listening. Isn't she?

Could she, Denise thought, not quite hoping, possibly talk her way out of this? She had enough ancient hymns and prayers memorized by now to come up with something reasonably authentic, and Babylonian demons were supposed to love flattery. Could she flatter Lamashtu so extravagantly that the demon thought her a worshiper and not to be hurt? Prove to Lamashtu that for all this human's knowledge, she was no threat?

No threat? How could anything as small, as fragile, as thoroughly mortal as a human ever possibly pose a threat to . . . *that*?

Oh God, but I am; I can translate Babylonian texts, and Lamashtu knows it through her human host.

Of course there were other scholars who could read Babylonian—but those scholars didn't work in the museum; they didn't even work in the same city!

And I, lucky me, I do. Not that it matters. You can't reason with a demon, can you? They're evil, and you can't reason with that!

There was only the one light left, and Denise knew with sudden dreadful certainty that when that last bulb went, so did she. Not only could she read Babylonian, she was the only person, the only human, who could recognize Lamashtu for what she was—yes, yes, and the demon must assume that Denise also had the knowledge to banish her as well!

But I don't have *that knowledge,* Denise's mind gibbered, *not yet!*

No matter. All in all, Lamashtu dared not let her live.

"I know why you've come down here," Denise said, desperately stalling. "You're down here because it's dark, safe from daylight. No daylight in the Tunnel, ever."

But while she was talking, she was closing her hand about a small but hefty limestone statuette, thinking, *at least Sedgwick's body is mortal.* If she could only get in one good blow—

The body was mortal, but the mind inhabiting it and the reflexes controlling it were not. Before Denise could do more than start to move, Sedgwick's hand snaked out to catch her wrist with enough force to make her cry out, forcing her fist open. The statuette fell harmlessly to the floor.

All right, damn you, but I am not going quietly!

Denise fought back, kicking, biting, clawing, got in a few of what should be incapacitating blows—all to no avail. She saw the ancient evil in Sedgwick's eyes, Lamashtu's eyes, and knew that she was about to die of Ebola—no, not disease, if there was any justice, Lamashtu couldn't deliver disease, couldn't use any of her dark powers, while it was still daylight out there, but there were a dozen other ways Denise could die and she was about to learn one of them right now—

Suddenly Sedgwick was torn away from her, hurtling with a crash to the floor. Ilaron stepped out of the darkness, his eerie eyes blazing, literally glowing in the faint light, and brandishing what at first looked like a silvery walking stick. But then Sedgwick sprang up, charging him, and Denise saw that what she'd thought was a cane was a sword, that silvery sword she'd seen in his apartment, because Ilaron used it calmly and efficiently to run Sedgwick through.

Denise didn't have time to notice more. In the next instant Ilaron was throwing himself at her, lips pressed fiercely to hers.

He's gone mad, been possessed—

But there was nothing brutal or erotic about this. It was almost like a ritual, an exchange of breath—

God, yes, Lamashtu is going to be hunting a human host, and I'm the only choice down here!

And Ilaron was defending her in the only way he could right now, hiding her presence, her aura, with his own. For a terrifying moment, Denise glimpsed Lamashtu over Ilaron's shoulder: lioness head, wide wings and all.

Then—the demon vanished. Ilaron released Denise, who gasped, "Where is she?"

"Somewhere down here. Lamashtu isn't strong enough to manifest fully, and she can't enter all those sunny museum halls without a living human body to host her. She couldn't focus on yours, there's none other down here, so she has to have entered an object, an artifact, something familiar to her from ancient days, pottery or bronze—"

Ilaron broke off, pointing sharply to a case full of ancient Greek and Roman oil lamps. "There! I *feel* her!"

"An oil lamp," Denise heard herself babble, "a genie in a lamp, how trite," even as she dived at the iron-mesh door to the case and slammed it shut, latching it, wishing the door had a lock. Magickless though she was, she could feel, actually feel, a wave of psychic heat, Lamashtu's fury at them both for so easily snaring her, at herself for having been snared.

"Is she—will she stay put?" *Oh please, please, say yes!*

But: "I'm not sure," Ilaron said after a thoughtful moment, so calmly that she wanted to slap him. "As long as the iron remains in place, yes. She cannot pass that barrier."

"Then . . ."

"One could hope that ensnarement would last forever, but more realistically she will be trapped only till someone sets her free or she can puzzle out an escape."

"We can't do anything?"

"What? If we open that door, she escapes. At least this way we have bought ourselves some time."

As for the bodies of the guard and Sedgwick: "A pity," Ilaron said, glancing at them with nothing of that emotion on his face. "A madman kills someone, then takes his own life. Your Mr. Atherton is *not* going to be pleased. A moment, please. You might," he added carefully, "prefer not to watch."

She most certainly preferred not. But when Ilaron returned to her side, as composed as ever, Denise couldn't help but ask, "What did you do?"

"Used the madman's knife to make his death wound look more credible. More self-inflicted. Less like the mark of a sword's point."

Again, there was not the slightest trace of emotion in his voice. Denise started away, toward the stairs, toward light and sanity, but she was shaking so badly that she could barely walk.

And Ilaron—whatever he was, whatever he'd done, the hand he suddenly put under her arm to support her was reassuringly warm and steady. "Take the papers you've gathered," he reminded her.

"Oh yes. God, yes."

She was not coming down here again. Ever.

Not surprisingly, Denise thought, she had no trouble at all in putting on a good show of hysterics for Alan Atherton and the police officers he had reluctantly had to summon. Being Alan, he had sneaked them in, of course, by back ways: "We don't want to alarm the public!"

Or hurt attendance figures.

Ilaron, meanwhile, had slipped away unnoticed. His presence there, Denise silently agreed, would have been just too coincidental.

Rather to her disgust, she realized that Alan, conveniently ignoring the fact that he had also ignored all of Ilaron's warnings about Sedgwick, was already trying to turn this tragedy into a publicity event.

"The public," he murmured to Denise, "*loves* a good, bloody scandal!"

At her involuntary wince, Alan looked at her as though surprised at the reaction. "Why, my dear, I'm sorry. How inconsiderate of me, and after all you've just been through. Are you sure you're all right? Why don't you just take the rest of the day off?"

Condescension dripped from every word. Denise, well aware that he was patronizing her and that she would lose valuable status points if she gave in, bit back what would have been a career-killing *I'll see you in hell first,* and said only a reasonably cool, "That won't be necessary."

She gave her carefully edited statement of what had happened in the Tunnel to the police: "Yes, we went down there to look up some records, no, I don't know how the—the madman got down there; he must have followed us. All I know is that h-he killed poor Jack Carlton"—the quaver in her voice at that point was quite real—"and then . . . well . . . he . . . died."

Was that going to be enough? It hardly sounded like a sufficient statement to her. Denise braced herself for the barrage of questions sure to come.

Ilaron stood motionless, half-hidden behind a museum column, coolly observing how Atherton and Denise dealt with the small coterie of police and the little pack of reporters that somehow seemed to appear like a host of *eriatil* on a victim whenever a crime occurred.

The bodies had already been quietly and discreetly removed from the Tunnel without, fortunately for the museum, having roused much public notice. And more fortunately for all, Ilaron thought darkly, without having made any contact with Lamashtu.

Now, if Denise could only escape this ordeal, all would be well.

I will do what I may.

Eyes shut, Ilaron sent out the faintest touch of persuasion . . . difficult to do this by daylight, difficult to include them all . . . impossible to do more than add the vaguest of veiling over human minds, add the slightest of hints. . . .

He broke off, gasping, struggling to catch his breath and trying not to make a sound, aware that he had drained the life from the nearest lamps, thankfully without having the bulbs shatter.

But it had worked. Ah yes . . . and yes, again. Judging from what he could overhear from where he stood, Denise was not about to be entangled in any legal difficulties.

Something strange was definitely happening here, Denise thought: No one was asking her for anything further. She quickly bit back what would have been some stupid babbling about, that can't be enough, you've got to need more, don't you want any more details? *Never volunteer, you idiot!*

But maybe it wasn't so strange at that. Although she was almost absently warned that she might have to go down to the station house later to file a more formal report, Denise saw from their expressions what the police had to be thinking: Cultist plus explosion equals bombing attempt on museum gone awry and last-ditch attempt by only survivor to cause trouble—case closed.

If only it was that simple!

To her horror, she heard Alan, still on the publicity trail, wondering aloud whether they could open the Tunnel to the public: wonderful publicity and all that.

Stifling an "Are you *insane*?" Denise settled for reminding him how potentially dangerous it was down there—"All those low-hanging pipes, the darkness and all, the insurance hassles," and prayed that was enough to keep him and any other potentially nosy sorts out of there.

"Now, if you'll all excuse me?" she added with a

faint and, she hoped, reasonably businesslike smile. "I have a department to run."

Good. She'd sparked Alan's sense of duty. He gravely waved her away, and Denise hurried off, all but racing through the halls to her office.

Perfect, Ilaron thought. The police, unaware of any mental magickings, were clearly quite satisfied that the case had just been closed without any of those inconvenient loose ends. Satisfied, he strolled out of the museum like any other casual visitor, sword once again disguised as an innocuous walking stick, and returned to his gallery, trying his best to act as though life was, indeed, back to normal.

"Ah, Ms. Daniels." His voice was perfectly bland. "Any crises in my absence?"

"No, sir. In fact, you'll be happy to hear that we've already sold the Anderson."

"Excellent! And you've already telephoned him?"

She beamed. "Of course. I don't have to tell you how happy *he* was!"

For all his impatience, Ilaron glanced at the small abstract with the "Sold" sticker with genuine pleasure. He sometimes included younger, unknown artists in the gallery if their talent moved him, Shannon Anderson being a case in point, and it was always satisfying to see his choices justified.

About Kerezur and Lamashtu as well?

"Excellent," he repeated shortly. "Truly. Now, I have some work to do, so kindly excuse me. . . ."

With that, Ilaron calmly walked on to his office, calmly closed the door—

And only then collapsed behind his desk, head in hands.

Ahh, that had not been easy! Casting that net of his will in the museum—not easy at all. Every time he thought he understood the difficulties involved in working magic in this realm, the realm reminded him anew.

And then there had been Lamashtu. Ilaron shuddered. Dealing with demonkind was never an easy thing! Particularly not when part of his being had so fiercely envied Lamashtu her dark freedom.

But he'd won that battle.

Nothing too tempting, actually, about a demon who isn't host of anything as darkly splendid as the wild cosmic forces, but of . . . disease.

As for his having slain the demon's host—so now, the fool had freely made the choice to welcome Lamashtu and had paid the price. Not even the slightest regret there.

But he could not be comfortable about having left the demon where she was, in such a ridiculously insecure trap.

And yet, and yet, I . . . just . . . cannot *come up with any safer solution.*

He straightened, considering the options, which were distressingly few and none of them agreeable.

Item: Simply destroying the lamp wouldn't hurt Lamashtu, who would merely move to some other object or, worse, living host.

Item: Dumping the oil lamp into the Central Park Reservoir just north of the museum *might* work—and then again, it might merely destroy the lamp and not Lamashtu.

Item: Locking the lamp in a safe or, for that matter, a safety-deposit box, just meant that the risk was postponed only until someone opened that safe or box.

Ilaron gave a silent snarl of pure frustration. He had certainly dealt with demons before in his native realm, but only when he had known their weaknesses; even then, it had been a risky business.

And I know almost nothing about Lamashtu.

No, he concluded reluctantly, like it or not, he could

do little. Although his realm hardly encouraged one to rely upon, let alone trust, anyone else, this matter was something that must be left to Denise. She was, he reminded himself sternly, bright, competent, quite well versed in her chosen field. And after all the events the woman had undergone in the past day and a half, she had definitely proved herself brave and strong as well.

You make her sound like one of those . . . ah, what do they call them . . . ? Girl Scouts! That forced a wry chuckle from him. *And what is it those girls earn? I was cornered by a flock once, all trying to make me purchase cookies . . . they earn badges of some sort Merit badges, that's it.*

So be it. Denise Sheridan, let us hope you quickly earn your merit badge in Demon-Banishing!

Sarah, after one quick glance at Denise's expression as she entered, sprang to her feet.

"What *happened*?"

"It's all right, Sarah. Honest. I'm not hurt."

"But—"

Quickly, Denise gave her the same brief, carefully edited statement she'd given the police. *I've got the cursed thing memorized.*

"Oh, but that's *horrible*!" Sarah gasped. "We were right, the Children of Sumer really were something to worry about, but who would have thought they would—he would—never mind that. You must have been so scared—and to see that—him—I mean—if there's anything I can do . . . ?"

"No. Truly. I'll be all right."

She hurried on into her office, closing the door firmly, and tried her best to bury herself in research and not think about the Tunnel, the demon, the calm, casual way Ilaron had run his sword through Sedgwick. . . .

Suddenly the sound of voices penetrated her laboriously built-up wall of concentration. Heart racing, she called out sharply, "Sarah, who's there?"

"No one much," Sarah replied, almost cheerfully. "A reporter, but I've already sent him away."

Of course there are reporters, Denise thought. *Crime scenes draw them like flies to the proverbial honey.*

Museum Security would be ushering them out by now, barring them from questioning the public or from getting into any private areas. But one of the lot had obviously slipped through the net, and been cunning enough to track her here.

"What did you tell him?" Denise asked warily, suddenly sure that the young woman had just involved Ilaron or done some other foolish—

"Oh, nothing much," Sarah assured her with a grin, then let her voice go "dumb blonde," chattering, wide-eyed, that, "There are so many weird people out there today and isn't it a shame that something like that should happen, and this is such a nice place to work and people should all come and visit. . . ."

Denise gave a shaky little laugh. "Clever! Thank you." Sarah might be green, but she wasn't all *that* naive!

But Denise's humor faded again as she returned to work. For all her determined willpower, it was difficult not to keep seeing what had happened down in the Tunnel, it was difficult not to keep imagining what had almost happened.

Poor Jack . . . he never did anyone any harm. I wonder if he has—had any family . . . And Sedgwick—

No, she couldn't feel any pity for him.

But what of Ilaron, killing with such quick, easy efficiency? That was the word for it, efficiency. No wasted time over any sort of emotion, not like a human—

God, she was glad the door to her office was closed.

Ilaron, she knew, would definitely not approve of this, but Denise put her head down on the cluttered desk and silently but sincerely sobbed.

At last she was finished, completely worn out. She didn't exactly feel better; her nose was stuffed up, and her eyes, she knew, must look terrible. But at least, Denise thought, she had gotten the worst of the tension out of her system.

Hey, I'm a New Yorker, I'm tough.

More or less.

Too bad she didn't keep some of that excellent brandy Ilaron had served—no, she wouldn't think about him right now.

All right. Enough of this. This wasn't the first time she'd seen violence, even violent death: a good many New Yorkers had. Lamashtu—well, that was something else again, but . . . Denise shook her head, amazed at herself. Underneath the shock and horror, it was stupidly, ridiculously *exciting* to know she had actually trapped a demon.

My Lord, woman, who do you think you are? Denise Sheridan, Ace Demonologist?

If she started giggling, she wasn't going to be able to stop. Denise determinedly took out compact, eyeliner and lipstick, and set to work. Sure enough, the very act of repairing her makeup helped to steady her. Made her look less like some hysterical kid, too.

Feeling at least a little more like herself, Denise resolutely returned to work.

The solution has to be here. It just wouldn't be fair *for it not to be!*

Oh, right. Since when, she reminded herself sternly, was life fair?

Damn. And damn again. Brandford Richards, whatever else he might had been, had clearly been one weird guy, determined not to waste a square inch of paper. So many small, cribbed notes in these texts . . .

yes, and no guarantee that even if she found the right information, it would be accurate.

And it had, Denise thought, *damned well better be accurate.*

Or that "damned" might apply quite literally.

NINETEEN

Scherzo Fantastique

Outside his office, Ilaron could dimly hear his staff continuing to run down the list of hotels, making their phone calls. They weren't really getting anywhere, nor had he actually expected them to; hotels in this city were bound to be protective of their guests' safety and privacy.

A knock on his door. Ilaron sighed. "Yes, Ms. Daniels?"

"Sorry as usual to disturb you." Was there just the faintest touch of sarcasm in that? "But Mr. Haddad is here to see you."

Curse it! I forgot all about him.

Khalil Haddad was a young man with an incredible extended family and, thanks to that family, art contacts in a good many corners of the Near East. While Ilaron and he had been doing business for two years now, Khalil was hardly under contract as an agent for the Highborn Gallery.

Which means that if I don't see him now, he'll just shrug and go off to sell whatever he's brought with him to some other gallery.

And while the young man never had any really major items to sell, the artifacts he brought were almost always genuine and always legal. Objects that were not *that* important, yet at the same time, frustratingly, too salable to lose.

"Tell me," Denise's voice echoed in Ilaron's mind, *"do you really enjoy running an art gallery?"*

The chickens, as the humans said, did have a tendency to come home to roost. "Send him in," Ilaron said in surrender.

Khalil was one of those ebullient sorts, a good-looking youngster with dark, curly hair and olive skin, all smiles and genuine cheer.

But he wasn't a fool, either. One look at Ilaron's closed face, and he said only, "Well. Let me show you what I have brought here today."

A nice little faience statuette of the goddess Bast, late dynastic Egyptian—quite genuine, Ilaron's touch told him.

"Quite legal," Khalil added. "We found it in the effects of my fourth cousin, poor old Ali Hamid Haddad, Allah rest him. And he got it from *his* great-uncle, Salim-the-Egyptian, who—"

He stopped short at a warning glance from Ilaron. Khalil's relatives could easily fill a small country, and their adventures an encyclopedia. "Ah. I see. So. We also found this," a string of attractive, multicolored glass beads, Venetian, perhaps eighteenth century, "this," a Luristan dagger blade, ordinary but in excellent condition, "and this."

Ilaron drew back with a hiss, nearly knocking the little bronze plaque from Khalil's hand. "What is wrong?" the young man cried in alarm. "What have I done? It is genuine, I would not cheat you!"

"No, no, it's nothing like that. Of course you wouldn't. I was merely . . . startled."

"Ah." A flash of white teeth. "It is ugly, yes?"

"Quite." Ilaron forced himself to take the little plaque, studying it. Genuine, yes, Babylonian, of course: no mistaking the engraved figure of Lamashtu glaring from it.

Oh you idiot. You heard Denise say that these were

very common amulets, you know that they are. And this one, like the others, is nothing but a warding-off charm. It has no Power to it at all.

Even so, the sight of that too-familiar image . . . he had to fight the temptation to hurl it from him and snap, *Get that thing out of my gallery!*

No. He was not some irrational human. "Very well. Tell Ms. Daniels that I will take the statuette of Bast and the . . . " for all his will, he had to force out the word, "plaque."

He waved Khalil away before the young man could go into his usual flowery speech of thanksgiving. Alone in his office, Ilaron sat with forehead resting on steepled hands, forcing himself back to calmness. He straightened, called up a very mundane spreadsheet on his computer, forced himself to study the figures, moved on to a Christie's auction catalogue, gradually relaxing over the images of Byzantine enamels. Ridiculous to have let himself get so overwrought over nothing, ridiculous to worry about what could not be helped or—

Another knock made him start. Stifling a curse, Ilaron asked, biting off each word, "Yes, Ms. Daniels?"

"I really am sorry to disturb you again so soon." That definitely *was* a touch of sarcasm. "But Mrs. Lansford is here and asking for you."

Darkness take it. "I assume you have completed the transaction with Khalil?"

"Only just. Shall I . . . ?"

"Make the dear woman comfortable." *And yes, Ms. Daniels, that* was *meant as sarcasm.* "I'll be with her shortly."

Mrs. Lansford—Mrs. Richard Lansford III or, as she so clearly wished Ilaron to call her, Ashley—was one of the gallery's steady customers, a woman who had a great deal of money and far too much free time.

She was not, frustratingly, the sort who could be fobbed off on an underling.

So be it.

Ilaron stalked from his office, deliberately dramatic, deliberately mysterious, to greet her. "My dear Mrs. Lansford."

She turned to him, a perfectly charming smile on her lips, something darker and considerably warmer in her eyes. Ashley Lansford was not as young as she would have liked, and desperately elegant, her hair a precise gold, her face and body fashionably gaunt, her clothing stark black. Ilaron knew perfectly well why she was so interested in his gallery and thought, *I might give you that taste of Darkness you so desire, were I such a fool—and were you not more useful to me as a patron of the arts.*

But he had no time this day for her veiled flirtations and sideways glances. "Mrs. Lansford—"

"Tsk. I've asked you *so* many times to call me Ashley."

"Very well, then. Ashley. You will pardon me if I— No! Put that down!"

She was holding the Lamashtu plaque. "I beg your pardon?"

The others were staring at him, too. Cursing himself for a fool, Ilaron forced all emotion back behind a mask of composure, explaining coolly, "That piece came into the gallery only this morning. It has not yet been properly . . . authorized."

Let her think that he hadn't yet checked its authenticity, that it just might be a forgery. The last person he wanted in even tenuous contact with Lamashtu was someone both wealthy and already half in love with cruelty: Should the demon free herself, she would race right to so tantalizing and useful a host. A host with money enough to take Lamashtu wherever the demon wished.

"A pity," the woman said, still holding it. "Such an . . . unusual engraving. What is it? A demon?"

"Of disease." Carefully picking his words, Ilaron added, "She specialized in destroying beauty."

"Oh." The woman quickly handed the amulet over to Ms. Daniels, then almost surreptitiously wiped her hands. But it took more than a momentary setback to discourage her. With a sly little up-and-down glance at Ilaron, she asked, her voice just a few degrees away from being a purr, "But do tell me . . . Ilaron. What else have you," a second sly glance, "to show me?"

Oh you fool, I could show you pain and pleasure to make you shudder with rapture—but I have no time for this nonsense! Ilaron knew perfectly well which artifact she actually meant to purchase, since she had made that decision quite clear on her previous visit. *And I will cut your game short here and now.*

With a flash of will, he increased her interest in the fragment of Assyrian relief till she purred over it and—at last!—took out her checkbook.

The relief that shows the captive woman. Of course you'd want it: the eroticism of cruelty. Another case in point for Denise's department to mount that Assyrian show.

As Ms. Daniels, with a wry glance at her employer, took over the financial side of the sale, Ilaron escaped back into his office.

His name was Bill Johnston, self-admittedly less than ace reporter, and he was middle-aged, disillusioned and tired of tromping around on these hard marble floors, tired of the whole business.

If the museum wants more customers, let them put down some carpeting, dammit!

All these years of looking for stories, for *the* story, the one that was going to make him famous, maybe even win him the Pulitzer—investigative journalism, why not?—and what had it gotten him? A freelance stint, not even a steady job, for the *Nation and World* which, despite the grand name, was just another checkout-counter tabloid.

What the hell. The paper paid, and paid more or less on time, that was the thing. Better than some he could name.

Of course, it paid more for features with photos, which was why he had a small camera on his person.

Right. But what good had that been so far? What could he have shot? The cops wouldn't let him (or any other reporters) near the crime scene, and the paper wasn't going to settle for some stock PR shot of the museum or even of that woman curator he didn't get to interview, thanks to that little blonde ditz of an assistant.

All right. Never mind wasting time resenting things. He needed an angle, that was all, an angle . . . try a little brainstorming here. . . .

No hope of getting an exclusive, and certainly not a scoop. Okay, no problem. Try a different slant. The Tunnel, now, that sounded nice and dark and mysterious. Get a photo of that, maybe even a bloodstain, faked if necessary.

Yeah. There was the angle, all right. Johnston thought sourly: *What Dark Power Lurks Deep Below the Museum? or something garish like that.*

Yeah, maybe. He could do something with that, build it into a real horror story. Good stuff. But how to get down there, get that shot?

At last after some consideration and a good deal of walking about on these damned hard floors, he realized he indeed did have an idea of how to get down there, right to the murder scene. Had to wait a bit, though.

Johnston found himself a seat away from the public eye and waited with weary patience for things to settle down. Once the cops were finally gone and the museum seemed to have returned to normal, he got up again and went in search of a guard.

Security guards were, Johnston knew, notoriously underpaid, and one of the guys here was bound to welcome a nice, friendly bribe.

Who knew? The day just might not be wasted after all.

Ilaron rubbed a hand over his eyes. *Why now? Why today? I thought Mrs. Lansford—dear Ashley—would be the last of it, but no, this seems to be the day for everyone to visit.*

At any other time, he would have welcomed such brisk business. Now, his concentration was broken again and yet again by this customer's needs or that purchase order requiring his signature. Even as he acted the role of a pleased, concerned businessman, Ilaron's mind was desperately turning over the dual problems of Kerezar and Lamashtu.

Yes, and Reschet. Reschet, who had almost certainly been unable to resist mentioning that fatal word, "art." If he had, it was just a matter of time before Kerezar saw "Highborn Gallery," noted its location near the museum, and had the puzzle solved.

While my side of the hunt is beginning to look increasingly futile.

Those hotels that would admit to having checked in a lone traveler that night either didn't have specific data or insisted on knowing who was calling first. And precious time was speeding by.

Ah, at last there seemed to be a lull out there. Alone in his office, relatively sure he wouldn't be disturbed, Ilaron fed into the computer the information on which hotels had acknowledged having admitted lone guests. Storing the data, he then pulled magical energy from the electricity about him and accessed the police records of that night, hunting for deaths by stab wounds.

Along with the magic, as always, came that momentary surge of power, dimming of lights, and startled complaints from the staff.

They are going to suggest that an electrician go over the gallery's wiring yet again. A tedious task and, of course, a total waste of time.

Ahh, no matter. Ilaron leaned forward, studying the screen. Yes . . . now there was a track of sorts. Stab wounds from a sword could hardly be confused with those from a mere knife, which was why he had carefully altered that death wound down in the Tunnel. The trail of death-by-sword wounds led north from the West Village . . .

The Theater District, Ilaron thought. *Of course. So many lives there, so much potential Darkness—*

But, alas, so many hotels on his list. Taking a deep breath, Ilaron began to narrow down the search by hotel size—

No! Too much Power had drained too much power. Without warning, all the lights in the gallery went out in a total blackout. Ilaron swore, literally enough, "Darkness take it!" and gave up his search in disgust.

"A moment," he called out to his distressed staff. "This time I'll take care of it myself."

He stalked out of his office into the darkened hallway, making sure the humans could follow the sound of his progress (the not-quite-silent, not-quite-sure steps of an ordinary soul who could not, of course, see perfectly well in the darkness), back to the fuse box. There, eyes warily shut against the blare of light to come, he made a great deal of flipping switches and—

That did it. The lights came flooding back on.

"Yes," he called out wearily before Ms. Daniels could even begin her query. "The usual electrician. By all means. Try to arrange a time that doesn't interfere with peak gallery traffic."

Stalking back to his office, Ilaron eyed his computer warily. . . .

No. The last thing he needed was to try again too quickly and this time burn out the whole system. At least he had gained this much before the blackout: He could finally make an educated guess as to Kerezar's location.

But, naturally, it was already too late in the day to go after Kerezar alone, since that would force Denise, the only hope of quelling Lamashtu, to leave the museum on her own. And that was hardly a wise thing right now.

And was there . . . could there be . . . just a touch more to his concern for her than the purely practical?

Bah, no. Utterly impossible.

Ridiculous situation, he thought, *utterly ridiculous. But even I can't be in two places at the same time.*

A sudden disturbance from the front of the gallery brought him fully alert, springing to his feet and opening the door.

"Ms. Daniels? What's going on out there?"

Her harried voice called back, "There's a group of teens outside, gang members, I think, trying to get in. We've tried to chase them away, but they just won't leave. Shall we call the police?"

"No. Wait."

This, Ilaron thought, was *not* normal behavior for such scum; like true creatures of Darkness, they didn't usually come boldly out in daylight. And they most certainly didn't make such a daring frontal attack.

They've been sent, but by whom? And why?

No need for it to be anyone as dramatic as Kerezar, not yet; this wouldn't be the first time someone had tried to rob the gallery. Ilaron thought of the last unfortunate who'd attempted it when he had happened to be present, and smiled coldly.

Yet it seems an odd way to "case the joint"—or is it? A distraction, perhaps?

The gallery had a heavily locked service entrance. Ilaron slipped back there and soundlessly unlocked it, then stepped back into shadow and waited.

Sure enough, a thin, wary, shaven head poked into the gallery. A teen started to enter—and Ilaron grabbed him, muffling the startled stream of oaths with a hand. He dragged the teen into one of the gallery's storerooms, shutting the door behind them with a foot, then threw the boy to the floor. Before the teen could move, Ilaron was crouching beside him, hissing, "Who sent you?"

"What the hell you talkin' about?"

"Who sent you?"

"Fuck off, man! I told you, no one!"

Of course the stupid creature would play brave—until Ilaron, suddenly inspired and in no mood for patience, removed his sunglasses and stared.

The change in his captive was astonishing.

"Another demon!" the teen yelped, squirming backwards on the floor as best he could, radiating sudden terror.

Ah, Ilaron thought. *Kerezar.*

The teen was babbling how he was in Satan's employ, didn't this Lord of Hell or whatever he was know that? Or—omigodomigod, they were in the middle of a Demon War, weren't they?

"In a way," Ilaron told him coldly.

The reek of fear was beginning to play havoc with his self-control. Even though Ilaron suspected darkly that he would be improving the human race by eliminating this creature, yes, and and the creature's fellows as well, he refused to give in to such perilous temptation.

Instead, he pulled the teen roughly to his feet, barely letting the boy's toes touch the floor, allowing all of the raging Darkness he was feeling to show on his face.

"You and your friends, boy, are never to come here again. Is that understood? Never come here again!" He punctuated the words by shaking his captive, a jolt for each word. "Further," Ilaron continued, "if you wish to keep your lives and souls, you are never to become involved in my affairs again. Is *that* understood?"

The boy's last attempts at defiance had already crumbled. He was so pathetically terrified by this point, not even trying to struggle, that the urge to kill was almost too strong to resist. Ilaron dragged the teen to the service entrance, opened it one-handed, then literally threw the boy away. He hastily locked the door, then took refuge from his savage emotions in the human way, slamming his hand against a wall.

Sure enough, the sudden blaze of pain shattered the blood-lust.

And of course, the noise brought his staff running.

"Mr. Highborn!"

"What happened?"

"Are you—"

"I'm all right," Ilaron told them, flexing his hand and thinking, *That was damnably stupid; I could have broken a bone.* "One of the teens was trying to break in, but I just frightened him away. Don't worry," he added with a thin smile, "I strongly doubt that the boy or his buddies will be returning. Ever. There's no need for the police."

"Just the same," Ms. Daniels said sternly, "we are all going to keep a sharp lookout, just in case. And if we *do* see them, Mr. Highborn, we *are* going to call the police."

Sharon and Kevin, looking fierce as two young hunting hounds, nodded.

"Agreed," Ilaron told them, a little overwhelmed at their reactions. *But then, I shouldn't be surprised. The gallery is, after all, their livelihood.* "And now, if you'll excuse me . . . ?"

He vanished into the small rest room, turned the tap on full, and put his aching hand under the cold water, wincing a bit. But his thoughts were far from mundane bruises.

What if the teens really do report to Kerezar?

Now that the Darkness was retreating from his mind, Ilaron realized what he'd done. Stupid, indeed! He'd let the boy go, too terrified to speak, granted—but the others hadn't been terrified, and yes, what else would the lot of them do but run right back to Kerezar and tell him, "Here he is!"

I should have killed the boy, killed them all—

No! Such wholesale slaughter—Ilaron shuddered suddenly, knowing how easy it would have been to begin it, to thoroughly enjoy it. He was precariously balanced enough as it was. Such a total fall back into Darkness would have destroyed him.

So. No need to consider that. It had not happened; it would not happen. As for Kerezar: Eventually he and Kerezar would, no, *must* confront each other.

I do not want this gallery to be the battlefield.

But what must be, must be—

No. No, it did not need to be thus. Not yet, at any rate.

On a sudden impulse, Ilaron returned to his office and found the computer up and running again. Warily, careful not to cause yet another gallery blackout, he tried one last search . . . and this time, Ilaron found victory.

The largest hotel in the Theater District, he realized. *Of course that's where he'd be: the safest place to hide, the safest place for a "foreigner" to go unnoted among the crowds. And the largest hotel in that area is that one: the Marriott Marquis.*

True, he couldn't actually access the guest registry; there *were* limits to what even magic could unlock. But that same magic snatched up a name, one name alone: Ahligar.

The name of a noble from Kerezar's court.

I know that Kerezar is here alone. Therefore . . .

Therefore, yes, that hotel was definitely where Kerezar was lurking.

Ilaron paused, considering. What he needed to do next would, unfortunately, mean involving Denise even further in his affairs. Would that increase her danger?

I hope not. But "hope" is all I can do. There really is no alternative to her further involvement.

Even so, even so, unless things fell into utter ruin, she would still be safer with him than she would be alone.

So it must be. He glanced at the hour. Yes . . . late though the day was growing, there was still more than time enough to act before nightfall gave the enemy full freedom to move.

And by then, Kerezar, Ilaron vowed, *the battle will have come straight to you.*

TWENTY

The Wild Hunt

Denise glanced casually at her watch, then glanced again more sharply in disbelief. Sure enough, it was already after four o'clock. She stretched stiff muscles, arms over her head, then yawned, thinking mockingly, *Gee, time flies when you're having fun.*

Ah well. It was beginning to look as though she'd once again be taking work home—

But she couldn't go home, could she? She had to go off with Ilaron.

Who is, Denise reminded herself sternly even as her heart gave a lurch, *the good guy. Even if he is so alarmingly calm about taking a life.*

A life? Not really. A demon's host. Not an innocent life at all; probably hadn't been much of the original human occupant left at all. And Ilaron had saved *her* life. She must keep remembering that.

Besides, dammit, Ilaron had no logical reason to harm her, and she had no logical reason to fear him. Even if he wasn't human and came from a realm that sounded pretty close to hell—no. She wouldn't even consider *that*!

Desperately, Denise returned to her research, telling herself that dithering like this was stupid. Worse than stupid, maybe much worse. She still had some time before she had to leave, so she would just look at this one more page before yet another person interrupted her, yes and this one. . . .

Denise froze. And stared at the page again. And yet again. Very, very carefully, she went over both the cuneiform and the transliterated script, now and again reaching for one of the volumes that made up the equivalent of a Babylonian-English dictionary, making sure that she had every word correct. This wasn't a complete text, no such luck! But something about it struck a chord in her memory . . . where had she seen . . . fairly recently . . . where . . . ?

Ha, yes!

Ignoring Sarah's startled questions, Denise practically raced for the storeroom down the hall, fumbling with the key, then hunted through drawer after drawer of the endless score of cuneiform tablets, most of them mundane business accounts or rote prayers, useless, searching for the one tablet she dimly remembered, thanking her memory for being so good with bits of trivia.

Yes, I was right! Here it is!

The tablet wasn't complete, the text inscribed on it just so much gibberish, and what was written on the page hadn't been complete, either—

But the words on one looked like they might overlap the other to form a whole.

I have the incantation. Oh, please, let me have the incantation!

If she dropped the tablet now—no, she wasn't even going to think of that, no self-fulfilling prophesies, thank you very much. Warren, the on–sick-leave technical assistant, always left rolls of that bubble wrap plastic in here, just in case . . . yes. Cutting off a good hunk of the stuff, Denise wrapped the tablet with extravagant care, then raced back to the office, package firmly clutched in both hands. Sitting at her desk, she just as carefully unwrapped the tablet, leaving it safe in a bed of plastic, then set about transcribing its text and that on the printed page. Working carefully despite the impatience quivering at the edge of her mind, making sure not to mistake a sign, she began combining the half texts into one whole.

There. Done. And she— She sat back for a moment staring in amazement at her handiwork.

I've got it. I've got the incantation. I've actually got the incantation to summon Pazuzu and, oh God, please, banish Lamashtu.

Right, but this was too important to leave without a backup. Denise quickly ran off two more copies on the little office copier, checked the quality—yes, all the symbols were quite clear—then stored the tablet in the office safe, the original page underneath the chaos of a lockable drawer in her desk (she rather doubted even a demon could find anything in that "I must clean it out someday" mess) and, with an innocent smile at Sarah, all the while hiding what she was doing, one copy at the very back of the card file.

And then Denise returned to her own office and sat back down in renewed, if dazed, satisfaction.

Whoa, wait. Only one problem left—and now that she had time to actually consider it, this might be a major dilemma: No one alive today knew how the ancient language had actually been pronounced. At best, she could only make a "guesstimate."

That has to be enough. Please let it be enough!

Ah well, nothing she could do about it. Not without time travel, and she doubted that Ilaron's magical repertory included anything quite *that* drastic. Her guesses would just have to be sufficient, Denise told herself, and began memorizing what she had written.

A tactful "Ahem" made her look up with a stifled gasp.

"Ilaron!" A quick glance at her watch. "You're early!"

"Not by much. I—"

"Wait, wait, guess what? I think I have the incantation to summon Pazuzu and banish Lamashtu!"

His eyes were, of course, hidden behind the usual sunglasses, but she caught a matching flash of excitement on his face. "Are you sure?"

"Well, yes. Pretty sure."

" 'Pretty sure' isn't enough." It was almost a snarl. "Not when a demon is involved."

Denise, in no mood for lectures, snapped right back at him, "I'm not a fool! I'm not going to try anything with a demon till I know *exactly* what I'm doing."

"Splendid. Truly." He held up a conciliatory hand. "And no, I'm not patronizing you or belittling your find—believe me, I'm not! It's only that there isn't time for this just yet. Denise, I must insist that we leave, *now.*"

Oh God, now what?

But there had been such urgency in his voice that she didn't even try to argue, just slipped the copy of the incantation into her handbag and snatched up her coat. "All right. I can just as easily complete my memorizing in your apartment as here."

"Ah, no. Not yet. Before we may go home, I'm afraid that we must pay a visit downtown."

"Downtown! Where? And in God's name, Ilaron, why? Who are we hunting?"

"Kerezar."

"*What?* What are you—"

"Denise, wait. I apologize for involving you in what is basically my affair, but . . ." He muttered something in a musical language she suspected was his native tongue, as though he'd suddenly run out of the English words he wanted. "This is," Ilaron said after that frantic moment of word-hunting, "quite literally the lesser of two evils for you. I cannot let Kerezar go, surely you understand that—but I also cannot risk leaving you alone. And surely you know why."

"I wish I didn't! Dammit, Ilaron! You're giving me great choices, just great. But . . ." She gestured helplessly. "What can I say? I don't *have* a choice, do I? I'd much rather be with you and the protection of— of your magic, even against a . . . being from your realm, than alone against a demon!"

His face showed nothing, but Denise could almost feel his relief.

Well, I'm glad one *of us is relieved about this!*

With a hasty "Good night!" to Sarah and an unspoken, *I really hope I can say "Good morning" as well,* Denise let Ilaron hurry her out of the museum, down the front stairs, and into a taxi. Breathless, she heard Ilaron tell the driver, "The Marriott Marquis Hotel. You know where that is? Good. We need to be there as swiftly as possible."

A shrug from the driver. "I try. You know, rush hour."

Ilaron sighed. "I know rush hour. Do your best."

As they settled back on the seat, Denise glanced sideways at Ilaron. He, without turning to her, asked, "What?"

"Why are you doing this?"

"Eh?"

"Why are you protecting me?" She kept her voice low so the driver wouldn't overhear. "You've saved me twice so far, from Sedgwick and from Lamashtu-in-Sedgwick, and now you're still doing your back-handed best to guard me. Why? And don't tell me it's just because you need my knowledge. You didn't have to give me all those hangers and that lovely perfumed soap in the guest room just to guard my knowledge."

Ilaron shook his head impatiently. "Protecting you seems only right."

"That," Denise snapped, "is the feeblest excuse I've heard."

After a moment, he murmured, "Agreed."

A pause. A very long pause.

Then, just when Denise was wondering if she would ever get an answer, Ilaron said, as though truly amazed at himself, "I've come to think of you as a friend." Not looking at her, he added, "It's a novel sensation, one that I would like to keep a little longer."

Whether that meant anything more than the flat words, Denise didn't know, and just then didn't really want to know.

Friendship. Good enough.

Their taxi was, as the driver had warned, creeping its way through the rush-hour traffic as though it would never make it all the way to Broadway and Forty-sixth Street. At least, Denise thought, they had finally made it *to* Broadway.

They and every other taxi in the city and every tour bus and every car driven by every idiot out-of-towner who hadn't believed the warnings about "Don't take your car into midtown!" All around them was a chaotic world of light and noise, the many gaudy signs of stores, fast-food restaurants, flashy billboards, that giant-sized Sony screen. Crowds of commuters and tourists packed the sidewalks, sometimes even spilling out into the street, and car and bus horns added their constant blares, with the shrill shriek of a siren, police or ambulance, adding its nerve-jangling counterpoint.

The Symphony of New York, Denise thought. *Never starts, never stops: The city that never sleeps or shuts up!*

Ilaron murmured suddenly, "How does he stand it? All this chaos. This very alien peril—how does he stand it?"

He? Kerezar, presumably. "You did," Denise reminded Ilaron.

"Indeed." A pause. "After a fashion."

With that, Ilaron fell back into an almost inhuman

quietness. Though he showed not the slightest outward sign of anxiety, Denise by now had come to realize that when he grew so very still he was at his most impatient. She could, she thought, practically feel the tension radiating from him: They must get to the hotel before the sun set.

That, Denise thought, *sounds like something out of a really bad vampire movie!*

She only wished that it was one they could leave.

Bill Johnston, Ace Reporter, the man thought with weary sarcasm. *Look at me, wandering around in this godforsaken Tunnel like what's his name, good old Indiana Jones.*

But Jones at least came up with treasure in every movie, while all he seemed likely to find down here was dust.

Get some photos, right. Make the big story, right. Too dark to get much but blurs. Just like the rest of my luck. One big blur.

Behind him, the guard was getting nervous. "You finished? Hey? You about done? I've got to get on with my rounds."

"Yeah, yeah, in a mo'. I just want to look around a little more."

"I've got to go, honest."

"So go! I'll be all right down here."

. . . over here, come over here . . .

Over there? Why did he want to look at some dingy case of . . . He blew off some of the layers of dust . . . of oil lamps. Heh. Right. Maybe if he rubbed one, a genie would appear and—

. . . and grant all your wishes . . . the story is here . . . "the big story," here, here it is, here is what you seek . . .

Something was in the case, something intriguing, but

he couldn't quite see what. Ha, no lock on the iron-mesh door.

. . . *all you need do to win that prize, that fame, is raise the latch, yes, raise the latch* . . .

Hell, yes, easy. He flipped the latch, opened the door—

—knew one last terrible moment of *God, no, I never should have*—

And was gone.

Lamashtu stirred in Johnston's body, stretching his limbs, hissed through Johnston's lips. So easy, so incredibly easy! The human's will had been weak, weary, full of vague, useless dreams He'd been already half-won even before he'd raised the latch, opened that cursed iron trap. He'd not even struggled, just . . . surrendered.

And as simply as that, she had been freed.

And he had been lost.

"Hey," the other human, the guard, called. "Hey. I can't stay anymore. I've got to . . . "

His voice faded as Lamashtu-in-Johnston turned to him. And, he knew. Some tiny trace of psychic sight awoke, and the guard knew exactly what he faced. Without a word, he turned and clattered up the metal staircase. Lamashtu started after him—

No. Wait. The senses of *place* and *time* were flooding into her, human *day*, and she hissed in sudden rage. Forget that little prey: He was nothing, less than nothing. What was he going to say? That he'd been down here against orders? Seen a demon possess a man? Perhaps in an earlier age he would have run screaming to a temple and been believed. Now? This, Lamashtu knew from her host's memories, was a far more . . . mundane time. The guard would be silent.

And now, now, it was already too late for what she wished to do, what she *needed* to do:

The woman has escaped me!

No. Not escaped, Lamashtu told herself. Never escaped. Merely postponed their meeting. The sun had nearly set and soon, the demon thought with a small thrill of anticipation, soon her full powers would return.

And then there shall be a most entertaining hunt—yes, and a most satisfying kill!

Slowly, calmly, Lamashtu climbed the stairway out into the museum, wincing within her host at the bright blare of daylight. But even with the interference of sunlight, Lamashtu could still dimly sense where the woman was going.

And so the demon went that way, too. If the distances she read from her human host's memories were correct, it would be a long walk for that host, but Lamashtu hardly cared about that. He need last only until nightfall.

And then she would need no human host at all.

"At last." It was the coldest of murmurs from Ilaron.

The taxi had finally arrived at the huge mass of the Marriott Marquis, with the theater and shops on its Broadway front practically hiding that it *was* a hotel, and pulled into the interior driveway.

But now, of course, Denise thought, as Ilaron paid the driver and sent him on his way, there was a new problem, one she'd foreseen and Ilaron, for once, had not.

"How," Denise wanted to know with an expansive wave of the hand, "do you plan to locate Kerezar amid all *this?* There have got to be more than a thousand rooms here!"

Was he angry at having been proved wrong, he who had been so sure he would somehow *feel* his enemy despite all odds? Not the slightest sign of annoyance crossed his face. "And with so much interference from iron and human auras as well . . . " Ilaron shook his head in surrender. "I admit it. It's nearly impossible.

"And I can hardly go up to the Front Desk and ask for him by name, or rather, pseudonym: The last thing I want to do is to prematurely announce my presence to him."

"Time to try my idea," Denise said.

They rode up to the eighth floor, the location, signs told them, of the front desk. The hotel's glass-sided elevators were set in a semicircle around a central square holding the more mundane, opaque-walled ones.

The ordinary ones are for the agoraphobes, I guess. Denise glanced about and winced. *Mirrors everywhere. Difficult for anyone to hide.*

But Ilaron, after a quick survey of the problem, sighed softly and went to stand at the innermost curve of the semicircle, hidden by the square, looking like a man waiting to be shot. Despite his relative immunity to the metal, he was clearly not at all thrilled about being surrounded by what was, for all the ornamentations of dark enamel and chrome, basically a curved wall of iron.

"At least now," he said through not quite gritted teeth, "I should be quite undetectable by magic. Don't just stand there! Go get this done."

Denise went to the front desk. All smiling charm, she asked in her finest Southern Lady manner—the result, she thought, of one too many Tennessee Williams revivals, "I wonder if anyone who was on night duty two nights ago might be here now? Yes? You see, I understand about hotel security and all that, but I really am trying to get in touch with a guest who checked in then. What's that?"

"A name, ma'am. Can you give us his name?"

Denise, all but fluttering a virtual fan, told them all, "Why, you know, it's the silliest thing, but I just can't *remember.* I think it was . . . mm . . . Ahligar? Mr. Ahligar? I can describe him, too, if that will help."

And thank you, Ilaron, for the description. "It *will?* Why that's just *wonderful!* Well, let's see now: He's a tall, slender, pale gentleman, *so* refined, with long silver hair. Handsome fellow, you know, and foreign, and oh, I guess he would have paid in cash."

Sure enough, there was a Mr. Ahligar registered, and someone remembered the description as well, a young man who looked barely old enough to shave, but had the theatrical hint to him that told her he was, like so many other employees in the area, probably yet another actor-wannabe.

"You must understand," he told her earnestly, "we can't just give you the room number."

"Oh no, of *course* not! I do understand."

He flushed slightly under the force of her smile. "But what we can do, ma'am, if you like, is telephone the gentleman, and if he's there and okays it, you can speak to him."

Denise beamed. "That would be just splendid!"

She waited, trying not to tap her fingers impatiently on the marble countertop. Would Kerezar answer? From what Ilaron had told her, Kerezar was clever and quick to learn; he must surely know what this human technology did.

At least, she thought, *the phone's likely to be plastic, not all iron, so he can handle it! Assuming he does—*

"Uh, ma'am? He's on the line."

Oh. God. "Why, thank you!"

With one last, very feigned smile for the young man—one actor to another—Denise turned away, put the receiver to her ear, and said a wary, "Hello?"

Her heart gave a great leap of panic at the sound of the equally wary voice at the other end of the line: It definitely had Ilaron's accent, only much more pronounced. It was a cold, precise voice, too, despite its music, making Ilaron even on his worst day sound downright sunny by comparison.

"Who are you?" it asked brusquely. "Why have you disturbed me?"

Why, indeed? Trying not to sound nervous—no, no, downright terrified—and shielding the phone from on-lookers, Denise murmured, "I am a human. My name . . . isn't important right now. But I know that you are called Kerezar. And I have some interesting news for you about . . . another of your kind. Are you interested?"

After a terrifying moment of empty air, the cold voice told her, "Continue."

Denise nearly tripped over her words in her hurry to get the message in before the wary Kerezar could hang up. "I don't want Ilar"—She cut off the name as though she'd let it slip by accident—"this other one around."

"Why," the voice asked darkly, "not?"

"Because he interferes with my dealings with"—(dramatic pause)—"Lamashtu."

Ha, that must have startled him! Denise heard the faintest hint of a sharply drawn-in breath. But when Kerezar replied, he sounded almost bored. "What is that to me?"

He was startled, Denise reminded herself. *Bargain— and quickly, before he recovers.*

"How," she asked with feigned calm, "do you think I knew your name and how to find you? Come now, Kerezar, you must admit that for all your cleverness, you are not yet an expert about this realm. And I am not exactly without Power." *Even if it belongs to Ilaron, not me!*

"Come to the point."

"Of course. Let me offer you a deal." No nerves now, keep the voice steady: "I will help you snare Ilaron if you give me free rein with Lamashtu."

"Why?" the cold voice asked without the slightest hint of emotion.

"Why do you think?" Denise all but snapped. "For Power, of course!" She paused dramatically, then added, trying to match his coldness, "Perhaps we can plot together. Would that not be interesting? Two realms united, as it were, ruled by two daring people."

"I see."

She could almost hear the contempt hiding behind his cold voice. He was as much amused at her presumption, she guessed, as genuinely interested. But he *was* interested in Ilaron.

And Ilaron told me that Kerezar never turns away from even the most unlikely of tools.

A moment of tense silence followed. Then Kerezar said without warning, "You must wait a bit, until sundown. Do you understand?"

"Of course," Denise assured him, heart racing.

Kerezar gave her no clue as to his room number— not that she'd ever expected him to be that trusting, or that foolish. "We will meet in neutral territory," he said, and it was a command. "The lower lobby, the side that faces west. Do you know it?"

The side, Denise thought, *that opens up onto that inner walkway, with no chance of any last stray beams of sunlight hitting you.* "I do. Very well. Till then."

Hanging up and giving the front desk staff one last, radiant smile and a fluttery wave, Denise hurried to Ilaron's side.

"He bought it. Or at least some of it. He's going to meet me in the lower lobby, on the west side, at sundown."

As she spoke, Denise saw Ilaron's face go very still. The face, she thought, of a hunter. Or a predator.

Yet: "I have my doubts," he murmured. "I do not trust Kerezar not to see through the trap—and I'm also not sure that it was wise to bring Lamashtu's name into this."

"You heard that?"

"My hearing is not *that* acute!" He gestured at all the mirrors. "I saw the name on your lips."

"What else could I do? I couldn't think of any other way to convince him!"

"Denise, please. I'm not accusing you. You did an excellent job. And no, I'm not patronizing you, either. But . . . " He shrugged ever so slightly. "What will be, will be, as you humans put it. And we will see what comes of this."

Kerezar stretched languorously, smiling a thin, cold smile as the night slowly came on, feeling his magical strength returning, new strength flooding his body.

"Lamashtu," he called softly on more than the physical level. "Lamashtu."

He was hardly arrogant enough to think that he could truly control her, not after the easy way she had tricked him.

He also didn't believe that any mere human could control her.

And yet . . . who knew what might be possible?

"Lamashtu," he said in the Unspoken Language by which one communicated with demons, "hear me. Lamashtu, heed me. I have that you wish to know. There is one here, mighty one, to interest you."

She already knew. He felt that wordless response thrill all through his body. Lamashtu was already forcing her host body toward the hotel. And Kerezar continued to smile his thin, sharp, humorless smile.

Entertaining, he thought. *One way or another, something will come from this night's work. One way or another, this should prove most entertaining indeed.*

TWENTY-ONE

Godot

Ilaron glanced sideways at Denise from behind the shelter of his sunglasses. They were both standing in the hotel's lower lobby, by a small counter at its western side. An innocuous enough place, but Denise looked tense enough to snap, simultaneously nervous and alert, like, Ilaron thought, a hunter about to take on some perilous, valuable prey—or, rather, a hunter eager to see if her snaring of that prey will work or if the prey will turn on her instead.

I think that she's starting, somewhere deep within her, to enjoy *all this. Like some novice mage who's cast his first successful spell and believes, therefore, that all magic is simple.*

A dangerous frame of mind.

Not, admittedly, that his was much better. Trying not to look at the hotel staff manning the little counter, Ilaron told himself that they were not growing suspicious; they could not be. They had to be used to seeing people waiting for others at such a convenient landmark.

Such an exposed landmark! "Denise, this is absurd," Ilaron burst out, just at the last moment remembering to warily keep his voice low. "He cannot fail to spot me."

"Agreed," she shot back, a sharp whisper, "assuming you keep waiting here with me. He *won't* see you if you go to stand behind that column. *As* we agreed."

"Perhaps, but . . ."

Denise glanced at him, eyebrows raised. "All that iron's really getting on your nerves, isn't it?"

How could it not?

But he said nothing, only glanced about, hunting for a better hiding place. There, perhaps, behind those ornamental plants—no. That was ridiculous; he'd have to crouch like an idiot, and that would *definitely* make the humans suspicious. Perhaps, instead, just outside, in the walkway behind them, between the two revolving doors—no, then his line of sight would be blocked. The column, then, except . . .

Except that he was not at all comfortable with anything to do with the situation. Not with the thought of a trap that might not close. Not with the thought of so many potential human complications: Almost as many tour groups seemed to be coming through these doors as had been passing through the main Broadway entrance. And, as Denise had guessed, he was most certainly not comfortable with so much iron surrounding him, even more than he normally faced, whole walls of the cursed metal, making him, in effect, magically deaf and blind.

At least Kerezar will be in even worse condition.

If he appears.

If he doesn't simply slip out another way. And there are too many other ways!

He could almost, *almost* see the front of the lower lobby, the eastern side that fed out onto Broadway, from here but, maddeningly, he couldn't get a clear view of anything.

"Ilaron? Ilaron! Will you please stop *quivering*? Face it, this isn't going to work, not with you looking like a spring wound too tight. Leave me here and go watch the main entrances."

"No! That would be—"

"Ilaron, please. It's going to be really difficult for

me to miss recognizing someone who, no matter how he disguises himself, is still going to look like a silver-haired Ilaron!"

He frowned, insulted. "Yes, of course there is a racial resemblance, but he is hardly—"

"All right, so he doesn't look like you. Spare me from male vanity! Just the same, I can hardly miss spotting him. And let's face it, it's not as if I were in any real danger."

"How can you say that? He—"

"I mean it! Look about you. What can Kerezar possibly do with so much iron and so many witnesses around? And," she added acerbically, "I am certainly not stupid enough to go anywhere alone with him, no matter how . . . ah . . . alluring he might prove to be."

Her logic was, unfortunately, flawless.

I cannot let Kerezar escape, Ilaron thought frantically, *yet at the same time I must guard Denise from Lamashtu, and that means—*

And that means nothing! Darkness take it, there's no choice!

Ilaron glared at Denise. "So be it. But first we shall agree on a time when, come what may, I will rejoin you."

"No argument there. Let's give it . . . what, a half hour?"

"That should be sufficient, yes." If Kerezar didn't appear by then, he surely wasn't going to appear at all.

"Right. Synchronize watches and all that, which should make it . . ."

But then Denise glanced up from her watch at him and sighed. "At least *try* to relax."

"How? Maybe you don't understand the full danger of the situation, but—"

"Don't underestimate me!"

"And don't you underestimate Kerezar! Denise, please, listen to me. You are a brave, competent human, I am not denying that—but you *are* human. You're very new to magic, to devious plots—"

"Am I? Haven't you ever heard of curatorial meetings and 'publish or perish'?" She held up a hasty hand. "All right, I was being facetious. Of course I know I'm a beginner, a mere novice compared to you. And I promise not to do anything stupid. Okay?"

"Words," he said, "are easy."

"Will you please stop that? I will be just fine. Everything will be just fine, and—" She stopped with a snort. "And I sound like an idiot. Pollyanna Sheridan—no, never mind, that's a book reference you really don't need. Just get out of here. Go hunting."

"And may I," Ilaron muttered fervently, "catch my prey."

There was, unfortunately, no such thing as one main entrance to the hotel. Thanks to the configurations of the hotel and its attached theater and stores, the facade was divided into three parts, with two openings on the far side of the driveway leading out onto Broadway. Worse than that, Ilaron realized, the driveway itself, cutting through the hotel complex as it did from north to south, created yet two more ways someone could leave.

For all I know, there may be even another exit through that underground garage. Wonderful. Like trying to catch the wind in a net.

He chose as central a position as he could find, between the two revolving doors leading out from the actual hotel onto the driveway. Even so, Ilaron found that he still had a difficult time keeping all four possible exits in clear sight, mostly because those cheerful and never-ending crowds of tourists and pre-theater diners all too frequently blocked his view.

If it wasn't for the iron, and the humans, I'd be able

to sense Kerezar easily and not have to stand here like—

Bah, might as well wish for a thunderbolt to strike him dead before me. If I must hunt like a magickless human, so be it.

And so, for that matter, must he.

But Ilaron was aware of the additional handicap of passing time; he had no intention of leaving Denise undefended for one second longer than was necessary.

Oh, indeed. I sound not like a hunter, but like some fool of a human lover!

And was this all just a waste of that so-precious time? Had he guessed right by waiting here?

Who could say? Kerezar was such a devious being that there was no forecasting which way he'd go—get off those elevators on one of the conference floors, and he could steal down an escalator, bypass a watcher, maybe even somehow slip out through the theater and not be seen at all.

Or, for that matter, he might just decide not to leave his room—

He had left.

He was here, standing on the far side of the driveway, and all uncertainty vanished from Ilaron's mind, leaving it cold and sure. For a time that seemed to stretch beyond bearing, he and Kerezar stood frozen, staring at each other through the crowds, each waiting for the other to make the first move. Kerezar's eyes, predictably, were also hidden by sunglasses, but even so, the hatred stabbing from them was blatant as two spears of ice.

Just as my hatred must be to him. And now shall we— But then reality struck him a sharp blow. *Now, curse it, shall we do nothing!*

No magic was possible, not here, not in the midst of so much iron. Judging from Kerezar's slight start, the same fact had just hit him, as well. No tangible weapons were possible, either, not in the midst of so many folk. The last thing either of them wished was police interference.

Oh, this was just too absurd! Ilaron started to laugh, Kerezar with him, both amused by the irony of this deadly predicament, this ridiculous stalemate, as only two of their cold race could be.

So. We can at least . . . talk.

Ilaron crossed the busy driveway, warily keeping his gaze on Kerezar even as he dodged a taxi and a limousine. On the far sidewalk, he and Kerezar cautiously narrowed the distance between them till they were standing just out of each other's reach.

"As the humans would say," Ilaron commented in chill, sardonic pleasantry, speaking in their native tongue since none of the humans could understand it, "fancy meeting you here."

"Indeed," Kerezar replied, just as coolly. "I was about to say how . . . pleased I was to see you again."

"I cannot say the same."

"How curt. You have learned much from the humans."

"As you, clearly, have not. Kerezar, listen to me. I have not come here to exchange easy insults. This does not need to go any further."

"Does it not?"

"Listen!"

But then they had to sidestep a busy group of package-laden Japanese tourists. When the humans, chattering happily to each other, had passed, Ilaron continued with fierce haste, "I swear this by the Triple Oath. Hear my words:

"I freely surrender all claims to the throne, I freely surrender all claims to my title, I freely surrender all claims to whatever else binds me to our realm. To *your* realm.

"I swear to that, my word, my life, my honor."

"I swear this by the Triple Oath." He took a deep breath, seeing the unchanged coldness of Kerezar's face, reading a hint of sardonic humor only another of their race could have found. "Is that understood, Kerezar? I do not want anything but this, to be left alone to live my own life—*here,* Kerezar, in *this* realm among *these* people."

"What, among humans?" Kerezar deftly stepped aside to avoid a family of camera-wielding Italians, dipping his head to one plump, giggling woman in insincere courtesy, then gave Ilaron a wry, sharp grin. "Among such noisy, foolish beings as those? I cannot accept that."

"I have just sworn the Triple Oath." Ilaron forced his voice to stay coldly tranquil. "Do you question the truth of that? You may bear witness of my oath back to your people, show them that your strength is undiminished, your honor unstained."

"The truth. I am to accept the truth from a heretic."

"I swore the Triple Oath."

"Indeed. But 'truth' is such a malleable thing. The truth in this matter, I fear, is that Ilaron has grown afraid. Soft. Weak."

"Give it up, Kerezar. I don't rouse to anger that easily."

"What, then, is Ilaron? Or rather, what has he become?"

"My own self. No more. And no less. Kerezar, were you not listening—"

"Tsk, he is already a thief. A traitor. Yes, and above all, a heretic. And now I am to believe he has, as well, become a . . . ah, what do these people call it? . . . a 'pacifist,' is that not the term?"

He said that in the human tongue; theirs had no such word or concept.

"Believe what you will. Only go. Rule your realm. Leave this one forever."

"I fear not." Kerezar feigned great interest in his hand, in the angle of his nails, a thinly veiled imitation of a predator sharpening its talons. "I find this . . . realm interesting," he added, glancing up at Ilaron again. "I will enjoy adding it to my own."

Slipped in with the veiled contempt was sudden blunt truth. About this one thing, Ilaron knew, Kerezar meant exactly what he said.

Oh, no. He shall not harm this realm, I swear that. This must end here and now, and to the Darkness with the consequences.

But even as Ilaron began a sudden lunge forward, Kerezar turned and—fled, fled out onto the street, heading downtown, pushing his way through the crowds, leaving startled, angry humans in his wake.

Damn him! He shall not escape!

Every latent instinct flared to life. The enemy was fleeing, and there was nothing more than this, the hunt, the chase, the hunger for the kill. Ilaron raced after Kerezar, dashing perilously across Forty-fifth Street, dodging cars, taxis, weaving through the crush of humanity—

Only to stagger to a halt halfway down the block, panting, shaking. Wait, wait, *wait!* There was no logic to this, none! Struggling with instinct, struggling against the savage hunting frenzy, Ilaron thought, *Running from a foe?*

Running was *not* Kerezar's way. Even exposure to this realm and its maddening iron would not have changed that.

This is a trick, a trap—yes, damn him!

Kerezar could only be trying to lure Ilaron away from the hotel.

Denise! Ilaron thought.

But the madness still burned in his blood, screaming

of: the chase, how can you stop when the quarry lives, the quarry flees, how can you give up the chase?

You idiot! You mindless idiot! Oh yes, the chase, by all means the chase, go ahead, yield to blind instinct—and let Denise die!

Raging and terrified in one, Ilaron turned and hurried back to the hotel.

What has Kerezar done? What can he have had time to do? And—am I already too late to undo it?

TWENTY-TWO

On Little Cat Feet

Lamashtu smiled with Johnston's lips. Aiie, yes, she was enjoying her first subway ride very much. So much nastiness, so much Darkness, all crowded in together! Wearing Johnston's body so very comfortably, she brushed up against a middle-aged white woman, a black teenager—

Foolish humans with your foolish hatreds toward your own kind, all those eons of your stupid hatreds for each other on the grounds of what? Appearance? Worship? Do you think to rival me? *Never that! For I alone make no judgments, I alone need no excuse save one: I slay because there is life!*

The rage was growing within her, the rage telling her to kill, kill again, kill all that lived, all that—

Yes, but Johnston's body was telling her that they had reached the proper station. Rage and sweet, sweet slaying must wait just this tiny bit longer. With one last reluctant touch to the shoulder of a businessman, Lamashtu abandoned the train.

For now. Once I have slain that human woman, that Denise Sheridan, then . . . yes. Then I shall return here.

But first, the hunt.

Denise stirred restlessly, shifting her weight from one foot to the other, back again, wishing they had put some chairs in this lobby. But it wasn't a real lobby, after all, just an entryway, and—

And she was starting to dither.

Where was he? Had she—no, impossible, she couldn't have missed someone who looked like Kerezar. Assuming that he would be using the elevators. Oh, he would, surely. But, assuming that he would, indeed use an elevator—*where was he?*

More time slipped by. Denise had just about reached the stage of checking her watch every minute, more and more sure that she'd been "stood up," when she noticed a man approaching her from the walkway outside—

No. Not Kerezar. This guy was human, and overall pretty nondescript. But what had brought him to her attention was the trouble he seemed to be having getting through the revolving door.

Oboy. A real *out-of-towner.*

But then he was through, and close enough for her to see his eyes. And Denise knew in that terrible instant:

Lamashtu!

Oh God, no, what was she to do, where could she go, what could she—Ilaron was nowhere in sight, and there were crowds all around, happy theatergoers, tourists—

I can't let Lamashtu massacre them, I can't!

Where could she run? Not outside into the crowds, that would be murder, yet she couldn't risk getting trapped on an elevator with Lamashtu—

The escalators! Yes, of course, they led up to the conference floors, and no one was going to be holding any meetings at this odd hour. Two floors, maybe three, would be empty.

Without hesitation, Denise raced up an escalator, the demon alarmingly close behind her, landed on the second floor—no, no, Level Three, whatever had happened to Level Two she couldn't say but—

No, no, this wasn't the conference floor after all,

this was the theater level! She was leading the demon right into what would very soon be a feast of humanity!

No!

Denise ran frantically for the next escalator, there along the far wall, sure the demon's hand was going to drag her back, raced up the escalator at full speed, panting, to the next floor—sure enough, Level Four, meeting rooms.

Now what? Now where? No one was up here, though a few brooms and mops showed that the cleaning staff was going to come through here shortly, one last clean-up before any stray theatergoers could wander up this way.

Ha, yes, yes! Denise ran full out for a conference room, one of those with a double set of doors leading in, snatching up a mop as she ran, and dashed through one set of doors into the room.

Saw this in an old movie—a Babylonian demon can't know about old movies, can she? God, but her host can, if there's enough left of him!

Seemingly not. Lamashtu was following without hesitation, a savage grin on her host's face, clearly delighted at having so easily trapped her prey—

Right, and prey armed with such a puny weapon as a stick!

The demon's arm reached for Denise—

But Denise ducked, darted out the second set of doors, then whirled, slamming them shut, ramming the mop through the double handles to lock them. Hearing Lamashtu crash futilely up against the doors, Denise grabbed a broom and nearly killed herself getting back to the first set of doors before Lamashtu could recover and reach them, slamming them shut, too, jamming the broom through the handles. A moment of tense suspense passed, another. . . .

Then, panting and trembling so badly her legs shook, Denise sank to a chair.

She'd done it. As easily as that, she had trapped Lamashtu.

After a while, Denise looked up, only now realizing that this floor was an open rectangle through which the elevator shaft passed. Oh, great. Anyone who'd been riding in those glass-sided elevators just now would have seen the chase.

In this city? Probably thought it was just part of some movie shoot.

Denise fumbled in her purse for the precious paper holding the incantation, wishing that she'd had time to memorize it fully. Now, though, if ever there was a chance to banish the demon, this—

A sudden hiss made her glance sharply up again. And realize with a groan that it must be fully night outside. Which meant that Lamashtu was now free to manifest without needing a human host. Oh, yes, the human body was still locked safely away behind those doors—

But the demon was out here with her.

Denise stared up at that fierce lioness head, the unfurling wings, the woman's body and taloned hands and feet—Lamashtu was beautiful and terrible and hideous at once.

And deadly. And totally without mercy. Denise raised the paper with not-quite-steady hands, wondering if she could possibly read the incantation cold— but a talon caught the page, tore it from her hand, ripped it casually to bits and tossed it aside.

Lamashtu, like a lioness, like a cat, liked to play with her prey.

I never was a cat person, flashed through Denise's frantic mind. She didn't have the incantation, she couldn't summon Pazuzu—

But I haven't come all this way to die now!

Ridiculous defiance.

It's the only one I've got.

She shouted out the first thing, the only thing, that came to mind, Babylonian, yes, a prayer in the Babylonian tongue, a magical prayer to the ancient gods, words that meant:

> "Oh Ea, Shamash, Asalluhi, great ones!
> You whose utterance is Life,
> You whose speech is Life!
> You who are Life!
> Wondrous are your ways, wondrous . . ."

A prayer thanking them for their mercy, their shielding of mortals from all evil, all demons. She didn't have to think about the words; she had the prayer memorized, having recently written a paper on it.

"Publish or perish," indeed! Please, please let my pronunciation be at least close to accurate!

It . . . was.

It was more than that. To her astonishment and utter relief, Denise saw Lamashtu recoil in rage and pain— Pain?

Of course—Lamashtu, the fallen child of heaven! The prayer was suddenly hitting home, forcing her to remember the glorious being she'd once been—and oh, how she was all at once yearning for what had been yet could never be again! The taloned fingers reached for Denise, then fell back, clenching futilely as Denise frantically continued her chant.

With a shriek of pure despair, Lamashtu suddenly— was gone.

Ilaron rushed through the crowded hotel lobby, dodging, twisting, narrowly avoiding collision after collision, not caring that he was leaving a storm of indignant complaints behind him.

The demon was here. He could feel her, feel the Darkness, and Denise was alone and unprotected—

And not here, not on the lower lobby. Where? Where? Ilaron turned fiercely this way, that, hunting, ignoring the bewildered humans around him and—

There! He raced up the escalator, brushing his way past yet more humans, nearly bowling them over, raced up the next level, no longer making any pretense at humanity, his "walking stick" now clearly glinting as a sword. No telling if it would work against that unfamiliar demon, no telling if he would be able to work any harm—

Denise! And Lamashtu—as the demon loomed over her, not yet aware of his presence, Denise was . . . chanting something? Chanting in a foreign tongue— Babylonian?—words that glinted with the smallest edge of Power—

Not enough, never enough!

Ilaron froze, suddenly realizing that the moment he moved, Lamashtu would sense him and strike out at Denise. All the demon need do was brush her, the smallest touch, and Denise would be dead. Lamashtu—

—gave a wail of despair, and was gone, swiftly as that, air rushing in with a "bang" to fill her space.

What did Denise say? Do?

Someone was sure to be hurrying up here to investigate that howl and noise. "Denise!"

She whirled with a gasp, then recoiled, staring. Ilaron realized how savage he must look, like a Dark Elf out of one of her books, sword gleaming, wild hair flaring free from its ponytail.

Curse it, yes, and there were those glass-sided elevators: The last thing he wanted was to put on a show for tourists.

Have they already seen worse? Have they seen Lamashtu?

No. If so, the panic would be already spreading. Or rather, humans saw only what they expected to see. A real demon? Naw. Special effects for the theater. Right, or just a trick of the light.

Still, no reason to give them any more of a show. Quickly Ilaron wrapped the sword back in its walking-stick illusion, brushed back his hair, forced his face back into its calm mask. No need to waste time asking if Denise was hurt; if the demon had touched her, she would already be dead.

She looks like a warrior expecting a battle to the death, then suddenly, unexpectedly, left without that battle.

The way I felt when I had to let Kerezar escape.

"Denise, come, we must—"

"I didn't banish her," she burst out, all but sobbing. "I scared her away for now, but I didn't banish her."

He'd already sensed that. "Better than nothing," Ilaron told her as levelly as possible. "At least now you know your pronunciation is close to accurate. We must leave—"

"She tore up the incantation. I had to say whatever I could, came up with a—a prayer, Babylonian prayer, to the old gods. Guess I gave her a—a—oh God, I don't know what. A guilt trip, maybe."

He had no idea what she meant. *But if I don't calm her, she will break.* "So be it," he said brusquely. "You did what you could, and it was well done, indeed. We may have lost one copy of the incantation, but the other is still safely back in the museum."

She blinked. "Y-yes. Yes. It is."

"And as I say, now you know that your pronunciation is accurate. Excellent. Now, come."

The brusqueness did seem to be keeping her from hysteria, but she was still very close to the edge of shock; humans simply were not used to true magic. Ilaron took her arm, quickly filling her in on what had happened between himself and Kerezar, not sure how much of it she was actually absorbing, and half-dragged her onto an elevator up to the eighth floor, ignoring the elevator's other occupants, thinking, *No knowing when or where Lamashtu will reappear.*

Denise had recovered enough by the time they got off the elevator to walk under her own power. Ilaron took her straight to the lobby bar, sat her down, and called for a waiter.

"The lady has just had a terrible emotional shock. I wish hot food and drink for her—yes, yes, whatever can be prepared quickly."

A flash of will ensured it.

"Ilaron, I—I can't."

"You can. And will."

When the hastily prepared soup, sandwich, and coffee arrived, Ilaron practically forced her to eat and drink.

And slowly he saw the color come flooding back into her pale face, saw the life return to her dazed eyes. Denise offered him half the sandwich, and Ilaron took it, realizing that by now he, too, could use some nourishment, as well as some time in which to recover.

Wonderful just to sit. Wonderful just to enjoy this almost peaceful moment between them: *Comrades in arms,* he thought, *that's the human phrase for it.*

Only that?

Of course only that. What else could there be?

What, indeed? Denise glanced at him, glanced down at her plate, and he . . . wondered. Comrades in arms who . . . weren't quite sure that there was anything more to what they were feeling than that?

Ah, nonsense. It was merely the novelty of *having* a comrade affecting him, of knowing he could actually trust someone not to turn on him or—figuratively or literally—stab him in the back.

Merely? Wasn't that amazing enough in itself?

Ilaron looked uneasily around, suddenly not quite sure of himself, seeing nothing but normal, busy, noisy humanity. A pianist had struck up the first notes of some amiable, non-intrusive melody . . . something, he guessed abstractedly, from a Broadway musical. The song "Memory," perhaps? Mm, yes. That was one melody humans did seem to love repeating over and over again. Odd to suddenly have that touch of normalcy. . . .

Denise gave the softest of uncertain laughs, and Ilaron glanced back at her in alarm.

"Denise?"

"Nothing. After all that just happened, to be just sitting here in such ordinary surroundings, listening to a song that's been done to death . . . weird, that's all. And I was just thinking that you must find the mundane human world boring."

"Right now," Ilaron retorted, "I would welcome the chance to be bored."

"Good point." She studied the dregs of her coffee, swirling them about in the cup, then put the cup down sharply. "What about Lamashtu? She's going to be back sooner or later, but . . ."

"But where and when are a mystery to me, too."

"I was afraid you'd say that."

"She was clearly badly shaken by that Babylonian prayer, but I have no way of knowing just how badly, or how long it will take for her to recover."

"Oh joy. Then we'd better get to that second copy and fast."

"It's past the museum's normal closing time. Are we going to be able to get in?"

Denise glanced at her watch, looked more closely, as though astonished to realize how little time had passed. "Not a problem. This is one of the museum's late nights; we should still have about an hour."

But without warning, they were no longer alone. Kerezar was there, seating himself with cool arrogance at their table, just out of either of their reaches.

"Good evening," was all he said.

TWENTY-THREE

The Peaceable Kingdom

Denise couldn't quite stifle a startled little gasp at this sudden materialization. An irreverent corner of her mind whispered, hey, look at this, another drop-dead gorgeous, dangerous guy at the table—

Gee. Aren't I the lucky one?

She glanced quickly from the newcomer to Ilaron and back again, thinking, silver hair instead of black, a slightly lighter frame, paler skin, but the same grace, the same cold, elegant look to their faces. Sunglasses on both of them, but Denise didn't need those removed to know she'd see the same eerie eyes on each.

Same race, no doubt about it. Guy's got gall, I'll give him that.

He also had an air of totally indifferent cruelty that sent a chill through her.

All right. Don't let him know he scares you.

Ha. Easy to say.

Biting back the impulse to snap, "Dr. Kerezar, I assume?" which probably wouldn't mean a thing to either of the men, Denise instead turned to Ilaron with a sweet smile and asked, amazed at how steady her voice sounded, "I take it that this is someone you know?"

That earned her a smile, cold, sharp, and thin as a blade, from Kerezar, and a bow so very graceful yet at the same time so very slight and brusque that Denise guessed she'd just been insulted.

Subtly mocking an "inferior," eh?

"Indeed he does," Kerezar said to her before Ilaron could speak, "though I doubt that he is pleased to see me. I am, as you must surely have already guessed, Kerezar."

Oh, you smooth talker, you! "I wish I could say that it was a pleasure to meet you."

The thin smile never wavered. "And you are that clever human who telephoned me, are you not?"

Under cover of the table, Ilaron sharply nudged her foot with his. The message was clear enough: Give nothing away. All right, that made sense, the stories all said that true names held Power.

And the fact that Kerezar is so free with his own name has to be another sign of his contempt. Toward me and Ilaron both. Thinks neither of us is a threat.

Well, two, or rather, three could play this game. "I am," Denise agreed evasively, then turned to Ilaron with an even sweeter smile than before. "Tell me, are all your people like this? So . . . rude?"

"Ah, no." Ilaron's face was bland. "We do not generally intrude on others' privacy or insist on joining a party uninvited. I'm afraid that somewhere in his wanderings from realm to realm, Kerezar must have learned discourtesy."

Kerezar showed no sign that he'd heard either of them. Ignoring Ilaron completely, he learned slightly towards Denise. "I must tell you, my dear, that I truly admired the way you dealt with Lamashtu. It could not have been an easy thing for you to chase away a demon. Of course," he added with delicate malice, "she hasn't actually been banished, but then, you knew that, didn't you?"

Not sure where this was going, and getting no guide from Ilaron, Denise warily said nothing. After the briefest of pauses, Kerezar continued, "I see. What a pity that such a clever young woman has chosen to join with Ilaron—such a treacherous heretic."

"I haven't found him such." *Damn, shouldn't have said that, shouldn't have given him an opening.*

And of course Kerezar took it. "Of course not." His voice was velvet. "How could you? He has probably shown you nothing but kindness, yes? Ah, a shame. The better to make a willing slave of you."

Denise opened her mouth to say, *Don't be so melodramatic,* but all at once she couldn't seem to find her voice. Kerezar's smile thinned: *Predatory,* she thought. *Ilaron, why don't you do something? Say something?*

But he sat motionless, watching her as though she was expected to know what to do.

I don't!

Kerezar continued, his voice still smooth, "My dear, do you know who sits beside you? Truly know?"

Somehow she managed to force out a choked, "I know all that I need to know."

"I think not. You believe him so charming and . . . gentle. A sad misunderstanding. But forgivable."

All right, try, get the words out: "Oh, please." It came out not as the sarcastic drawl she'd intended, but as a half-strangled gasp. "Is this where you tell me what a monster Ilaron truly is?"

"Ah, you do *not* know." Kerezar's voice was smoother than velvet now: silk, Denise thought, rich, dark, gleaming silk. Poisoned silk, if there could be such a thing—probably was, in his realm. Poisoned silk, poisoned air, poisoned minds . . .

"You do not know," Kerezar continued, caressing each word, "that this is the one who used to delight in the hunt, the kill. You really should know. You must. For this is the one who brought slow, slow death to his prisoners, the one who gloried in the Darkness, the one who showed never a trace of your . . . gentle human mercy."

As he spoke, Denise felt reality slide away, losing her in a mist . . . a mist through which she could see Ilaron . . . a cold, foreign Ilaron clad in eerie black armor, his face . . . terrible, all warmth lost, all hope, all joy save the dark joy of cruelty . . . Through the mist, she saw hints of horrible things . . . glimpses of elegant, refined, brutal torments made all the worse for being utterly indifferent, made all the worse for Ilaron's being the hand wielding the blade, the flame, Ilaron's the hand causing such horror . . . such cruelties beyond anything merely human . . .

. . . and through it all, Kerezar's voice, smoothly conjuring those images, vague glimpses of the past, all the harsher for seeming so very true.

"Think of that, my dear," he purred. "Think of him in the throes of cold, cold ecstasy, watching, tasting, feeling his victims die screaming. There is your . . . friend, my dear. Think of that."

No. It was the smallest thought of defiance.

No. A little stronger.

No, I will not think of that. No, I will not believe him. No, I will not fall for this.

She knew, somewhere in a corner of her mind untouched by mist, she knew that Kerezar's main intention was to create a rift, to tear her from Ilaron's protection. *What protection can there be from such a being—no! No, that is Kerezar's will, not my thoughts . . .*

Kerezar. There was something more to this than the mere wish to separate her from Ilaron. Something more . . . something . . .

Yes. He's enjoying *this.* The realization was like a dash of ice water. *Cold, cruel, detached pleasure, but yes, he knows his words are hurting me, and he likes that, yes, yes, he likes causing pain, seeing me hurting—*

Damn him for a pervert, no!

But Kerezar's voice continued its cruel croon, and she couldn't find the way out of the mist.

But . . . something he said . . . a word . . . if only I can remember . . . one word, right at the beginning . . .

I have it!

The mist was thinning, as though her growing anger at Kerezar for doing this, at Ilaron for not stopping it, was shredding it, and—

I am not Ilaron's slave, I am not Kerezar's slave—I am not anyone's slave!

And the mist was gone. She was herself again, mind free, realizing with a shock that whatever had just happened to her had taken almost no time at all. A quick wary glance at Ilaron showed him sitting tensely silent, watching her as though trusting Denise's judgment but all too aware of how susceptible humans were to Faerie glamour.

Well, thanks so much for the vote of confidence, but a bit of help would have been far more useful!

Kerezar was still talking, but Denise, no longer even slightly enthralled, held up a silencing hand. He stopped, blinking in surprise.

"I applaud you," she drawled. "Very nicely done. Almost had me convinced."

"But surely you—"

"But surely I never did believe that Ilaron was a—well, you probably don't even know what a choirboy is. Let's just say that whatever he did or might have done in the past is his affair. And it *is* the past. The important thing is that he sought to change, to escape that . . . place . . . you still call home. And that he did and you didn't speaks in his favor."

"Ah, he does have you enthralled—"

"Oh, give it a *rest!*" That came out before she could find a more diplomatic way to word it. *What the hell, go for honesty!* "I'll grant you this," Denise continued, more urbanely, into the sudden, startled silence. "I *might* have been swayed, but you made a bad choice of a word right at the beginning.''

That made even Kerezar start, and the faintest hint of distaste crossed his face, as though the very idea of a human criticizing him was repulsive.

No, Kerezar, you're *the repulsive one.*

"The word," she told him shortly, "is 'heretic.' You see, it's been used a great deal in human history, far too often, in fact—and always by those trying to dominate others.

"Sorry, Kerezar. You, as the saying goes, blew it from the start."

"Ah well, then you will die with him." The calm indifference in Kerezar's voice was more chilling than any emotional outburst.

But Ilaron finally roused, leaning forward—and, incidentally, nudging Denise's foot again in the process: Don't interrupt.

Go for it. And about time, too.

In the next moment, she was glad for his warning. Because what Ilaron asked coolly was, "Do you see? My people are loyal to me."

The faintest of frowns crossed Kerezar's face.

Struck a nerve, did we? Why? What did Ilaron say? Or imply? Wait, wait, that "my people"—someone as nasty as Kerezar would never be able to believe Ilaron is anything as innocent as an art dealer.

What, then? Does he think the gallery's a front? That Ilaron is secretly a—a what, a crime boss? Ha, yes, I bet I'm right!

"Do you understand, Kerezar?" Ilaron continued. "You failed to fully comprehend me before. I have not *sunk* to this realm, Kerezar. This *is* my realm, these *are* my people, and I will not permit invasion. Is *that* understood?"

I was *right. Ilaron the Godfather.*

"Do you issue formal challenge?" Kerezar countered. "That is forbidden you, traitor. All there is for you is to be hunted, punished, tormented without the mercy of madness or death. Is *that* understood?"

Oh Lord, were they going to fight it out here and now? In front of everyone?

But without warning, Ilaron casually flipped a knife—no, Denise realized, a *bread knife* at Kerezar. Of course it wasn't sharp enough to cut, but it was made of stainless steel.

Steel, iron—ooh, that must smart!

Sure enough, Kerezar was springing up with a startled yelp of pain. Ilaron coolly shouted, "Thief! Stop him!"

Kerezar, shooting him a quick flash of open hatred, fled. The hotel had security guards, of course, and those guards were already roused from having investigated the mysterious wail and explosion on Level Four—and, presumably, Denise thought, from having found the body of Lamashtu's late host.

Ilaron, looking smug, sat comfortably back to watch the chase. "This should be entertaining," he noted.

"Entertaining!"

"Iron elevators, iron emergency exits—yes, and armed with those nice, loud security alarms that he won't dare trigger. Oh, nice leap! Tsk, point deducted for crashing into that flower stand. Look at him struggle with the roses—ha, there he goes, headed for the restaurant. No way out, unless he plans a suicidal leap through plate glass—no, I thought not."

"Ilaron!"

"Aren't you enjoying this? I certainly am. One doesn't often see such excellent street theater. Ah, but there he goes, around behind the front desk, heading backstage with the staff. Finally found the one unalarmed door—yes. He's gone. A pity. But it was a fine exhibition while it lasted."

Concerned hotel staff were swarming their table.

Ilaron treated them all to a charmingly urbane smile. "No matter," he assured them with a casual wave of the hand. "Truly. Nothing was taken. It was merely an unsuccessful attempt. No, no, of course I'm not blaming anyone here! This *is* New York, after all, and a hotel is not and should not be a fortress."

He got to his feet, Denise, wondering what he was doing, with him. "At any rate," Ilaron concluded to the staff with another of those cool, so very sophisticated smiles, "you've just given that thief the fright of his life. I doubt that he shall ever dare to return." He suavely took Denise's arm. "And now, I bid you all a very good night."

As he and Denise rode down in an elevator, she accused, "You did that deliberately."

"Of course. Kerezar and I couldn't fight, not here and now; I didn't have a chance of defeating him without being free to use magic or my sword. But humiliation is *such* a handy weapon. Let Kerezar be the one off-balance! And let him live with the shame first of having been struck with a blunt weapon, a weapon without honor, and then of having to flee like a slave."

"Don't sound so smug. You've made an enemy—"

"I already *had* an enemy."

"Well, yes, I admit that sounded stupid. What I meant was that if he hated you before, he's *really* going to loathe you now."

"The feeling," Ilaron said, "is mutual."

"Yes, but now we don't know where he is!"

"We will."

"But Kerezar won't be returning here!"

Ilaron shrugged. "He wasn't planning to return here anyhow."

"How could you know that?"

"That, my dear Denise, should be obvious: He knew that *I* knew he was lodging here."

"How can you be so *calm* about it?"

"What good would anger do? I *will* settle matters with Kerezar. In time. But, as your human adage puts it so nicely, 'first things first,' and first must come the banishing of Lamashtu. Oh, and thank you, by the way."

He'd lost her completely. "For . . . ?"

"For that vote of confidence against Kerezar."

"Oh, right! I kept waiting for you to say something. Defend yourself. Help *me!* Yet—you just sat there! What if I had turned on you instead?"

"I trusted your judgment. Besides," he added in genuine bewilderment, "what good would denials have been?"

"You mean, what he was saying about you was— no. Never mind." *Alien. He really is alien. Can't see that I just might have failed. Or been revolted. I still could be, if I let myself, but . .* "I told him that your past was your business, and I meant it. Still do."

He turned, stopped, looked straight at her. "You lie beautifully."

"Ilaron!"

"But you accept me as I am now, so thank you again. Now, come, let us—"

He gasped out something astonished-sounding in his native tongue. And Denise gasped as well. They had just stepped out onto Broadway.

And Broadway, Broadway and all the world outside, had become blaring, blinding utter chaos.

TWENTY-FOUR

Take the "A" Train

The world outside the hotel was nothing short of insane, Denise thought, like a scene from some end-of-the-world disaster movie, a wilderness of noise, light, shouts—chaos worse than ever was normal for the area. Ambulances and police cars, sirens blaring, seemed to be blocking every street, every corner, and traffic was at a standstill. Ilaron managed to corner a policeman long enough to ask, "What happened?"

A shrug, a wave, a hasty, "Something in the subway."

A woman rushing uptown added something about, "Epidemic!"

Two teenagers, breathless with excitement and shock, contributed a quick, gory description of sudden death. "Right there, man, I saw it! Right there! Fell over, blood all over him—I just ran, man, didn't wanna even breathe!"

Sudden death? A disaster in the subway? Epidemic? All at once the scattered bits rushed together, and Denise gasped, "Lamashtu!"

"Exactly."

"My God, Ilaron, don't you see? She was in a human host, she must have used that host to take the subway to here. The subway! How many people did she . . . oh my God, my God, Ilaron . . . "

His hand closed on her arm, just tightly enough to keep her from collapsing. "We can do nothing for them. Do you understand me? We can do nothing. Save avenge their deaths."

"R—right. Damned right. But—but how are we going to get out of here?"

It took a great deal to panic New Yorkers, but rumors of the Ebola virus loose on the subway system were certainly enough to do the trick. The police had blocked off the Times Square station down at Forty-second Street, as well as Broadway and several side streets, and frantic crowds were forcing their way uptown on foot, crashing into the inevitable curious idiots (*the type,* Denise thought wildly, *who wait on the beach to watch the tidal wave come in*) who were trying to get farther downtown.

"Hopeless," Ilaron muttered, and she wasn't sure if he meant the situation or the humans. His firm hand on her arm steered her through the crowds, across Broadway, weaving through the motionless herd of swearing, horn-blowing drivers, and heading east.

Toward Sixth Avenue. Of course. Ilaron had certainly lived in this city long enough to know there was no chance of catching a taxi anywhere on the West Side, not under these circumstances.

But all at once what had happened hit her with full force. All at once Denise could have stopped where she was and wept, weighed down by a sudden dark surge of guilt. "Ilaron . . . ?" she murmured. "Ilaron, those people . . . those poor people . . ."

"Are not your fault."

"Aren't they? It's because of *me* that Lamashtu came here, because of me that she—that she killed those people."

Ilaron's mind was clearly as much on Kerezar as Lamashtu. "Did you summon the demon?" he asked brusquely. "No? Did you set the demon after you? No, again? Then there is no reason for guilt."

"But I can't—"

"It was almost certainly Kerezar who gave the demon access to this realm; you should put your foolish feelings of guilt on him."

Ilaron's implacable logic wasn't exactly comforting, but at least it was turning her misery into something else. "Well, damn him! And—and—"

"If you are about to curse me as well, don't bother."

"How can you be so utterly, lucidly, *cold*?"

His expression never changed. "I am as I am."

"But—those were lives!" Denise protested, hurrying to keep up with his longer stride. "Or don't human lives count as important to—"

"Don't be ridiculous. I do not disregard the lives of any sentient beings. Not any longer. But as soon blame *me* for daring to leave my realm—" His glance flicked sideways. "Is that it? Do you blame *me* for Lamashtu's appearance?"

"No, of course not!"

"Then we are agreed that neither of us is at fault. And let us drop this foolishness!"

They made it as far as Sixth Avenue, still wildly arguing morality and responsibility—

They stopped. Stared.

"Oh, hell!" Denise muttered and Ilaron hissed what was probably his language's equivalent.

Traffic on Sixth was completely snarled, predictably, now that Denise thought about it, reflecting the chaos over on Broadway.

"So be it," Ilaron snapped. "There is still another possibility."

With the air of an aristocrat fallen on hard times, he led the way north to the Forty-seventh Street subway station. Denise, not daring to look at that elegant, indignant face, nearly choked on her sudden, frantically suppressed laughter.

Aww, poor Ilaron! Forced to travel like a common

human! Lord, if I start laughing now, I'll never stop. And he—he will never forgive me.

It was difficult to stay hysterical down in the dingy, very mundane reality of the subway station. Now it was Denise who had to take charge, since Ilaron clearly was on unfamiliar territory. She quickly got them tokens, telling Ilaron, "The B train, that's what we want. The F would get us over to Lexington, where we'd have to change trains and wait for the—"

"Which is the quickest way?"

"The B, I guess. It'll get us closest to the museum: Eighty-first Street and Central Park West—do you know that area?"

He nodded. "From there we can catch a taxi across to the museum."

Optimist.

They were lucky, Denise thought. They'd just missed a B train packed to the doors with overflow crowds avoiding the presumably totally shut-down Broadway lines, but a second train pulled in, wheels squealing, only a short while after, and yes, it, too, was a B train. She and Ilaron boarded what, thanks to the first train and the fact that the rush hour was pretty much over, turned out to be a nearly empty car.

Fortunate, Denise reflected. Ilaron was plainly not in the mood to be a peaceful straphanger!

At least the car was relatively clean, almost no refuse on the floor, the sides almost unmarked by graffiti. It was standard issue, lined with two rows of plastic seating, each row one solid strip indented at regular intervals.

Poor Ilaron, Denise thought. *Not even the luxury of a separate seat.*

She glanced at her silent companion, who was sitting as though trying to make as little contact with the plastic as possible, looking decidedly out of place amid the mundane surroundings. Handsome even now, though, even while he was radiating that *I am an aristocrat so don't bother me* air.

Like to take him down to the East Village, Ludlow Street, maybe, one of the scuzzier jazz clubs—no, decadence he knows. Her mind shied away from the rest of that thought. *It's just the common, working class stuff about which he hasn't got that proverbial clue.*

Uh-oh, here came trouble. A would-be troublemaker, anyhow, a scruffy teenager trying to panhandle through intimidation. Ilaron grew very still, and Denise tensed, not sure what he was about to do.

Oh please, not more violence, not more death . . .

But all Ilaron did was calmly remove his sunglasses to look at the teen, no more than that. Denise stifled a snicker as the panhandler wannabe's eyes widened in shock, and he scurried off without a word. Ilaron just as calmly replaced the sunglasses and settled back into *I am not here.*

Then, without warning, he came back to life, turning so sharply to Denise that she nearly started. "I . . . have been curt with you," he said. "Unjustly so, when you have undergone so much trauma in so short a time."

An apology? From him? Well, well, well! "You don't have to—"

"Please. No platitudes. Let me finish. I . . . Denise, I have no words for this, not in this tongue, but . . . the iron, the noise, so much of both out there, facing us on every side . . . I . . . " He shook his head. "All of it, jumbled so closely together, all that was very nearly more than I could endure."

"Oh. I . . . oh." God, she hadn't considered that. It must have been very near to hell for him, wall-to-wall cars, wall-to-wall iron, and noise, and flashing lights that must have blazed right through his sunglasses' protective lenses. Fortunate that so much of a modern subway car was plastic and—and whatever composite metals they were using nowadays rather than solid steel, or he probably would have cut and run.

And here he was, actually trying to apologize to her, actually showing unfeigned concern—

"I'm sorry," Denise blurted. "I should have realized. All that—it was asking a lot of you, too. I mean . . . " That sentence wasn't going anywhere. "I can't imagine what . . . " That one wasn't working, either. Her brain seemed to be going on sabbatical.

"Oh, hell," Denise said helplessly. "Tell you what, Ilaron: If we ever do get this whole stupid business settled, we'll go to some nice, friendly bar and get ourselves most unscholarly drunk."

That surprised him to the point of a genuine burst of laughter. "That," he said, just barely forcing his face back into its usual cool mask, "is the most unusual offer I've heard in quite some time. And, my dear Dr. Sheridan, I must say the idea does have its appeal. It does, indeed."

Kerezar stood alone and unnoted in a shadowy alley as far from the chaos of Broadway as he could get in so short a time, struggling to catch his breath and his self-possession. Oh, he had easily enough eluded those human hounds, no problem there at all. But the wild blaze of iron, light, noise—

No. Focus. Control. Eliminate the simmering rage at Ilaron; it was foolish, perhaps even perilous, to allow his mind to be distracted by . . . pettiness.

Oh yes, what had just happened to him had been nothing short of outrageous, a triple insult. But Kerezar told himself, *I am in control, I shed the humiliation . . . it is past, it cannot stain me. I shed the humiliation . . .*

Of being hit like a slave with a blunt weapon, an honorless weapon, of being hunted by humans like some—some common, degenerate thief—

No. The humiliation *was* past. Clever of Ilaron to work such a scheme, but nothing more than that.

It will not save him.

Yes. Calmness. The savage mass of iron that was all those vehicles could not be ignored, a weight almost heavy enough to crush him, but with it . . . yes, ah yes. Kerezar stood listening to the chaos he could still hear even this far away, then slowly, warily, moved back toward it, drinking in the fear and anger, drawing to him the surrounding haze of Darkness.

Yes, yes . . . a rich enough tangle of emotion almost to let him sense Ilaron despite the iron, the crowds . . .

Kerezar's eyes snapped open. Where would Ilaron be headed in such haste? His home? His gallery?

No . . . he had left with the human woman, the one who Lamashtu found so fascinating. Ilaron wouldn't want to risk drawing Lamashtu to either place.

The museum, then . . . ? So close to the gallery, so full of art and antiquities . . . yes . . . of course. What more logical site to fight a demon than a great storehouse of information about the past?

There, now, the calming disciplines were working. His mind was clear once more. But how, Kerezar wondered, did one reach The American Museum of Art from this place? Too far to walk, definitely, yet Ilaron could hardly have expected to catch a taxi, not in all this confusion.

But a city this size surely had other means of transportation.

All I need is the smallest bit of information. And that can easily obtained from the hotel—

No. With the tiniest flare of quickly suppressed anger, Kerezar remembered that he could hardly return to the Marriott Marquis.

No matter. I will learn what I need. This, all this, is unimportant.

*No matter how Ilaron flees from me, it will mean
nothing. For I will win.*

Their small talk had soon drifted into silence. Ilaron
quickly slid back into his inhuman stillness, doubly
unnerving in a subway train speeding its way
through darkness.

Oh Lord, now what? Denise thought, not quite sure
she wanted to know. But she couldn't not know, either! Not sure if she was going to get a response, she
asked warily, "Ilaron . . . ?"

He turned to her so sharply Denise nearly flinched,
his face unreadable. "There is something left unset-
tled, an item that is disturbing me."

"Ah . . . Kerezar?"

"Precisely."

"Well, yes, I'm sure the two of you are going to,
ah, have it out eventually." A quick, ridiculous image
of Ilaron and Kerezar facing each other like two gun-
fighters in the Old West—no, no, they'd be using
swords or magic— "You made that very clear," Denise hurried on, "but—"

"You miss my point. Yes, under more normal conditions, we would already be 'having it out,' as you so
delicately put it. Were Lamashtu and the need to banish her not involved." He gave a sharp, humorless
laugh. "A backhanded compliment to me that Kerezar
would be so sure I would *want* to banish her before
dealing with him—that I've become so clearly part of
this realm."

"But . . . ?"

"But in my former realm, Kerezar was always amazingly swift to adjust to changing situations. I don't
know how quickly he can adapt to these surroundings,
especially since he has no immunity to iron. But there
is a web of Darkness in the theater district, twined

through all the dark corners, persisting even now that the district is facing . . . what . . . that change . . . "

"Urban renewal?" Denise hazarded, and he nodded.

"Urban renewal, yes. Even so, enough predators and prey still remain to feed the Darkness. And unlike me, Kerezar has no need or wish to bar that Darkness from his mind."

"He's feeding off *it*?"

"In a manner of speaking. What I meant is that by now, even surrounded by iron, even tired and humiliated from the chase, Kerezar is probably thinking quite clearly. And if we could decide to go this way, then so can he deduce our decision."

"So quickly?"

"Do not," Ilaron warned, "underestimate him. I told you such before."

"You really expect him to follow us there?"

"I am planning on it."

Denise looked at him directly. "Planning."

"Oh come, give me some credit for forethought."

I don't want to know, I really don't want to know. Yes, I guess I do at that. I'd better, at any rate. "You can't be expecting to confront him in the museum."

"Hopefully not. Near it . . . well now, what happens, happens." The faintest of smiles. "The lure should be nearly irresistible to him."

The lure. Us. Great. "If you have it all worked out, then what's worrying you? He *couldn't* have gotten there before us."

"No . . . not he. Still . . . he does have helpers. Young humans, the type who have, whether consciously or not, sworn themselves to the Darkness. I have had, shall we say, dealings with one of them. And no, such creatures aren't what worry me. Especially since I think that by now most of them will have fled Kerezar; there are limits to what even such as they can endure.

"And yet, and yet . . . I don't know what other aides he may have caught for himself. You have experienced for yourself just how persuasive Kerezar can be."

Is that *why you kept silent when he was bespelling me? So that I'd have firsthand experience?* "Yes," Denise said, carefully without expression. "So you don't know who's helping him." That was a deliberate reminder to him that he wasn't perfect, either.

Ilaron didn't deign to notice. "Or where they may be waiting . . . " A quick shrug. "Foolish to worry about what cannot be known. Ah, but here is our station."

And, Denise added to herself, *not a moment too soon.*

Kerezar stood leaning on the concierge desk of another hotel—he had no interest which it was—studying transit routes, in particular a subway map, and being advised of traffic conditions by yet another earnest young woman.

"Yes, yes, I see," he told her as she chattered, though most of the traffic information she was giving him was so much arcane babble. "The easiest route would be up the West Side Highway, then across *here* or *here*. But what if I wished to use public transportation instead?"

"Well, the subway *would* be the quickest way."

Indeed. Ilaron and his human companion were most likely to be in a hurry, which meant that yes, they would have headed for a subway station. Kerezar listened to the earnest young woman's talk of trains and stops.

"There's really nothing that stops right next to the museum," she babbled.

"The most direct route?"

"I guess that would be this . . . see? The B train.
You'd still need to get across Central Park, but there's
a crosstown bus. The only other way means changing
trains, and you'd still wind up over on Lexington, a
good walk away."

Would Ilaron and the human really want to switch
trains? No. Logically not since that would make them
dependent on the vagaries of subway schedules that
might leave them quite a distance from where they
wished to be. The fastest route would be this more
direct one . . . yes. The one that would, he mused,
tapping the map thoughtfully, let Ilaron and the
human out on Central Park West, on the wrong side
of the park—

"Oh, wait!" the oh-so-helpful young woman cried.
"Did you hear that? The traffic report? You really
don't want to drive it, sir. The Eighty-first Street
Transverse is closed, an accident I guess, which is
going to tie up the others, too."

Oh? Information which Ilaron and the human
would not have possessed. Very valuable information!
"I see. Very well, then, my dear. Thank you *so* much."

Leaving her blushing with pleasure, Kerezar went
his way. So now . . . Ilaron would almost certainly
expect him to follow. That didn't mean he need take
the most obvious route. Particularly since the fastest
way across Central Park for Ilaron and the human
would be to walk.

Splendid, he thought.

Denise and Ilaron surfaced from the subway system
at Eighty-first Street, quickly getting their bearings.
On one side loomed the Gothic conglomeration of
buildings that was the Museum of Natural History—
the "Other Museum," as Denise and her colleagues
called it—on the other was the dark mass of Central

Park, and the nearest transverse through the park was—

"I don't believe this!" Denise wailed, looking at police sawhorses and flashing lights.

But why not? Murphy reigned supreme in this city, and this was just another typical New York transit problem. Nothing supernatural about it: The transverse had just been closed down because of a perfectly ordinary accident.

Ilaron glanced about impatiently. "No matter. We are near enough now to walk the rest of the way."

"Through the park?"

"No one," he said without the slightest hint of expression, "will bother us."

Ah, right. What's that tongue-in-cheek quote? "Yea, though I walk through the Valley of the Shadow of Death, I shall fear no evil, for I am the meanest son of a bitch in the valley."

Besides, the sooner we get to the museum and that precious incantation, the better.

Leaving the hotel and the chaos behind him, Kerezar walked west and west again, hunting for the most isolated of the warehouse region. Too much traffic here, too, drivers trying every route to avoid the tie-ups in the Broadway area . . .

Yes. A small, barren courtyard, possibly intended for deliveries of some sort. No sign of activity now, although the yard was guarded by a wire fence topped with vicious-looking barbed metal. Kerezar avoided that, glanced at the nearby wall . . . yes. He was up in one graceful surge, catching hand- and footholds in the ancient brick, leaping out over the fence, clearing the barbs, landing almost soundlessly, going to a crouch.

No one had seen or heard, no one would see.

Now to locate his young human tools . . . not physically, of course, since they could be anywhere in the city. But by tasting their blood, he had established a useful psychic link.

What he must do would not be without risk. If Ilaron was aware that Kerezar was opening his mind, leaving himself, however briefly, defenseless—

But if Ilaron was in an iron vehicle hurtling along iron tracks—no, there could be only the slightest danger from him.

Sitting in shadow, shutting out his base surroundings, Kerezar sent his consciousness out and out . . . hunting . . . finding . . . yes . . .

Ah, look, poor little fools, feel their auras. Not too many of them left for his use: The others had fled the Darkness, cutting their link to him. Ilaron's doing?

No matter. All the weaker ones, those who could be turned by fear or some long-denied inner flame of Light, might have fled, but those who remained . . .

Wonderful! Those who remained were doing their own petty hunting, and where they hunted—

Perfect. Rousing from his trance, Kerezar smiled inwardly. Few though they were, the human tools would be sufficient. More than sufficient. Nothing but Darkness was in those remnants, nothing that could be salvaged by the Light or stolen from Kerezar's will.

"You are," he murmured, "about to prove your truest worth to me. You are, in fact, though you know it not, poor little tools, about to give your all to me.

"And in the process, I fear, you are about to be . . . discarded."

He got to his feet, swarming back over the fence, then brushing off his clothes.

Now, Kerezar thought, he had his own swift journey to make. But unlike that of Ilaron, who was about to face some definite inconveniences, it was one that would not be . . . interrupted.

TWENTY-FIVE

Up in Central Park

Denise glanced uneasily about in the darkness, then almost stumbled over a rock, stubbing her toe in the process, and hastily turned her attention back to what little she could see of her footing.

By now, she guessed, they must be about halfway across the park, but even though it was difficult even in the heart of Central Park to get too far away from the civilized world, Ilaron seemed determined to do his best. Or rather, Denise thought, he was in such a determined rush to get to the museum that he was ignoring the meandering, carefully planned, nicely paved paths and, as a result, was missing most of the city's carefully placed lighting as well, striding boldly and surefootedly across the landscape, through the shadows, Denise in tow.

"Ilaron!" she panted. "Slow down, will you? Or let go of me. Remember I'm only human, I *can't* see in the dark!"

"I will guide you."

"If you don't pull my arm off first! Ease up, all right? Getting there a few moments later can't possibly matter."

Ilaron said nothing, but his grip did loosen a bit. Enough, Denise thought, for her to at least get the circulation going in her arm again.

Going to have finger-shaped bruises, though. Bruised

toes, too. Why didn't I think to wear walking shoes? Or at least sneakers?

Because, Denise answered herself, _I never expected to be doing cross-country running in Central Park, that's why! Foolish me!_

She risked another glance around.

No sign of trouble. Maybe I'm just letting anti–New York propaganda get to me.

Right. And that woman who was raped here the other day was just a fantasy.

The park shouldn't be that dangerous, though, really. The hour wasn't particularly late.

Uh-huh. And that rape took place when, six or seven o'clock? Not "particularly late." Just after hours, the wrong time of night to see anyone else. Except predators.

And maybe a few suicidal joggers.

Of course, any would-be rapists would first have to get past a sword-wielding Dark Elf—no, right, he wasn't an elf, all right, a Whatever He Was.

Damn. She was really getting out of breath. Getting pretty tired of being dragged along like a child, too.

Besides, the air wasn't so good, either, growing unnervingly still and heavy. Must be an inversion layer, or whatever they called it on the Weather Channel. (_Television!_ she thought with a pang of nostalgia. When was the last time she'd had a chance to watch something nice and thoroughly trivial on television?) A quick glance up showed nothing but darkness, with thick clouds rolling in over the western skyline like something out of a horror movie.

Great. Just what we needed. We may not meet any predators, human or otherwise—not, thank you very much, that I'm complaining—but we're about to get drenched in a storm. Some demon-hunter: Denise Sheridan, Drowned Rat.

Eerie out here, no denying it, with lots of what was

so charmingly called light pollution—a pollution she would have welcomed a little closer—radiating from the buildings rimming the park yet none of it quite touching where she was. Surreal, almost, those lights out there and the darkness in here. Even though she knew Ilaron and she were right now smack in the middle of Manhattan, the rest of New York, with its noise and light and life, seemed a world away, and the park, by contrast, seemed alarmingly quiet.

Too quiet. Ilaron suddenly came alert, sword whipping out, a blaze of silver.

"Ambush!" he snapped, and threw her to one side.

But it was already too late. There was the sharp crack of a gun, Ilaron's grunt of pain—

A gang! was Denise's first frantic thought. *No, no, not just that, these are Kerezar's allies.*

They had to be, because she could hear them laughing in terrified glee, shouting, "The demon can be hurt!"

"Yeah, just like Satan promised!"

Satan? That *had* to be Kerezar!

"The motherfuckin' demon can bleed and—"

The demon could strike. Denise saw a blur of motion, a flash of silvery metal, heard a scream. Gun and hand together went flying, and one teen fell, shrieking terrified, agonized obscenities that were quickly cut off. The other teens attacked in blind panic with clubs, knives—no chance to use any more guns, not with such a swift-moving predator upon them. They hadn't a chance of moving as quickly, as gracefully, with such deadly purpose, as Ilaron. Denise stood in horrified fascination, unable to move, to look away, as his sword glinted now silver, now liquid black, blood's red turned dark in the darkness. The attack suddenly turned into a rout as the terrified survivors tried to flee.

Oh God, he's going after them, he's going to kill

*them all, butcher them—they'll be dead and he—he'll
be damned to the Darkness, all that love of music, art,
that lovely, gentle smile, damned and lost—*

Without thinking any more clearly, Denise rushed
to block his path. Ilaron loomed over her, taller,
surely, than he should be, surrounded by a Darkness
greater, surely, than the mortal night, and his eyes—

Ilaron's eyes were terrible, cold and cruel—but what
made it the most dreadful was that there was nothing
in them of any blank killing frenzy.

He knew exactly what he was doing.

And in that moment, Denise realized that she was
as frightened as ever she'd been when facing Lamashtu. No, more, definitely more. But the very ratio-
nality in Ilaron's eyes, terrible though it was, let her
risk it, let her stand her ground and shout in his face:

"Are you going to kill me, too?"

For a horrible instant, she was sure the answer was
going to be *Yes!* But at least Ilaron stopped dead,
staring at her, bloody sword still alarmingly raised,
and . . .

And those terrible eyes were suddenly shocked,
then no longer terrible at all, the eyes of a man all at
once overwhelmed with unbearable self-horror and
anguish.

"The Darkness," he gasped, lowering the blade,
staggering, almost falling against her, suddenly
shrunken back into himself, all but sobbing the words
out in the force of his horror. "The Darkness nearly
had me. Utterly. Totally. There was nothing, *nothing,*
but blood, death, blood and the joy of it and the killing, the killing—the terrible, wonderful joy—killing—
and I could find no way out of it, no way—"

Denise slapped him as hard as she could, paused,
slapped him again, raised her hand for another blow.
But his hand moved in a blur of speed and caught her
wrist, not quite hard enough to hurt.

"Enough." His voice was not exactly steady. "Enough. I am in control again."

Denise wasn't quite sure of that, seeing how badly he was shaking. She was doing a bit of trembling herself, and right now was in no mood to be soft or soothing. "I suggest," she all but snarled, "that we get out of this—this battlefield before someone sees us. Besides," Denise added sharply, remembering the gunshot, "you're hurt!"

Ilaron waved that off. "The would-be assassin had terrible aim; he did little more than tear skin."

His good arm linked in hers, Denise not sure which of them was supporting whom, they managed to struggle out of the park onto Fifth Avenue. Then Denise's nervous energy gave out and she had to stop, clenching her teeth to stop their chattering. She'd seen violence before, bloodshed, the whole nine yards of it. Hell, she'd even seen a building blow up just the other day!

But she'd never seen anything like . . . that. The flash of the sword, the sight of that boy's hand, severed, flying off like some stupid, cheap special effect, the screams and blood, all that blood, staining the bright blade black—

Stopping under a streetlight, Denise glared up at Ilaron, not sure if she wanted to scream or be sick. And he? His sword was a walking stick once more, not a trace of blood on it. And he, he looked too clean, too unstained, with only the rip in one sleeve and the dark stain surrounding it to show that a bullet had grazed him—with only that one sign that he had even been in a battle.

No, dammit, no, it's just not right! *"What are you?"* Denise exploded.

"You know what. Kerezar spoke truly."

If he'd said that in self-pity or arrogance or even as a challenge—

But there was nothing in his voice save an utter, hopeless weariness. And his eyes . . . were the eyes of a damned, defeated soul.

"No," Denise said in sudden, surprised defense. "There's a hell of a lot more to you than that. The love of art, of music—Yes, and the man that Kerezar described could never have fought so long and hard for his freedom."

"I'll take that for a compliment." There was the faintest, weariest tinge of humor to his voice. "And no, before you ask, I . . . I have never done anything so . . . so . . . anything like that before. Not in this realm."

God, I should hope not! But his anguish was real, so very real. And it was weirdly reassuring that he could be *feeling* that anguish, that he was not the immoral, no, no, the downright evil being that Kerezar had claimed—that Kerezar, without a doubt was.

Sentimentality, she suspected, wasn't going to help. And so Denise said only a brisk, almost cheerful, "And you're not going to do anything like that again, are you?"

That forced the softest of startled chuckles from him. "I wasn't planning to, no."

"Ilaron . . . " She had to say something more, she must. "Ilaron, humans can be prodded beyond endurance, too. We break, we lose control, sometimes we kill."

"Every race has its criminals."

"Not just criminals." *Vietnam . . .* a voice whispered in her mind, and she wondered, *What was the name of that village? My Lai? Yes.* "All of us. Even the good guys. Listen to me, Ilaron. Once this country went to war, where and when doesn't matter. We were supposed to be on the side of Good, the side of the Light. But it was a long, bloody, hopeless war, more so than they usually are, I guess. And it was our soldiers who one day lost control, the good guys on the side of the Light, who massacred a village full of unarmed farmers.

"Do you see? The Darkness can seize us all."

Of course the situations weren't the same: Few humans, she thought with a flash of sardonic humor, came from a realm that was quite literally a part *of* the Darkness, and Ilaron knew it. But a flicker of relief crossed his face just the same, and he murmured, "Thank you."

"I—"

"Denise, wait. Hear me. I owe you a great debt. A debt beyond measure. This time . . . this time, I could not have pulled back from the Darkness alone."

A little embarrassed by his sincerity, she muttered, "Oh, well, it's, uh, don't worry about it. Call it repayment for the times you saved me."

But Ilaron shook his head and continued, with a strange, intricate bow, "You are my Light, lady. You are my Light. I am your Shadow."

Then, in a perfectly normal voice, he suggested, "We had better enter the museum before it closes."

"Uh . . . right."

What just happened there? What did he just say without out words? I don't know, I don't want to know, I just want this all to be over and life to get back to normal. If it ever can be normal again.

It seemed almost anticlimactic to be simply walking up the steps to the museum without the slightest of problems. But they made it all the way into the museum unchallenged. And then:

"Evening, Dr. Sheridan."

She nearly gasped, nearly whirled about, just in time recognizing this as nothing more than an offhand greeting from a guard. Struggling to look matter-of fact, Denise smiled briefly at him, nodded, hardly wanting to stop for a conversation, hoping that nod would be enough.

But the guard, a chatty guy named . . . ah, she couldn't remember right now, Dave Something-or-other, insisted, "Getting here kinda late, aren't you? Museum's gonna be closing pretty soon. Gonna have to let someone know if you're staying after that. Sign out and all that."

"I know. Thank you."

But chatty Dave insisted, "Remember, you haven't got much time."

I am not going to see that as an omen. "I know," Denise repeated. It came out, amazingly, sounding perfectly ordinary. Perfectly sane. "And thanks again. Don't worry: We just have a little work to finish up."

Right. Just need to banish a demon, that's all.

Getting to her office seemed to take an eternity, particularly since they couldn't race full out the way Denise was aching to do. Instead, they had to . . . walk, just walk through all that maze of hallways, walk as though nothing in all the world was wrong.

But finally they were there, climbing the last little flight of steps, opening the office door. Denise locked the door behind them—and then she and Ilaron both collapsed onto the nearest chairs.

"I'm afraid that I can't offer you anything but water," she said after a minute.

"Water," Ilaron said gladly, "will be fine. Splendid, in fact."

Wincing slightly, he slid out of his jacket and gingerly rolled up the sleeve of his shirt. Denise drew in her breath in a gasp of alarm at the sight of the ugly, bloody welt crossing his arm, but when she tried to help, he waved her away, cautiously dabbing at the wound with the water.

"There's no real damage here. Truly."

"But that's your, ah, sword arm!"

"I've noticed," drily. "Though fair to tell, I didn't notice during the . . . when I . . . "

"When you got shot."

"Yes. And no, don't fuss! A bullet's sheathing is lead, not iron. And it's far more important that you start memorizing that incantation."

That she was able to concentrate on it, a part of Denise's mind noted wryly, was a credit to Academia.

Or maybe it's the human being's shock overload system kicking in.

Denise surfaced with a jolt as the lights dimmed, brightened, dimmed again. "Closing time . . . ?"

No. Ilaron was prowling about the room like a sleek predator, murmuring under his breath—spellcasting, Denise realized.

He stopped, listened with what she suspected was other than physical hearing, then nodded in satisfaction. "Don't look so alarmed, Denise. All I've done is Ward us, which means that no one will notice that we're still here. Have you mastered the incantation?"

Suddenly newly uneasy, she nodded.

"Good. Because," Ilaron continued as calmly as though reporting on the weather, "I sense, quite strongly, that we are going to need it—and very soon."

Denise stiffened. "How can you be so sure? About the 'soon' part of it?"

That earned her an almost scornful look. "Did you really think the attack on us was by chance?"

Denise hadn't wanted to think about that at all, but she warily countered, "I'm not naive. I could hardly have missed that it was a deliberate trap. But what—"

"Exactly. One that wasn't meant to succeed."

"Oh, right. Ilaron, they could have killed you!"

"Those? Even with that gun, they were hardly dangerous enough to pose a true threat. No, those stupid young would-be demon-slayers were *sacrifices,* sacrifices sent by Kerezar."

"Are you sure? They couldn't have been acting on their own? Trying to prove something to him?"

"Bah, no. It was part of his plan, no doubt of it, an attack so feeble that it was meant to be a humiliation!"

"Damn," she said, voice absolutely flat. "And here I thought that only humans got involved in macho duels!"

"It was also," Ilaron added sharply, "definitely meant to buy Kerezar some time. Which he has used to good advantage."

"He's *here*?" Denise cried. "In the museum?"

Ilaron held up a hand, standing tensely as a hound scenting elusive prey. "Ahhh, yes, I was right. He is, indeed. Where Kerezar may be, the demon—whom it would not be wise to name right now—will follow.

"And now," he added, so calmly that the words lacked all melodrama, "I think the time has come for a confrontation."

TWENTY-SIX

The Warriors

"He's *here*?" Denise repeated helplessly. "Kerezar? He can't be!"

"Denise—"

"I mean, not *here!* I thought you had a plan!"

"So did I. But I'm not prescient. I could not factor in the time wasted by the closed transverse or the . . . delay in Central Park. Kerezar, obviously, knew of the former and created the latter."

Still horrified, she argued, trying to make him see her point, "But you *can't do this,* not here! A museum isn't the place for a—a confrontation, for violence, not with all these priceless, fragile art treasures!"

"I would not wish it, either. But things are as they stand, and I can hardly say to Kerezar, 'Will you please just step outside?' "

"Yes, but what about you? You're wounded—yes, yes, I know," she added before he could say anything, "it's not serious, but it *is* an injury, and to your sword arm, too—and you're still tired from the—from the battle!"

Just then, with perfect timing, the lights went out. "We don't," Ilaron said shortly, "have a choice."

"Wait! Just let me find . . . " Denise rummaged blindly through her desk's drawers, then straightened in triumph. *Ah yes, I knew there was a flashlight in here!*

Ilaron, whose eyes, judging from their eerie glint,

were already adjusting to what to him wasn't true darkness, was watching her with interest. "What have you found?"

"Just a flashlight." But there had been something odd in his tone, and she asked in surprise, "You can't tell me you've never seen a flashlight before!"

Her own eyes were adjusting as best they could, enough to show him shrug, wincing slightly as the motion pulled at the bullet graze. "I knew such things existed, but I obviously never had a use for one. And so, no. I never have."

"And," they added together in sudden sharp realization, "neither has Kerezar!"

"Wait," Denise added, "before we get optimistic about this, cover your eyes." She'd seen those idiot movies in which a character's flashlight so inconveniently and coincidentally flickered and died just at the wrong moment. "I need to test the batteries—ha, yes, good. Nice and strong."

She switched the light off with a click, feeling for all the world like Luke Skywalker.

"Useful," Ilaron said succinctly. "Don't use it unless you must, and," he added fervently, "in the name of Light, warn me first!"

"But do you know where Kerezar is?"

"Not specifically. Nor he, me. Yet. That each is within the museum is all we can know for now."

"Somewhere within a multiple-storied, four-block-long building. One of the largest museums in the world. Terrific. Ah, what's wrong?"

"I just realized what a lovely target I make, fair of skin and wearing a white shirt that will blaze in the dark like a flare. And—what are you doing?"

"Wait . . . can't do anything about your skin tone, but I think there's something . . . guard your eyes again. I need a light."

By the flashlight's beam, Denise searched through the office coat closet—yes.

"Here. Ira, Dr. Ira Meyers that is, the one who's off on a research sabbatical, left this sweater behind. He's tall and lanky . . . it should fit, if you're not too fastidious about style. *And* it's black."

He pulled the proffered sweater on without a word, and they set warily out into the dark museum. Denise knew that there must be guards scurrying frantically about, hunting for the source of the problem, but they seemed strangely removed, distant. The Warding? Probably. And probably Kerezar had cast a Warding of his own.

The museum was an eerie place without light, and even the familiar galleries just outside her office seemed alien. Only Ilaron's guiding hand on her arm kept her from crashing right into the Tiffany lamp in its display case on the central pedestal.

"Gently," he murmured.

But the blackout wasn't total; here and there, patches of emergency lighting glowed faintly. *Kerezar may be good,* Denise thought, *but he isn't perfect.*

"A warning," she whispered. "The guards have almost certainly called the head of Security, the police, and Alan Atherton."

"We'll be done before any of them can get here," Ilaron said grimly.

How could he be so sure? Where *was* Kerezar? Somewhere in all this vast mass that was the museum, stalking them even as they were stalking him. Or so Denise had to believe; she had to take on faith that he was there at all.

If Ilaron's so sure, there can't be a doubt about it. Can there?

And the art—Kerezar wouldn't want to harm even human art, would he?

Don't be an idiot. You met him, felt his will. Kerezar will do whatever he can to win.

But he wouldn't be familiar with the layout of the museum, there was that small advantage. While she . . .

I boasted once that I could find my way around this place blindfolded. Never make promises you can't keep.

Her eyes were finally fully adjusted to what little light there was. She could faintly make out Ilaron's pale face, and guessed from his grim frown and the lack of that by-now familiar tingling along her skin that he was using very little magic.

Right. Magic blazes like a homing signal, I should know that by now.

Unfortunately, that had to mean that Kerezar also wasn't using much magic: no convenient beacons blazing from him, either.

They continued their wary stalk from room to room, now prowling through part of European Art, each neoclassic statue in turn tearing at her nerves by looking jarringly alive.

Too many rooms. Too many hiding places. Never did like those "jump out and go boo!" movies.

A voice said softly, "Ilaron."

Denise almost screamed in shock, just in time getting both hands over her mouth. "Illusion," Ilaron said in her ear. "He is not in this room. He merely wishes us to stay in one place long enough for him to locate us." Then, a touch more loudly, "A pretty trick, Kerezar. Have you been playing with your toys again?"

"Have you?" the eerie whisper returned. "Did you enjoy the welcoming I sent you?"

"Toys, indeed," Ilaron retorted. But all the while, he was turning his head this way, that, hunting. "Broken toys, now." Silently, he signaled Denise: *Come. This way.*

"You shall join them," the whisper continued as they moved on. "You and your little human pet."

Denise stopped dead. Why should she be surprised that Kerezar might know she was there? Why else would he be speaking in the human tongue?

As though he'd guessed her reaction, Kerezar told her, all but purring, "Little human, hear me. This is your world, this museum; I realize that. If you stay with the heretic, I shall begin to break the pretty things around me."

"Can he hear me?" Denise murmured to Ilaron. "Yes? Good." She told Kerezar, "Go ahead. They're alarmed, all of 'em, alarms that *don't* depend on the power grid."

A second's silence. Did he get her point? Did he not *care* that the noise would bring every guard in the museum? Armed guards? A second more. Then: "Ah, she attempts to bluff!"

"Is it a bluff? Go ahead, then, try me. Set off the nice alarms. See what happens. *I* know. I've seen it. Remember that chase back in the hotel? This one will be worse—and *so* much more humiliating! The humans will mock you, Kerezar."

Heart racing, she glanced at Ilaron, catching a quick flash of white teeth in an approving grin. Kerezar . . . said nothing, and Denise and Ilaron moved on.

Point to our side. I think.

Keep going, keep hunting. Never stay still long enough to leave a psychic spoor or whatever it was Ilaron and Kerezar were hunting. Ilaron, of course, moved like a shadow. Denise . . . did her best. But she was uncomfortably aware of being a liability. No human could hope to be as swift, as soundless, and he could definitely have been hunting much more quickly—and quietly—without her—

But I also know I'm not going to sit here in the darkness like some sacrificial goat.

Even if Ilaron would let her. And even if there wasn't Lamashtu to consider. Of course she couldn't simply leave the museum, either. At the first sign of trouble, the heavy security doors, which, like most of the alarms, were not on the main electrical circuits, would have all slammed resoundingly shut, sealing the building.

And that's another signal that's going to go straight to the police. Great.

As Ilaron might have put it, what was, was. Besides, Denise thought, suddenly recognizing where she was, there were other weapons than magic. Ilaron and she were cutting back through the American Wing, entering that section devoted to the Colonial period. The guards, she'd heard, didn't like to patrol this area: They found it too unnerving. Nothing as melodramatic as ghosts, no, it was something about a sound happening *after* a man had left a room, making him jump out of his skin . . . ha, yes! She whispered in Ilaron's ears, "Old floorboards. Delayed creak. If he's anywhere near . . . "

The briefest of nods; he'd gotten the message behind those cryptic words. Together, they moved warily, silently, across the ancient floor, the wood giving slightly underfoot but not making a sound, Denise trusting Ilaron to not let her collide with anything. Stopping on the far side of the room, they crouched behind an old armoire, waiting . . . waiting . . .

Sure enough, the old floorboards came back up with a delayed "crack" that sounded sharp as a pistol shoot to Denise. And—yes! There was Kerezar at the far end of the room, sword glinting in his hand, come to investigate, sure that his foe had finally made a mistake.

No mistake. Ilaron, his own sword drawn, lunged without the slightest preamble.

Not a sound from either foe. Kerezar merely

brought his own blade up to parry, and the swords rang out as they clashed together, disconcertingly musical. Those swords, being of no Earthly metal, glowed eerily of their own accord and flashed brightly each time they came together.

Denise could guess why Ilaron had chosen swordplay rather than sorcery: *He doesn't want to risk damaging the art. Even now, he cares—oh, dammit, he's got to win, he has to win!*

The enemies drew back, circled, graceful and wary as stalking cats, closed once more. Another clashing of blades, striking dazzling silver sparks.

This is a ridiculous place for a duel, all that furniture just waiting to trip someone up—no!

As Ilaron twisted aside, his sword arm struck the edge of a chest. Denise heard his choked gasp of pain, saw the sword fall from what must have been a suddenly numbed hand.

He hit the bullet wound!

Small wound or no, that would have *hurt*. And even Ilaron couldn't recover swiftly enough. He dived for the blade, rolled, sword in hand—but before he could regain his feet, Kerezar was there, swordpoint at Ilaron's throat.

"Eyes!" Denise yelped.

No time to see if Ilaron had understood. Denise, flashlight in both hands like a gun, switched it on—catching Kerezar full in the face. He screamed in pain, recoiling—but where a human might have fled, he unexpectedly lunged with inhuman speed, lashed out blindly with his sword. The flat of the blade connected solidly with the flashlight, tearing it from Denise's hands. It smacked against a wall and, predictably, went out.

Leaving all three of us half-blind. What the hell. If Kerezar wins, I'm dead anyhow.

She threw herself into the darkness at where she

guessed he must be. Good aim! For one brief moment, she was grappling with Kerezar, alarmingly aware of his inhuman strength, trying to kick him where it would do the most good, wishing she had her keys in hand—then he tossed her aside with a snarl. She hit the floor so hard the back of her head banged painfully against it, sure she was dead as Kerezar's glowing sword flashed up—

And was blocked by Ilaron's blade. The two swords locked, right over Denise's dazzled vision. She scrambled frantically back out of the way, colliding with something solid, the chest that Ilaron had struck, wriggled her way behind it as her readjusting vision traced Ilaron, Kerezar, both still too near-blind from that blaze of light to risk closing with each other just yet.

But then both foes whirled as one, staring. Denise, staring with them, saw nothing but darkness, but . . . yes! She heard voices, saw a distant flare of light— guards! And they were coming this way.

With an angry hiss, Kerezar sprang away into darkness and Ilaron dived down beside Denise, huddling behind the chest with her, fairly radiating his fury over the interrupted fight.

As long as he doesn't turn on the guards . . .

No. He had enough self-control not to move, save to shield his eyes as the two humans, flashlights glaring, made their wary way through.

The flashlight! If they see my flashlight . . .

But: "Nothing here," Denise heard one of them mutter, and the guard grunted agreement. "Wish they'd hurry up and get the damned lights back on."

"Yeah. Just be glad whatever happened happened after closing. Can you imagine herding crowds out in the dark?"

"Hah. Must have been one hell of a blackout. Like the time Con Ed or whoever it was cut the main power cable. Remember that?"

Snickers from both.

I don't care what you remember! Denise thought, glancing uneasily at Ilaron. *Just take your reminiscences and go!*

Sure enough, they were moving on, amiably complaining to each other. Ilaron remained absolutely still until the last trace of the guards' voices had faded, then uncoiled to his feet, pulling Denise up with him. "Are you hurt?" he asked brusquely.

Denise gingerly touched the back of her head. Sore spot, nothing major. "No. And . . . you?"

He flexed his arm experimentally. "No. I could wish, though, you had not used that flashlight."

"If I hadn't, you'd be dead!"

"There is that." Ilaron bent, scooped the flashlight up, handed it rather gingerly back to her. Covering his eyes, he asked, "Does it still work?"

"Wait . . . yes. Amazingly." Switching the light off again, Denise said suspiciously, "I thought you told me we were Warded."

"We were. And still are. Not, it would seem, perfectly. The guards could not hear the swords. They would have seen us." Each word was bitten off sharply. "This is the second time I have had to let Kerezar go." It was close to a snarl. "It will not happen again. Come."

"Not perfectly." "They would have seen us." Wonderful. If anybody sees me stalking around in the dark with a guy wielding a sword, that's the end of my career.

And if Kerezar or the demon saw her first, she might not have to worry about having a career. At least Kerezar wasn't likely to blast her suddenly with some great and terrible magic—not when he'd be leaving himself wide open in the process to instant retaliation from Ilaron.

But there was other than outright magic. As they

came warily out into the main hall, with that vast sweep of wide stairway leading up to the second floor, Denise felt, sensed . . .

But if Kerezar really was there, why was he lingering? Why didn't he—ha, the flashlight! He was afraid of moving and getting another agonizing blast in the eye!

"Up there," she whispered in Ilaron's ear. "I could almost swear . . . hiding behind that column . . ."

"Human intuition," he whispered back without a trace of condescension, "and, yes."

They started warily up the stairs, a slow, silent step at a time. Somewhere overhead, thunder rumbled ominously as the storm moved in.

Good sense of drama, a panicky little part of Denise's mind noted, *really good. I could live without drama right now.*

They had just reached the landing when Ilaron shielded his eyes. "The flashlight, *now!*"

Denise switched it on, aiming blindly up the stairs. There was a frantic flurry of motion as Kerezar dodged—

And in those few seconds of confusion, Ilaron went rushing up to the top of the stairway to meet him and eliminate Kerezar's advantage of higher ground. Denise hastily switched the light off so that she wouldn't dazzle him as well.

Damn, now I can't see anything!

But after a few panicky moments, her eyes began to adjust once more. Denise realized, in fact, that she could see reasonably well—because the two foes had their swords drawn once more, and the swords were blazing. Part of her mind wished there was even better light, because what was happening now was one spectacular duel up and down the sweep of stairway.

God, Hollywood would love this!

Nothing to trip either foe now, nothing to interrupt

them, nothing but flashing blades and skill, superb skill, and inhuman grace and reflexes. Hatred burned from both, a cold, clear, definitely inhuman hatred that hardly handicapped either, Kerezar utterly determined to take Ilaron, Ilaron just as utterly determined to survive. Perfectly matched, perfectly balanced, lunge, thrust, parry, a step lost, a step gained, no more than thin trails of blood darkening the blades—God, no, this couldn't go on for much longer; she'd read somewhere that real sword fights never lasted long, and never mind Hollywood. And this, this was *too* perfect, *too* even a match. Sooner or later one of them was going to make a mistake.

Yes, she realized suddenly, or else what was left of their Warding was going to collapse and they'd be overwhelmed by guards—some of whom, Denise remembered in horror, were armed.

No . . . ah, no . . .

All at once it was Ilaron who was giving way, Ilaron who was starting to weaken.

The bullet wound. Denise gripped the flashlight so tightly that her hands hurt. *I don't care how he denied it, that's got to be affecting him. Oh God, Ilaron . . .*

He slipped, staggered down a step, caught his balance precariously as Kerezar cut at him, parried, lost another step, another, slowly giving way, and Kerezar pursued, fierce as any predator scenting the kill. Ilaron parried, parried again, steadying his sword with both hands, no longer able to do more than just defend himself, being driven slowly back against the side of the stairway.

The flashlight—

Nothing.

No, dammit, I don't believe this, not now! This isn't some stupid movie!

She shook the flashlight frantically, slapped it, got only the faintest of glows. Dammit! The batteries had been old, after all, and the thing couldn't have been helped by being thrown against a wall.

There's nothing I can do to help him, nothing!

"So be it, traitor," she heard Kerezar say quietly. "You have lost."

His back literally to the wall, his sword held in hand shaking with exhaustion, Ilaron cried out—but not in despair. His voice betrayed his weariness, but the will behind it was strong, pure and bright as silver. And what sent a little shiver up Denise's spine was that he called out not to the Darkness, but:

"Hear me, Powers of Light! I give myself to you, I swear myself to you!"

With wonderfully dramatic timing a roar of thunder shook the building, and for a startling second the museum blazed blue-white with lightning. Denise saw Kerezar falter, staggering back, eyes wide.

He thinks Ilaron's using strange new magic, magic of the Light!

No magic. With one clean lunge so fiercely, terribly beautiful it took the breath from Denise, Ilaron ran Kerezar through.

TWENTY-SEVEN

The Tempest

Time seemed to freeze.

And then Ilaron pulled his blade free. For a moment more, Kerezar stood motionless, staring, as though refusing to believe what had happened, what had just been done to him. But then a second flash of lightning showed his cold, beautiful face suddenly convulsed with pain.

"Lamashtu!" Kerezar shrieked, head thrown back. "Lamashtu! Lamashtu, *tha'ea lithatach!*"

He fell, tumbling down the stairway. But before he could strike the midway landing, Kerezar—

—disappeared, air rushing in with a "bang" to fill the space where he'd just been.

Denise hurried up the stairs, warily shying around the spot where Kerezar had just vanished, up to where Ilaron stood panting, leaning on his sword.

"Ilaron!"

"I'm all right," he gasped. "Just scratched a bit . . . winded . . . no more than that."

"There's a bench at the top of the stairs. You can catch your breath there before—"

"No! No time to rest. I might have killed Kerezar, I at least badly wounded him before he fled—but you heard that last shout."

"Oh . . . God. He called her."

"You have it. That was a genuine summons to Lamashtu. And she," he added, straightening in alarm, staring starkly up, "is definitely manifesting above us."

"The roof!" Denise gasped. Even while every survival instinct was screaming to her to *Get the hell out of here,* she knew running wasn't going to save her. And it certainly wasn't going to save anyone else, either. *What a time to be heroic!* "Come on, I know how to get up there."

No hope of using the little elevator to the side of the stairway, not without a key she didn't have, but there was a small, half-hidden staircase, and Denise and Ilaron breathlessly climbed up to the top floor, above where visitors ever went, up to the maintenance level just below the roof, but:

"Damn!" Denise gasped, just as breathless as Ilaron by now. "Forgot about this."

A locked iron grating sealed them off from the floor and the roof above it.

"We just do not have time for this!" Ilaron snapped, and brought his sword down with all his force on the lock. Iron and alien metal screamed—but it was the lock that shattered. "Huh. Half feared I'd lose the sword instead."

They hurried up onto that top floor, then up a final narrow stairway, stepping onto the flat roof, the wild winds all around them, staggering them, the thunder booming theatrically.

Between one flash of lightning and the next, Lamashtu was there, towering in her fury. For what seemed forever, Denise simply could not move. In the hotel, she'd thought she'd seen Lamashtu in the demon's full fury, but that, oh that had been merely a shadow of . . . this. This was the essence of horror, wild, primal hatred, primal rage, the lion's head open in an endless roar, the woman's body smeared with filth, encrusted with blood. Blood darkened the clenching talons and widespread wings, and so strong

a reek of decay and death encircled Lamashtu that
Denise nearly choked, fighting not to retch.

No time for that! she snapped at herself. *Unless you
want to be her next dinner, it's* Showtime*!*

Don't worry about pronunciation, don't worry about
anything, just say the words, say the incantation, the
banishing of Lamashtu, the summoning of Pazuzu:

> "Ga-e pazuzu dumu ha-an-pa,
> Lugal li-la hul-a-mesh,
> Hur-sag-ta kala-gla mlu
> Hus ba-an-e-de!"

and:

> "Lamashtu, remove your claws!
> Release your prey before the hero's magic
> strikes you!
> The doors are open for you, the doors are
> open—
> Away!
> I conjure you, I conjure you by Ea, by magic—
> Lamashtu, begone!"

and again:

> "Ga-e pazuzu dumu ha-an-pa,
> Lugal li-la hul-a-mesh,
> Hur-sag-ta kala-gla mlu
> Hus ba-an-e-de!"

And—

Nothing! Not even the slightest stir of Power, not
even the slightest flinch from Lamashtu—nothing!
Nothing save Lamashtu's laughter.

"Come, little one, come," the demon taunted, holding up her sagging breasts in her hands in horrible
mockery of maternity. "Come, let me hold you, let
me suckle you at my breast!"

No use to run, no use to plead. Denise knew in that moment of ultimate despair what had gone wrong: She had the words, she had the will—but she simply didn't have the innate magic that would bring the spell to life!

But even as she knew she was about to die, Denise felt Ilaron step behind her, felt his arms enfolding her, reassuring in their warm strength. Oh well, if she must die, at least it wasn't going to be alone.

But then she heard him murmur, "Again. Cast the spell again."

Shaking with a sudden surge of unexpected hope, Denise began her chant again. And Ilaron joined his Power to her incantation, Power flaring through her body, hot as flame, wild as the storm around them— and this time magic flared into existence. With a fierce rush of wind, Pazuzu was there, the demon-god prince, Pazuzu, son of Hanbi, King of the Winds, and Denise shrank back against Ilaron, as much in awe as terror.

For Pazuzu was hideous and wondrous in one, his face that of a savage beast, his body that of a powerful naked man, his double pair of wings wider, more splendidly plumed than Lamashtu's own. From him radiated no stench, nothing but the sharp tang of ozone, the scent of the storm itself, from him radiated the storm's fury at seeing this, his darkest enemy.

The two demons circled, snarling their rage—and then Pazuzu lunged at Lamashtu. Their battle was a whirlwind that hurled Denise and Ilaron off their feet.

We're going off the roof!

But Ilaron twisted, sent them both tumbling away from the edge, then pulled Denise to him. They huddled together, heads down against the force of the wind and the grit stinging them. Denise gladly buried her face against Ilaron's chest, aware of his heartbeat under her cheek, calm, regular—

How can he be so calm? How can even he be used to something like this?

She dared look up, just in time to see Pazuzu form again, shrieking in savage joy—then a new roar of wind pinned Denise and Ilaron helplessly against the roof, gasping for air. Just when Denise was sure she was going to be smothered, the wind and demons both were suddenly, jarringly—gone.

"Pazuzu?" Denise panted.

"Pazuzu," Ilaron said breathlessly, "triumphed."

She and he struggled back to their feet, and Denise shook her head in wonder. Surely there should be *some* difference to the world. Instead: Nothing but an ordinary, utterly normal stormy night.

"It worked," she said. "It did. Ilaron, it actually worked."

"So it did," Ilaron agreed wearily. "Be glad that Pazuzu was too delighted to attack his enemy to bother with us. And be glad that he won. He has banished Lamashtu from this realm, and neither shall return."

"How can you know that?"

The faintest of ironic chuckles. "I have had some experience with demonkind."

"And . . . Kerezar? What about Kerezar?"

Ilaron shrugged, then winced, hand going to his sore arm. "I admit that I'd be happier if I knew Kerezar was dead. But then again, my . . . *his* realm is hardly charitable to the wounded."

He left that statement deliberately unfinished.

It was over, then, Denise thought, stunned to think of it. As suddenly as this, the demon was gone, Kerezar was gone, the mysterious disease was gone, and there would be no more victims slain by swords.

"I . . . uh . . . think we saved New York," she said.

Ilaron hesitated, considering, then grinned. "We did, didn't we?"

But then he winced again at an incautious movement of his arm. Worried, Denise cried, "Oh here, let me see!"

"It's all right," Ilaron insisted, as she tried to see the wound. "Your absent professor won't want this sweater back, but there's nothing that won't heal. . . . "

His voice trailed off as Denise looked up and they found themselves looking into each other's eyes. And for a moment, neither moved, neither knowing quite what to say or do.

The moment shattered. Denise drew back with a shaky laugh. "You know," she said, boldly linking arms—careful to make it his uninjured arm—with Ilaron, "we make a pretty good team."

He considered that. Then, to Denise's delight, she saw that lovely, genuine smile appear on his weary face.

"We do," he agreed. "We do, indeed."

AFTERWORD

A Few Disclaimers

This is, of course, a work of fiction, and The American Museum of Art does not exist. However, any similarities between it and a certain major museum on Fifth Avenue in New York City may not be accidental. The picture of museum life is as accurate as the author (who used to work in that certain major museum) could make it, although the employees are, again, all fictional.

The Tunnel, however, certainly does exist. It lies beneath the Metropolitan Museum of Art, and is exactly as the author (who has, indeed, had a spider run across her foot) depicts it. The peril of those low-hanging pipes is also true; someone once did nearly brain himself on one.

Lamashtu and Pazuzu and their feud exist, too—at least in Mesopotamian mythology. The "holy charm" plaques featured in the book exist as well; examples can be seen in many museums and in books on Babylonia. The author isn't advocating the conjuration of either being, by the way, nor are the "spells" in this book, which are the author's own renderings from various sources, intended to be complete or "how-to" sources!

Thanks go to Oscar White Muscarella of the Ancient Near East Department of the Metropolitan Museum of Art for sharing his information about Lamashtu and the means for banishing her.

Thanks also to the Marriott Marquis for permission to use their hotel as one of the "sets."

For those who wish to read more on the subject, and to see examples of some additional Babylonian charms, the following three books are easily available:

Black, Jeremy and Anthony Green. *Gods, Demons and Symbols of Ancient Mesopotamia.* Austin: University of Texas Press, 1992.

Dalley, Stephanie, trans. *Myths from Mesopotamia.* Oxford: Oxford University Press, 1989.

Foster, Benjamin R. *From Distant Days: Myths, Tales, and Poetry of Ancient Mesopotamia.* Bethesda, Md.: CDL Press, 1995.

ENCHANTING REALMS

☐ **SCORPIANNE by Emily Devenport.** Lucy finds herself with a new identity on a new world at the brink of rebellion. Even here, she cannot escape the nightmare memories of the assassin who strikes without being seen, the one who has sworn Lucy's death, the stalker she knows only by the name Scorpianne.
(453182—$4.99)

☐ **THE EYE OF THE HUNTER by Dennis L. McKiernan.** From the best-selling author of *The Iron Tower* trilogy and *The Silver Call* duology—a new epic of Mithgar. The comet known as the Eye of the Hunter is riding through Mithgar's skies again, bringing with it destruction and the much dreaded master, Baron Stoke.
(452682—$6.99)

☐ **FORTRESS ON THE SUN by Paul Cook.** When a lethal illness strikes his people, Ian Hutchings demands aid from their captors on Earth. Receiving only a denial that such illness exists, Hutchings has no choice but to find his own answers. As time runs out, the prisoners uncover one astonishing clue after another in a conspiracy of stunning proportions. "Highly inventive and engaging."—Robert J. Sawyer, Nebula Award-winning author of *Starplex*   (456262—$5.99)

☐ **THE ARCHITECTURE OF DESIRE by Mary Gentle.** Discover a time and a place ruled by the Hermetic magic of the Renaissance, by secret, almost forgotten Masonic rites, a land divided between the royalists loyal to Queen Carola and the soldiers who follow the Protector-General Olivia in this magnificent sequel to *Rats and Gargoyles*.
(453530—$4.99)

Prices slightly higher in Canada.

Buy them at your local bookstore or use this convenient coupon for ordering.

PENGUIN USA
P.O. Box 999 — Dept. #17109
Bergenfield, New Jersey 07621

Please send me the books I have checked above.
I am enclosing $_____ (please add $2.00 to cover postage and handling). Send check or money order (no cash or C.O.D.'s) or charge by Mastercard or VISA (with a $15.00 minimum). Prices and numbers are subject to change without notice.

Card #_____ Exp. Date _____
Signature_____
Name_____
Address_____
City _____ State _____ Zip Code _____

For faster service when ordering by credit card call **1-800-253-6476**

Allow a minimum of 4-6 weeks for delivery. This offer is subject to change without notice.

ROC

THE BEST IN SCIENCE FICTION AND FANTASY

☐ **LARISSA by Emily Devenport.** Hook is a mean, backwater mining planet where the alien Q'rin rule. Taking the wrong side can get you killed and humans have little hope for escape. Larissa is a young woman with a talent for sports and knives. She's beating the aliens at their own harsh game until someone dies. (452763—$4.99)

☐ **STARSEA INVADERS: SECOND CONTACT by G. Harry Stine.** Captain Corry discovers that the U.S.S. *Shenandoah* is at last going to be allowed to track down the alien invaders who are based beneath the sea—invaders who had long preyed upon Earth and its people—and this time they were going to bring one of the creatures back alive! (453441—$4.99)

☐ **MUTANT CHRONICLES: *The Apostle of Insanity Trilogy: IN LUNACY* by William F. Wu.** It was a time to conquer all fears and stand up against the tidal wave of the Dark Symmetry. Battles rage across our solar system as mankind and the Legions of Darkness fight for supremacy of the kingdom of Sol. But though there is unity against the common enemy, the five MegaCorporations that rule the worlds are fighting among themselves. The struggle for survival goes on. (453174—$4.99)

*Prices slightly higher in Canada   **RCF9X**

Buy them at your local bookstore or use this convenient coupon for ordering.

PENGUIN USA
P.O. Box 999 — Dept. #17109
Bergenfield, New Jersey 07621

Please send me the books I have checked above.
I am enclosing $_____ (please add $2.00 to cover postage and handling). Send check or money order (no cash or C.O.D.'s) or charge by Mastercard or VISA (with a $15.00 minimum). Prices and numbers are subject to change without notice.

Card #_____ Exp. Date _____
Signature_____
Name_____
Address_____
City _____ State _____ Zip Code _____

For faster service when ordering by credit card call **1-800-253-6476**

Allow a minimum of 4-6 weeks for delivery. This offer is subject to change without notice.

![RoC logo]

FANTASTICAL LANDS

☐ **AN EXCHANGE OF GIFTS by Anne McCaffrey.** Meanne, known to others as Princess Anastasia de Saumur et Navareey Cordova, has a Gift which no lady, much less a princess royal, should exercise. For Meanne has the ability to make things grow, and to create the herbal mixtures that will soothe and heal. Promised to a man she can never love, Meanne flees, seeking shelter and a new life in a long-deserted cottage in the woods.
(455207—$12.95)

☐ **THE JIGSAW WOMAN by Kim Antieau.** Keelie is created from the bodies of three different women to be a plaything for her doctor. Not satisfied with the life given to her, she sets out to find one of her own. From ancient battles and violent witch hunts, to Amazonian paradise and Sumerian hell our heroine spirals through epic distortions of history and magic, finding that her salvation lies not in the promise of the future, but in the lessons learned in the past.
(455096—$10.95)

☐ **DELTA CITY by Felicity Savage.** Humility Garden must once again fight the god Pati, whose cold-blooded ruthlessness made even his followers bow to his whims. But Humility would not be cowed into submission and vowed to retake Salt from the Divinarch. "Humility is as bold as the author herself."—*New York Times Book Review*
(453999—$5.99)

☐ **HUMILITY GARDEN by Felicity Savage.** Young Humility Garden's only dream is to escape her squalid homeland. She is about to embark on a journey that will teach her the secretive ways of the ghostiers, the language of the gods, and the power of eternal love.
(453980—$4.99)

*Prices slightly higher in Canada

RCF50X

Buy them at your local bookstore or use this convenient coupon for ordering.

PENGUIN USA
P.O. Box 999 — Dept. #17109
Bergenfield, New Jersey 07621

Please send me the books I have checked above.
I am enclosing $_____ (please add $2.00 to cover postage and handling). Send check or money order (no cash or C.O.D.'s) or charge by Mastercard or VISA (with a $15.00 minimum). Prices and numbers are subject to change without notice.

Card #_____ Exp. Date _____
Signature_____
Name_____
Address_____
City _____ State _____ Zip Code _____

For faster service when ordering by credit card call **1-800-253-6476**

Allow a minimum of 4-6 weeks for delivery. This offer is subject to change without notice.

ROC

JOURNEY TO FANTASTICAL REALMS

☐ **KNIGHTS OF THE BLOOD created by Katherine Kurtz and Scott MacMillan.** A Los Angeles policeman is out to solve an unsolved mystery—that would pitch him straight into the dark and terrifying world of the vampire.　(452569—$4.99)

☐ **KNIGHTS OF THE BLOOD:** *At Sword's Point* **by Katherine Kurtz and Scott MacMillan.** A generation of Nazi vampires has evolved with a centuries-old agenda hellbent on world domination, and the only way LAPD Detective John Drummond can save himself is to grab a sword and commit bloody murder.　(454073—$4.99)

☐ **A SONG FOR ARBONNE by Guy Gavriel Kay.** "This panoramic, absorbing novel beautifully creates an alternate version of the medieval world.... Kay creates a vivid world of love and music, magic, and death."—*Publishers Weekly*
(453328—$6.99)

☐ **GABRIEL KNIGHT: SINS OF THE FATHERS by Jane Jensen.** Gabriel Knight's inexplicable attraction to a beautiful woman surrounded by voodoo lore and mystery leads him much too close to an ancient curse and its deadly threat. To escape its diabolical evil, Gabriel in a race against time and vile magics, must find the key to his survival—a key hidden in a shocking family history. "The interactive Anne Rice."—*Computer Gaming World*　(456076—$5.99)

*Prices slightly higher in Canada

Buy them at your local bookstore or use this convenient coupon for ordering.

PENGUIN USA
P.O. Box 999 — Dept. #17109
Bergenfield, New Jersey 07621

Please send me the books I have checked above.
I am enclosing $＿＿＿＿＿＿＿＿＿ (please add $2.00 to cover postage and handling). Send check or money order (no cash or C.O.D.'s) or charge by Mastercard or VISA (with a $15.00 minimum). Prices and numbers are subject to change without notice.

Card #＿＿＿＿＿＿＿＿＿＿＿＿＿＿＿＿ Exp. Date ＿＿＿＿＿＿＿＿＿＿＿＿＿＿＿＿
Signature＿＿＿＿＿＿＿＿＿＿＿＿＿＿＿＿＿＿＿＿＿＿＿＿＿＿＿＿＿＿＿＿＿＿＿＿＿＿
Name＿＿
Address＿＿＿＿＿＿＿＿＿＿＿＿＿＿＿＿＿＿＿＿＿＿＿＿＿＿＿＿＿＿＿＿＿＿＿＿＿＿
City ＿＿＿＿＿＿＿＿＿＿＿＿＿＿ State ＿＿＿＿＿＿＿＿＿ Zip Code ＿＿＿＿＿＿＿＿

For faster service when ordering by credit card call **1-800-253-6476**

Allow a minimum of 4-6 weeks for delivery. This offer is subject to change without notice.